EMBER'S MOON

FIONA LAWLESS

LAWLESS BOOKS

CHAPTER 1

$\mathcal{O}$nce upon a time ...

"$\mathcal{T}$his way, Your Highness." Kit's mother's attendant led him to her chamber. "The king and queen expect you."

Of course, they do.

As the crown prince and heir to the throne, stately duties had been piled on Kit since birth.

What ribbon needed cutting today?

Which trade partner's daughter must he squire around?

Kit coughed behind his hand as he tried to appear composed in the royal couple's stuffy rooms. They reeked of medicinal incense. To combat the smell, his father had the servants place large vases with his mother's favorite flowers around in a vivid display of seasonal colors. The effect was a sort of tournament of the senses.

Currently, the court physician's quackeries were the clear winners.

The royal chambers were large, with teakwood floors and a massive bed with purple draperies. The French doors—which were always kept closed because his mother was never warm enough—led to a balcony where, on state occasions, the family greeted their subjects. Queen Bella Maria Filomena sat in a softly upholstered chair in her favorite shade of lilac. King Leander sat on the chair's arm with a hand on her frail shoulder. The queen was still the most beautiful woman Kit had ever seen despite the changes to her appearance wrought by age and illness.

He forced himself to study her.

This can't be real. Kit didn't speak the words aloud, but they must have shown on his face. His mother's eyes softened sadly though she tried to smile.

"It's all right, sweetheart," she said. "Come closer. Let me get a look at you."

I refuse to believe the evidence of my own eyes.

I refuse to believe the despair written plainly on my father's face.

My mother cannot be dying.

If she was dying, it was his fault, or so everyone told him because his mother had been ill since he was born. It was only her grit and determination that had kept her hovering in the liminal space between living and dying. She'd teetered on the very brink of death more times than he could count and then made miraculous recoveries.

She always got better. Always.

How dare those deathwatch beetles with their black garments and their somber faces make dire predictions now.

The queen held her hand out. Kit knelt at her side and took her hand between his. Her hand seemed so fragile; her fingers too cold.

"Here's my beautiful son." The queen eyed him with a sigh. "It's good to see you looking so well though I'm afraid you won't be able to say the same about me."

2

"Mother—"

"It's time to listen, son," the king admonished. "Hear your mother out."

"Time is not on my side, sweetheart. Though we have the finest physicians in the world, I'm not expected to make a recovery this time." Her voice was barely audible, her breath labored. "I've made a list of things I don't want to leave unfinished. Above all, I must see you mated and happy. Have you not found a single omega who pleases you?"

"No, Mother. I—" He clasped hands in his lap nervously. "I'm afraid I haven't found my true mate yet."

She nodded though it looked like the effort cost her. "We must hold a ball. Your father will invite every worthy omega in the kingdom. If we can accomplish this, I'm certain you'll find your true mate. I need—" She broke off, coughing.

"It will be done, Maria." The king gave her his handkerchief. "You have my word, my darling."

"I must see you settled and happy, Kit." She relaxed into the cushions with a fond look at Kit's father. "I cannot rest until I know you've found the kind of joy that your father and I have shared all these years."

"Mother—" Briefly, horribly, Kit wondered if avoiding marriage might keep her alive long enough for her physicians to find a cure, or—

"Stupid boy." She seemed to read his mind. "It's the Goddess's will, not mine, that keeps me here."

He frowned. "I don't understand."

"Kit. Your mother is in great pain." The king's face paled. "She's holding on to see you find your mate."

Kit's heart lurched with his rising anger. How dare they put that on him. He already blamed himself for her suffering. Now was her relief suddenly somehow in his hands as well?

He turned away to hide his burning eyes. "What if I never find my omega?"

"You will. I promise." His mother tried to sit forward and failed.

His father rearranged her cushions.

Kit could barely stand to look at her. He winced as she tried to move again.

How had things gotten this bad without him seeing it?

"The Goddess created your perfect mate." She coughed sharply. One of her maids rushed forward with a cup of water. "We have to look for that person. Please, Kit. Your father will hold this ball, and you—you must at least try, whether you're ready or not. I'm almost out of time."

"Some alphas die without mates," he reminded her. "What if you hold this omega ball and I still don't find the one meant for me?"

"You will." She had closed her eyes. "Your omega is out there, darling. Your happiness ... I feel it in my heart."

She touched her chest with her free hand then let it fall to her lap as if even that exhausted her.

"We should concentrate all our efforts on making you well. That's more important. Don't you think so?" he asked his father.

"There's no point, my darling." His mother held her hand out to him and he clasped it between his own. "My time with you is almost over. I'm so sorry if it saddens you or places you in a difficult position."

"You're worried about *me*?" He leaned over her hand and began to cry despite his age, despite the promise he had made to himself that he wouldn't listen to their gloomy predictions. He didn't know what he'd do without his mother. She was the one person who knew him, who understood him, who loved him unconditionally. She was his father's rock. The beating heart of the very kingdom she served.

With the queen gone, would his father even survive?

Theirs was a mated love match. They were the ones who had inspired him to hold out for his true mate. Sadly, his parents' dream was impossible for him. How could he bear to let them down?

Only few minutes passed before his mother fell asleep. His father had dropped the mask of confidence he'd worn for her. Despair enveloped both of them.

Kit patted his mother's small, pale hand and gave it into his father's keeping. "We'll talk more after I've had a chance to think."

"There will be no more discussion," the king said woodenly. "I will arrange the ball, and you will grant your mother's dying wish. Choose an omega, or I swear I will make your life a misery."

Kit stared at him, aghast. "But, Father—"

"No more *stalling.*" This was his king talking, now. "You must succeed. For your mother's sake, you *must* take a bride. If it's the only thing I can do for her, I will make you choose a mate, and you'll live with the knowledge we did the only thing your mother asked of us before she passed into the Goddess's hands."

"Fine." Kit left the room without saying more. What could he say?

How could he tell them he would never love *any* omega they brought before him? Omegas were *women*, and his body knew— his wolf and his heart were absolutely certain—he could only love a man.

How he wished there were an omega who could fulfill his impossible wishes. He could go to this ball and choose some omega he'd never find love with. That would please his father, but it wouldn't give him the life his mother wanted for him. It would violate the very essence of her wishes. He'd never have a love like theirs.

No one *cared* about what he wanted, he thought petulantly.

He'd do anything to please his mother. He wanted her to be happy. He'd have to at least pretend to go along with their plan ... Perhaps the end result didn't matter?

A terrible idea came to him.

An idea that had worked a time or two in the past because he and his first cousin Oliver favored each other in both looks and mannerisms. They'd exchanged places more than once, at school and for a lark at certain social gatherings. A simple illusion charm was all it would take.

Kit bit his lip in indecision, but his wolf perked up.

If he had to pick an omega, he was quite certain any omega from his father's list would do. He'd have Oliver go to the ball and look over the girls his father thought worthy. He'd tell Oliver to find him a girl everyone in the kingdom could admire, someone nice, someone biddable, someone Kit could get an heir with. Once they had that, Kit could leave her to her own devices.

Most omega girls would love to be queen someday, right?

Yes … it could work. Oliver would help him. He was always up for mischief.

Perhaps he could please his parents *and* avoid this debacle altogether.

CHAPTER 2

*B*efore the toe of a boot connected—not unkindly—
with his ribs, Ember was dreaming of his mother
and the nursery at Carlysle Manor. He breathed in the warm,
musty smell of it: his toys, his schoolbooks, and the rocking
horse he'd named Griffin. He dreamed of his mother's gentle
smile, his father's kindness, and his tutor's praise, which had
once made him feel so confident and proud.

Before Old Tom awoke him, he'd been able to escape into
the past, leaving his current circumstances far behind.

"Get up, you lazy bones. Can't believe you slept out here
again when you've got a fine bed inside the manor to welcome
you at night." The caretaker must have been suffering aches in
his bones because he wasn't normally that grumpy.

"Beauty foaled last night. I stayed to watch over her and
make sure everything went smoothly." Ember let his dream fade
as he brushed stray bits of straw from his hair and rose to his
feet. "What's gotten into you this early?"

"Early? The girls will be down to ride in half an hour, you
know." Tom followed him to Beauty's stall where the beautiful
mare and the foal were bonding. Beauty was a gorgeous horse.

Great conformation, good balance, flawless in performance. He'd paid for a prize stallion to cover her, and if their sound breeding held true, the foal would be a valuable asset.

Ember had a lot invested in these two. Someday they'd add much-needed cash to the family coffers.

"Oh, now. Isn't he handsome? Gonna be a fine addition to the stables." Tom looked on approvingly. "Got Beauty's coloring. She's a prize, son, and now we know she's going to be a fine broodmare."

"I think she's my favorite horse but don't let that slip to the others. Mother and baby seem to be doing fine. Can you lead them out to the paddock, so I can muck out in here?"

"Guess so. Be better than heading back to the house, that's for sure."

"Did something happen?"

"Great rumblings." Tom removed his cap and scratched his balding head. "The ladies are in a lather about something, and that means there's bound to be work involved."

"So you fled," Ember teased.

Tom raised a haughty brow. "I'm just one man."

"I'll ask if they need anything." Ember's stepmother had let the gardeners go along with most of the staff, but she'd kept Old Tom. He was married to their cook, Victoria, who was far too valuable to replace. But that left Tom, ancient and immutable as the stones that made up the old garden walls, with the work of ten men. As he'd aged, he'd been forced to call upon Ember to do more and more of the heavy lifting.

Behind them, the horses rustled restlessly in their stalls.

"I'll take these two and leave you to your work for now, Don't keep the young misses waiting for their ride or we'll never hear the end of it." Tom led Beauty and her foal outside.

"Goddess, no." Ember smiled. "We can't have that."

Ember got Lucy's mare, Biscuit, watered and fed first, then took care of her stablemate, Velvet. As always, they greeted him with warmth and trust. They bumped him with their noses and begged for treats. All he could scrounge for them today was a couple of wild carrots, but they crunched them and smiled with their eyes as he brushed them carefully from their necks to their tails.

Velvet and Biscuit were lovely dainty gray Lyrienne mares whose coats shone like pearls in the misty dawn of the late summer morning. Ember spoiled and babied them shamelessly.

Every morning, he spent his time crooning soft words to keep the horses calm because as soon as they heard his omega sisters' voices, they'd get excited, stamp, fidget, and strain at their bits, impatient to be off with their riders.

"Mother said we'll have to wear the gowns we have as there's no money for the seamstress." Ember heard Eleanor's voice first. "She says she thinks I should wear my blue gown from last year because it will bring out the color of my eyes, which is very fine, don't you think?"

"Yes, of course," Lucy agreed readily. "Your eyes are a wonderful shade. Periwinkle, I think."

"Thank you, I'm told it's quite unique."

"I'm to wear violet," Lucy lamented. "Though I want to wear the pink gown. Mother says pink makes me look too young. Do you think so?"

"Of course, darling. Pink makes one look like a schoolgirl. I promise if you want to fill your dance card, you must trust Mother to know. She has high hopes for both of us. Imagine what it would be like to be married to a prince!"

Light laughter filled the air as his sisters rounded the path. Both were beautiful young women. They wore fashionable, if worn, velvet riding habits and jaunty little hats. Feathers bounced insouciantly as they moved, making them look like extravagant little songbirds. Each day, they dressed to the nines for riding despite being limited to the Carlysle lands and therefore unseen by anyone but their family and the servants.

Stepmother Lenore said it was all about training them to be elegant young ladies, an activity that didn't require an audience. Though he was the eldest sibling, there had been no such training for Ember. The work required to run an estate the size of Carlysle didn't leave him much time for it anyway.

"Morning, ladies." Ember sketched a bow. "Biscuit and Velvet are very anxious to be off."

"Oh, Ember. Good morning," said Eleanor. "We're equally anxious to ride. Thank you for having our mounts ready."

"You're entirely welcome." He held out his hand to aid her as she ascended the mounting block.

If it occurred to his sisters to wonder why their elder brother—the Earl of Carlysle since he'd turned twenty-one a month before—spent his mornings in the stables to groom and saddle their mounts, they never questioned him about it. Ember didn't feel the need to explain. They lived in the country, and they got along fine without formality.

He couldn't blame his sisters for their ignorance.

Ember's mother had died giving birth to his much-anticipated baby sister, who had also succumbed. His father had been so distraught over their loss that he'd quickly remarried a foreign princess. She had brought two little girls with her, who also bore the hereditary title "princess" as they came from Rhielôme, where royal titles were passed down through the female line as well as the male. Ember's father had then left on a foreign trade mission and died shortly after. His death was seen as a terrible tragedy but had been all but forgotten by the time the next wave of gossip crested.

The girls had only had their mother's guidance. Where Ember slept, where he ate, or what their mother expected of him due to their straightened circumstances probably never occurred to them.

He assisted Lucy next. "Ready, Lu?"

"Oh, quite. Thank you."

"Old Tom said something happened to put everyone in a dither this morning. Care to share?"

"Yes!" She widened her eyes. "You can't imagine all the fuss. The prince is looking for a mate, and every worthy young omega in the kingdom has been invited to a ball. Everyone is talking about it."

"That must be very exciting." And expensive, he thought.

"Mother's having fits because the dressmakers will all be busy night and day," Lucy confided.

"Lucy," Eleanor chided.

Lucy flushed deeply. "I don't suppose I should have mentioned that."

"What does our brother care about fashion? Don't prattle on."

"Sorry," Lucy offered as he led the two horses to the bridle path.

"No worries." Ember gave her a smile. "It happens that I love fashion talk."

"Oh, you." She put her gloved hand on his shoulder. "I wish—"

"Come on, Lucy. Don't dawdle." Eleanor gave a kick to her horse's flanks and tore off. Lucy shrugged apologetically and raced after her.

Ember watched the two girls until they rounded the corner, out of sight.

The seamstresses were busy? More likely, his stepmother, Lenore, had said that to save face because in no way did Carlysle have funds in the coffers for fancy dresses. It truly grated on Ember that he couldn't provide better for his sisters, but Lenore had done everything she could to keep the estate afloat for years. He couldn't fault her. His father had simply left them cash poor.

"There goes trouble," Tom muttered from a nearby fence where he was making repairs.

11

"Perhaps." Ember turned to get the other horses fed and groomed. "But perhaps one of them will win the prince's heart."

"Right." Tom gave a laugh. "Imagine a prince falling for one of the girls and then meeting their mother."

Ember tried and failed to hide a laugh. His stepmother could be called temperamental, but that was because she was ambitious on their family's behalf. She had no scruples when it came to seeing her daughters married well. She'd move heaven and earth to see one of them married to Prince Christopher and seated on the throne one day. While Ember might not admire her driven nature, he couldn't argue that his sisters would make proper little queens.

"Best watch your back, Ember. If she manages to wed those girls off to royalty there'll be no more hiding what you are."

"I know that." Ember turned to him. "I don't look forward to it, but if Nora and Lu marry well, I'll do my duty."

"The omega Earl," Tom spoke with a kind of wonder. "The whole world will find out. Doesn't that scare you just a little?"

Ember frowned deeply, unused to hearing Tom speak so plainly. "Is that how you think of me?"

"Don't get your back up," Tom said gently. "Your father never gave a toss about your status, and your mother adored you. But the mistress? To her, a male omega is like tits on a rock. She's only interested in things or people she can use to get what she wants."

Tom had a fair point. "That's … a very unpleasant thought."

"Yeah, well. Unpleasant it may be but untrue? It might be prudent to have a couple of plans in place. That's all I'm saying."

Ember had been working on that. As an omega—the only male omega born in hundreds of years, as far as he could tell—he had a gift with livestock animals, especially horses. His skill for training the beasts was unusual because horses had to actively work against their best interests to allow a predator on their back. Animals didn't fear omegas, and as a man, no one questioned whether he had the right to work where he pleased. Well, no one except Lenore, who didn't take his work very seriously. If he worked at anything but being an earl it meant they were in *trade,* which somehow humbled and diminished his father's name.

He didn't care what she called his work as long as the Carlysle horses were getting the recognition they deserved. With Beauty producing a foal like Beau, the future looked very bright indeed. Carlysle's horses, in fact, were becoming so well-known they were coveted by their neighbors, who often brought obstreperous animals to Carlysle for help. They brought them to Tom in the belief that he was the Carlysle horse whisperer. Ember kept himself hidden from all but his family to keep gossip to a minimum.

The horses were Ember's dream. They were his plan. Even Lenore would have to reevaluate her thinking if his "hobby" put cash in the Carlysle coffers.

For most, the reclusive Earl of Carlysle was *eccentric,* but Tom was right. Since his parents' death, isolation had become his day-to-day reality. He kept to himself, and he used the stables as a place of refuge because it was there that he felt most at ease.

People didn't know he was an omega, an unnatural act of creation, powerless beyond the borders of his own land. Ember had been hiding who and what he was all his life, but if his sisters married well, if his stables were to become lucrative, eventually he would have to show himself for what he was despite his fears.

He groomed the horses and took them to the paddock so he could muck out the rest of the stalls. Unfortunately, that meant that when his sisters returned, he was sweating and covered in filth.

"Phew, Ember." Lucy giggled. "You must have a bath at once. What would Mother think?"

Nora scoffed. "She'll be glad to have a tidy stable, of course. Don't be a ninny."

Dear Lucy. She thought he needed to be reminded to bathe like a recalcitrant farm boy.

"I promise, Lu, I'm going to clean up as soon as I walk your mounts."

"See that you do," Nora said righteously. "Honestly, you'd think an omega would be more fastidious."

"Oh, Nora." Lucy winced. "Don't scold him. He works with horses. It's not Ember's fault the work is filthy."

"Have a good day, ladies." He waved as they walked away, lifting their skirts carefully to avoid the churned-up earth.

"The work is filthy," Tom mimicked. "My Victoria prays for you, boy. I hope you know that."

"I appreciate her kindness, but I need a full copper tub and some of her rosemary scented soap more than prayers right now."

"I'[l walk these two, go on. You've more than earned it."

Ember gave a backward wave as he followed in the direction his sisters had gone. He veered off when he approached the house, heading toward the tradesman's door at the back of the kitchen, where he scraped and removed his boots before entering.

"Hello," he called to Victoria and her beta assistant, Geoffrey. "Any chance for a bath?"

Victoria backed away from the oven she was tending. "Of course, Lord Carlysle. I'll have the lad heat water as quick as a wink. Wash your hands, and I'll get you something to eat while you wait."

The beta—who was maybe sixteen, a few years younger than Ember—drew two pails from the pump and dumped them into a massive copper pot on the stove. How he lifted that was a mystery, but he'd managed since he was a boy.

After Ember cleaned his hands, Victoria gave him a plate of bacon, eggs, and roasted potatoes. The smell was heavenly.

"Thank you." He took his food to the table where the staff ate their meals. "This looks delicious."

"Stay where you are. I'll have coffee and fresh bread for you in a minute."

"I'm not going anywhere."

She bustled around gathering what she needed before sitting across from him. "Did you see the young misses this morning?"

"I did. They rode out at the usual time."

"Did they tell you about the prince's ball? I've never seen such excitement. Course, there's only one prince, so it's bound to cause a fuss, isn't it?"

"One would imagine," he said between bites. He hadn't been aware how hungry he was until he sat down, and now he didn't want to be rude, but the food had all his attention.

"Seems like every noble will be there, even some foreign ones. Every unmarried young man looking for a wife will attend."

"Really."

She eyed him. "You could find yourself a bride there too."

"Right." He laughed then realized she was serious. "I'm not in the market for a wife."

"You could be." She got up and brought back more crisp roasted potatoes. "Here you go, love. I know they're your favorite."

"Thanks. You're a wonder with the spuds."

She blushed. "So? What do you think?"

"About what?"

"Finding a wife." She crossed her arms. "You're the earl now. You need to think about starting a family."

He rolled his eyes. "Who'd want an omega husband?"

"Any girl would be glad to have you. You're an earl, and Carlysle Manor is lovely."

"I'm an anomaly," he reminded her. "Or an abomination."

"Stop that." Her cheeks reddened. "My cousin Louisa says male omegas are rare because they're destined for greatness."

"She'd be the only one who believes that."

"Your parents thought so. They had high, high hopes for you."

He bit his lip. "They did?"

"Of course they did. They'd hate to see you hiding like this. Practically living as a stable hand in your own home. If you must fight for your destiny, lad, then fight. Don't give up before the battle starts."

"It's not like you make it sound—" Heels clicking along the slate floor caught his attention.

"Ember, dearest." His stepmother's demeanor felt stiff—as though she'd had to take a deep breath before entering the room. "I thought I might find you here."

"How may I help you?" he asked.

"I'm sure you've heard of the prince's ball by now." She lifted one perfect eyebrow. "Everyone is talking about it."

"I've heard," he answered carefully.

"The girls are to be presented, of course. We'll need to take the carriage. I don't suppose it's in any condition to make the trip?"

"It hasn't been used in several years." Their coach had hardly been used since his father's death, and even then it had needed work. Was the chassis sound? At the very least, it would require new paint. Ember doubted Old Tom was up for such a physical task. Geoffrey could help, maybe.

"The ball is set for the next full moon, so you have a fortnight. It must be ready by then. And I'm sorry, but I've thought this through, and you'll have to stand in as coachman."

"Missus." Victoria gasped with outrage. "Lord Carlysle is master here. Should he not be the one to present his sisters?"

"Would you ask Ember to make his first official appearance at a ball? Everyone who is anyone will be there."

Victoria frowned. "But—"

"Ember, would you really want to go?" Lenore asked. "Perhaps we could hire—"

"No," he answered quickly. "I'd be happy to drive you."

"I don't blame you." Lenore glanced Victoria's way. "Ember can't possibly look for a bride among the eligible omega girls. He needs a beta mate. Perhaps a burger's daughter? An unhandsome but wealthy young lady who can't possibly expect to marry a noble alpha but wishes to advance her family's standing."

"Hm." Victoria probably knew Lenore was right, but it didn't seem to sit well with her.

"As the earl, he should still be there to present his sisters."

Lenore sighed. "If not for the unfortunate circumstance of your status, of course I would ask you to present the girls. I'd like you to be our coachman, if you're willing. We can't afford to hire anyone and I wouldn't trust anyone else anyway." Her smile seemed genuine. "You'll look so very handsome in the Carlysle livery, Ember. I'm afraid we really need your help with this."

Lenore was right about one thing. There was no one else he trusted to drive his sisters either. "Very well," Ember agreed. "I will play John Coachman for the night."

If only to see his sisters safely to the social occasion of the season, he would do it. Being a coachman might even be exciting. He'd get to watch the nobles leaving their carriages in the first stare of fashion. He'd get a read on their horses.

"Thank you." Lenore relaxed. "I knew you would do it. You're a pragmatic man and a very good brother. My girls couldn't ask for better." Before Lenore turned to leave, she gave him a considering look. "Please bathe before then. You smell like the barnyard."

As usual, her exit line ruined her kind words.

"There goes the very devil." Victoria huffed her indignation as she rose and muttered darkly all the way to the oven, where she removed loaves of hot, fragrant bread. "Even when she's trying to be nice, she misses the mark."

"It's fine. She wants the girls to arrive at this party in style. I'll ogle the pretty aristocrats in their finery and come back and tell you all about it."

"Course, you will." She set a hot loaf of bread before him along with a thick crock of fresh butter. "And the woman's right. You will look handsome in the Carlysle colors. You wait and see. You'll turn all the young ladies' heads before the prince can even mark their dance cards."

"Of course, I will." With a good-natured eyeroll, Ember took up a butter knife and helped himself to a thick slice. "So long as I bathe before then."

CHAPTER 3

*V*ictoria's kitchen lad, Geoffrey, filled the tub with hot water and placed a folding screen before it to provide Ember with some privacy. The temperature was perfect, and Ember didn't mind spending a few minutes just enjoying the way the heat sank into his bones.

He'd soaped himself up and sponged off when Victoria came by with a soapy mixture in a small bowl.

"Use this on your hair." She handed it off without looking. "I make that for the misses. It leaves their hair soft and shining."

"It smells like almonds."

"That's right. There's oil of almonds in there."

He sniffed the mixture again. "And ... cherry blossoms?"

"Right you are. Almonds and cherries are kissing cousins. You'll smell delicious after washing with that."

"I'm sure the horses will think so."

"Go on and try it. You've got nothing to lose."

"Just my head if they should decide to eat me." Nevertheless, he used her concoction. It did make his hair feel softer, which was nice considering that no matter what he did it would dry into the dark, thick curls his sisters would kill for.

A loud noise came from the dining room before Jemmy—
one of his sisters' pet spaniels—ran by with a satin slipper in his
mouth.

He knew what that meant, and he had just enough time to
stretch a towel over the tub before his sisters came his way.

"Jemmy, no! Naughty, naughty puppy." Lucy cornered the
pooch with one foot clad only in a stocking. She skidded to a
stop on his side of the screen. "Oh, goodness. Nora, guess who's
taking our advice."

He felt his cheeks catch fire. "Ladies. I require privacy."

"You're blushing, Ember," Eleanor said from behind Lucy.
"Sister, do you suppose he'll catch that towel on fire and live up
to his name?"

"Don't tease him." Gentle Lucy disapproved of teasing. "We
shouldn't be here. Mama will have our heads."

"It's not like he's some shockingly masculine alpha." Nora
tossed her braid over her shoulder. She could be a plainspoken
girl. "Look at him. There's not a hair on his body."

"You don't know that," he scolded.

"We're all omegas here, so it's fine." She absolved him.

They scooped up Jemmy but didn't seem to want to leave
until Victoria came and shooed them out.

"Out, girls." The cook pointed the way. "This is highly inap-
propriate behavior. I'd hate for your mother to see you gawping
at Ember like that."

"Ember, why don't you ever use your bath?" Lucy asked as
she turned to leave. "It's so much finer, and you can lock the
door."

"And bathe where no one can see?" Truth was, he hated to
make Geoffrey carry his water up the stairs. "Plus, I'm too dirty
to set foot in the house, as you've pointed out more than once."

"I don't mind," Geoffrey said.

"Everyone, go away." Ember raised his voice. "I need to dry
off."

Could a man not get a bath without it becoming a spectator sport?

"We're going. But honestly, brother," Eleanor called over her shoulder. "It's not as if you've got anything very shocking to hide."

"Nora!" Lucy admonished.

"He's an omega, Lu. He couldn't have, could he?"

"He's still a man." Lucy gave her a shove. "Leave him be."

"All right, but how dreary." The two girls carried their misbehaving dog with them when they left.

"Well, I never." Victoria huffed. "The way those two go on. I should like to know what their mother would think about all this."

"For Goddess's sake, don't tell her. She'll blame me. She'll probably insist I bathe in the horse trough in future."

"I keep telling you, it's your house! You should bathe in the master's bath." Victoria's cheeks burned.

"You're right and I know it." Ember couldn't help wanting to avoid all the women in his life. "I'm the earl, time I acted like it."

With the screen firmly in place, he donned garments that smelled of sunshine and spring grass. He felt like a new man as he donned his good boots and went outside again.

The coach house for an exploratory visit. Long out of use, the wooden bar had swollen. The huge double doors required extra muscle to open. A loud, eerie screech told him he'd do well to oil the hinges.

Once inside the building, it was plain that the roof had rotted in places. There were owls in the rafters. They'd probably gotten fat on the same mice that had nibbled the padding on the coachman's bench. The carriage's once-black paint had suffered weather damage, and the inside was a mess, but it seemed the framework and wheels were still sound. Ember could probably fix the coach up by the full moon if he worked very hard.

Outside, he heard Old Tom whistling an off-key tune.

"Looks like you have your work cut out." Tom squinted as

his eyes adjusted to the gloom inside the carriage house. He ran his hand over the body of the coach. "You'll be heading to town for supplies to fix her up, yeah?"

"Tomorrow, yes. First, I need to patch the coach house roof. Best to get that done before I try rehabilitating her." He gave the coach a thump to see if the wooden doors were sound. Most of the damage was cosmetic, just as he'd thought.

"Just like Her Ladyship letting things go to this extent."

Ember shrugged. "My father didn't exactly leave a fortune behind."

"No, but your stepmother's priorities—"

"Are none of your business, Tom." Ember lifted a brow.

"Except now she needs her carriage, and it's you who's got to risk life and limb to patch yon roof because she's turned off all the servants and I can't clamber up a ladder like I used to."

Ember gave a sharp glance Tom's way but felt himself soften. Tom and Victoria were like family to him, and like family, he hadn't really noticed how much they'd aged. It occurred to him that they might not actually be up to their jobs anymore. Thank goodness Victoria had Geoffrey for the heavy lifting.

Tom, though … Tom only had him.

"I'll get it done first thing, once the horses are cared for tomorrow." He told the old man. "Then we can take the wagon to town together for supplies."

Tom swallowed hard. "I don't want to let you down, Lord Carlysle, I won't be much help."

"I understand. It's not really your job, is it?"

"I'm a dab hand with paint. I can do that."

"Can you?" Ember smiled. He hadn't been looking forward to that.

"Aye. I'll take care of that if you'll let me. I promise, the coach will shine like a beacon."

"Goddess, I hope not."

Tom laughed and clapped him on the shoulder. Then he

sobered. "It's a crying shame to see the place go to ruin like this. When the master was alive—"

"Tom, do you truly not understand the position Lenore was in when my father died? She made economies in order to focus on the future of Carlysle. Her girls are expected to marry well. Their deportment, their lessons, and their clothing are investments that could pay off handsomely. You know that's how this works."

"But you're the earl. Should that not rate some consideration?"

"No, because marriageable young omegas are a valuable asset, and I'm"—he waved his hands—"not. I'll probably have to marry well below my station. What woman would have a penniless omega?"

"Your status is not your station, boy. You're the Earl of Carlysle."

"Yet the very best I can do, according to Lenore, is some burger's daughter whose family is looking to climb the ladder by marrying upward. To them, I'd be a purchase, like a fine horse or a fancy carriage." He kicked the coach's wheel. "To everyone else, I'd be a punchline What's worse than living off some social-climbing merchant's girl?"

"If it comes to that, at least pick a girl you can love." Old Tom wore a serious expression. "Life is made vastly more bearable by love."

Ember snorted. "I never knew you were a romantic."

"Oh, aye. Victoria caught my eye and held it back in the day. She's a beauty, and she'd got a saucy wit. I fell so hard. Chased her until—as they say—she caught me. Been married nearly forty years."

"That long?" Ember gasped. "What's your secret?"

"Besides not dying?" Tom smirked. "She claimed my heart the moment our eyes met."

"That's nice." Love either worked out, and you called it fate, or it ended in disaster. Starry-eyed optimists—be they human or wolf—believed in love. Ember didn't.

"You'll find your mate." Tom gave his shoulder a shove. "Probably when you least expect it. It's destiny."

"Then why are there so many unhappy people in the world?"

"Because destiny isn't easy. A man's free to fight his fate. Suppose I thought Victoria was too much work. Suppose I went off looking for a more-docile lass."

"Knowing Victoria? She'd have hunted you down and killed you on the spot."

"Aye, she would have," Tom agreed. "If you don't grab hold of love when life offers it, the windows of heaven close. Nothing will go right after, mark my words."

"Old Tom, I'd have never taken you for a moon calf."

"Fine. Hush." The old man rolled his eyes.

"All I know is that I need to get this coach fit for a couple of fairy-tale princesses by the full moon."

Tom frowned. "Make a list of the things we'll need and I'll go into town for them."

"While you're there, pay close attention to the wealthier young merchants' daughters. See if you can find a nice one for me. I might even steal a march on my sisters."

"Oh, I'll keep that in mind, Lord Carlysle," Tom said dryly.

～

*T*hat night, as Ember drifted in the liminal space between awake and dreaming, he'd come to the conclusion that among all the wolves and humans of the world, titled and common, he occupied no concrete space. There was no advantageous marriage for him. He'd either have to choose with an eye for satisfying someone else's notions of propriety, or he'd have to wait and see if the Goddess had a mate for him.

He came into contact with so few people these days, it was

more than likely that he'd never meet his Goddess blessed, or true mate if one even existed. He supposed he should begin preparing himself to find them. He should open his mind and his heart to the possibility, at least.

Had the Goddess created someone for him?

If he went into the world, would he on the precipice of destiny or disaster?

He rolled over and tried to sleep, but he was restless. He had a fortnight until the full moon. Fourteen days to prepare the carriage for the ball. Tom would paint it black as midnight again, and Ember would polish it with beeswax until the wood shone like fine furniture. Since the ball was at night, it would pay to fix the lanterns. Lenore would want him to repaint the Carlysle crest on the doors. *His* crest, not Lenore's, not his sisters', but *his* to share or withhold if he chose.

He loved his sisters. He wanted to give them the fantasy of a lifetime. He wanted them to feel as confident, safe, cared for, and loved as Ember's father would have made them feel, but how could they if they were forced to wear old gowns and arrive in a coach that had looked worn ten years ago?

How could they feel cherished if the Earl of Carlysle didn't value them enough to make a sacrifice for them?

Weak moonlight filtered through the windows. It was just enough to see the outline of his hands.

Whatever Tom said about him being the earl, whatever value Victoria wanted to put on his name and title, the title was meaningless without the wherewithal to keep up appearances.

Ember wanted a brilliant world for his sisters. He wanted to build his stables' reputation throughout the kingdom. He wanted to wrest control of his home from Lenore.

What was his fate, and where did his destiny lie?

Ember had to create his own destiny.

He drifted to sleep with the determination to figure out how.

CHAPTER 4

*T*he following morning, Ember knew what he had to do. He went to the stables, as was his habit, and spent some time with Beauty and Beau, giving them an extra ration of oats and grooming them carefully before leading them out to the pasture.

Beauty stood guard over her foal while he gamboled over the dew-soaked grass then grazed patiently while he nursed.

After a long while, Beauty came to the fence, where she inspected Ember for possible treats. He pulled a small apple from his pocket and held it out for her, his throat burning as she delicately took it from him.

"You probably won't understand what I'm doing." He rubbed her nose while she ate. "I don't know if it's the right thing. It already hurts."

She ran off to chase Beau around, oblivious to Ember's heartache. She and Beau seemed so happy playing in the sunlight. They were healthy. Beautiful. They had not a care in the world.

None of that would change, he would see to it.

Kelleher Hall was their nearest neighbor, and Lord Kelleher

had coveted Beauty for years. If Ember was going to sell Beauty to anyone—and he had to do it for his sisters' sake—Lord Kelleher was the perfect choice. He cared for his stable in much the same way Ember did, although he had plenty of servants to take the burden from his own shoulders. Kelleher was a fair man. He'd pay a high price and treat Beauty and Beau well.

Ember's heart ached at the thought of losing them. He loved all of his horses. For ten years, they'd been his best friends. Each one was unique and special in some way that only he knew because only he had spent the time to get to know their likes and dislikes, their quirks, their mischief.

Beauty, though … she had always been his favorite mare.

He'd long thought of her and her progeny as the future of Carlysle.

Now Ember understood that *he* was Carlysle's future. His decisions. His character and his sacrifice would create Carlysle's future. Carlysle was family, and his would thrive because of his actions—not his buildings, or furnishings, or livestock.

"Tom," he called to the old man. "I need you to take a note to Kelleher straightaway."

"Can it wait? I'm fixing to cut some firewood for Victoria."

"No. It must be now. Wait for his reply, will you? He'll probably follow you back. I'm offering Beauty and Beau for sale."

"You what?" Tom stared at him as though he were mad.

"You heard me." He gave Tom the note he'd written at dawn that morning. There was no turning back now. "I'd like to get this business done before noon today. Don't dawdle."

Tom shot him a hurt look, and he was right to be hurt by Ember's curt tone. Ember couldn't find it in himself to reach out to the man just then. His heart was breaking. Perhaps he'd have the opportunity later and perhaps not. It didn't matter.

The only thing that mattered just then was moving forward.

*J*n the early afternoon, Lenore searched him out. He was in the kitchen eating a late luncheon at cook's table, where he always hoped to avoid confrontations. Unlikely, given that Lenore had a cool, unhappy expression on her face that meant she was disappointed yet again.

"Ember, I understand you plan to send Tom to purchase supplies in town. I don't have to tell you, I'm sure, that funds are quite dear right now. As much as I would wish otherwise, there's virtually nothing in the way of cash for expenses."

"As to that"—he pulled a fat purse from his pocket and laid it on the table in front of her—"I want you to have this for the girls. I believe there's enough there for ballgowns and whatever fripperies a young woman needs for a ball. Fans and the like."

"I don't understand." Her shock was palpable. She sat heavily and hefted the purse before loosening the strings and looking inside. Ember was delighted to see he could surprise her. "Where did you come by this money?"

He didn't tell her. He was still a little raw about it. "Last night it occurred to me that this is a once-in-a-lifetime opportunity. Nora and Lu deserve the chance to meet every eligible alpha, and we know the king has likely invited every titled man in the kingdom. I believe we must throw all our resources at this opportunity. No sacrifice is too great for my sisters."

She cupped the purse with both hands. "What have you done, Ember?"

"Lord Kelleher has long coveted the mare, Beauty. This morning I sold her, along with the new foal, Beau, for enough money to fix up the coach and dress the girls as you see fit."

"My Goddess." Her face paled. "Thank you. You can't begin to understand what this will mean for Eleanor and Lucy."

"I believe I do." He flushed under her direct gaze. "Their happiness means a lot to me."

She cleared her throat, obviously moved by his gesture.

"Nothing has gone as I planned since my arrival at Carlysle. If the girls marry well, we have a chance to make things right. *You* will have the opportunity to live the life your father planned for you."

"You mean for me to publicly take my place as the Earl of Carlysle?"

She nodded. "Should your sisters find husbands at the prince's ball, their connections will be yours too. If they marry well, that means protection for you. Aligned with a powerful family, no one will dare look down on you for your omega status. And I promise we won't squander the chance you've given us. This ball is practically a gift from the Goddess."

He lowered his gaze. "Understood."

"You've given me more than enough to have footman's livery made as well." She took a deep breath and then released it. The tension left her shoulders. "I'll ask Geoffrey to play the role. One last indignity for the family, agreed?"

Why not? He lowered his gaze. "Yes, ma'am. Tom and I saved back some coin to get the coach ready. We'll take it into town and see it's done well."

"Really? You're going to town?"

"I feel it's the responsible thing to do."

"I see." She narrowed her eyes. "Now that you're a mature man, it will be obvious to everyone what you are. Tom will protect you as best he can but don't lose sight of your objective. Promise me you'll be careful, Ember."

"I will."

Once she left the kitchen, he frowned, troubled by her warning.

Surely he was safe enough in Carlysle Crossing? Even if every man there thought he was a freak of nature, they wouldn't act against the earl.

Victoria moved from the stove the moment Lenore left the kitchen.

"I can't believe you sold Beauty." She widened her eyes. "I thought she was your favorite. Tom says she's the cornerstone of all your plans?"

"It's for the best. You said it; the girls deserve to be presented as Lord Carlysle's sisters, not urchins. Appearances matter," he reasoned. "Is what Lenore said true? Will Tom really need to protect me?"

"Well, now." She sat beside him and took his hand as if he were still a boy. "If you were an omega girl, there would be no question of you going out in public until your debut and then only under a chaperone's care. No one in town will have ever seen an male omega. It pays to be cautious."

That still didn't make sense. "Why worry, though? I'm not some young girl. I can take care of myself."

Her lips quirked into a smile. "It's because you've come of age, and you're pretty as a peach. Best keep social interaction to a minimum. Don't call attention to yourself. Let Tom do the work for once and listen to his counsel. He's well aware of the dangers facing unwary omegas."

Ember still didn't understand. His status was different, unique. He didn't want everyone to know he was an outlier but he couldn't see how being a male omega could be dangerous for him.

Lenore kept Lucy and Eleanor under strict lock and key at Carslyle, but Ember assumed her rules were meant to protect them. Omegas were wolves in that they each had wolf's nature. But unlike alphas and betas, omegas couldn't shift. A young omega was therefore defenseless in a world where wolves and humans alike might wish to take advantage.

Ember couldn't shift either, but he was no delicate girl.

Unfortunately, he wasn't as manly as an alpha either. Perhaps that's why Lenore and Victoria were concerned. He favored his lovely omega mother. He had her dark curls, her brown eyes, and her delicate physique. Until very recently—

perhaps his nineteenth summer—he'd been as hairless as a child. It was only recently that he'd noticed his body maturing. Even then, as Eleanor had loudly proclaimed, he wasn't much of a specimen.

Perhaps what they were saying was he wasn't masculine enough to bargain for goods and services without being taken advantage of?

That stung.

How was he to assume his role as the earl if people thought him lacking? Ember was still mulling over the problem when he met up with Old Tom.

"Good news about the sale, eh?" Tom said. "If you're paying for the work, I'm confident you can have the coach looking splendid in no time."

Ember nodded though he winced at the memory of parting with his precious Beauty. It had been painful to let the two horses go even though he'd known he was doing the right thing.

"I'll get Jasper and Juniper and meet you at the coach house. A good trial run will give them the opportunity to relearn how to work as a team."

"That's right," Tom agreed. "Those rascals haven't had to pull a coach in years."

"They were used to pulling the coach at one time. With prac-tice, they'll be fine. A trip to town will also tell us if there's anything we haven't planned for with regards to the coach."

Goddess forbid there were structural problems, rotted axels, or unsound wheels. It wasn't just their family's standing at stake. He wanted his sisters safe as well as successful in their husband hunt.

A successful ball meant good things for everyone. *At last.*

∼

om worked some magic on the aging tack, identifying the pieces most likely to survive a trip to market and putting the others aside to make necessary repairs. Ember already knew those things needed replacing. He'd planned a careful, leisurely drive for that reason.

Jasper and Juniper seemed eager to be put in the traces, even after such a long time. They'd been quite young the last time they drew the coach.

"I'm glad we're taking the horses out like this," said Tom. "Seems like Jasper has forgotten everything he ever learned about teamwork."

"They'll settle down once we're on the road."

Ember had absolute faith in all the Carlysle horses. He knew better than anyone their capabilities, their likes and dislikes, their fears. They'd been his only friends through much of his life.

Halfway to town, Ember slowed the coach to a stop, clicked, and gave them their heads. From that moment onward, Jasper and Juniper moved forward in perfect unison.

"Told you so." Ember grinned at Tom.

"You've a talent with the beasts, boy. Everyone knows."

"Not everyone." Most people assumed Tom was the Carlysle horse whisperer. Until today, he'd allowed Lenore to keep the business aspect of their stables on the quiet. Being *in trade* was the kiss of death, according to Lenore. Plus the less it looked like they needed money, the higher the price they could ask. "I think after this morning our secret's out. Lord Kelleher knows I'm the one who looks after the horses."

Ember laughed happily at the image of an earl as a horse trader.

"Blast. Lenore won't be happy about that."

"Don't see why earning a living is frowned on," said Ember. "I feel quite proud I have a skill I can exploit on my sisters' behalf. How's that different from hunting when what I bring home goes to feed them?"

"Filthy lucre, my lad. Everyone wants it, but no one can be seen trying to earn it."

"Goddess forbid people are seen to be working." There was no shame in it for him. The Goddess made him an omega. That was why he was gifted in his work with animals; they didn't fear him as they would an alpha. If the stables earned funds for the Carlysle family, he'd call it a blessing.

Out on the road with the sun on his shoulders, and a bright fall breeze rippling through his hair, Ember grew certain this was his moment.

Today he planned to make his ambiguous *gift* pay off.

CHAPTER 5

$\mathcal{E}$mber drew the coach to a stop at the livery stable, where they could leave the coach and horses while they made inquiries. Excitement built within him as he and Tom strode through town; he was awed by the scene before him. The town had grown in size, the number of people in the marketplace probably double what he recalled.

He quickly got caught up in the hectic pace. He had to wonder: if this was what their local town was like, what must it be like in the city of Moonrise Bay, the capitol city of Helionne? What would it be like for the girls in Spindrift Palace, the royal family's home on Mount Ehrenpries, where the prince's ball was to be held? Ember hardly believed he'd get to see both the palace and the city for himself.

Tom had a list of things to purchase for Victoria, so while the two of them saw to that, Ember allowed himself to study the modestly dressed young ladies around him. Were these the girls Lenore was referring to when she mentioned "wealthy merchants' daughters?" At the mercantile they were served by the owner's daughter. She was well spoken and dressed fashionably. Her manners were impeccable.

Of course, she didn't recognize him. None of these people had seen him in more than ten years. But the way she stared at him—the way she blushed and batted her eyelashes—made him uncomfortable inside. It was as if she knew something he didn't.

As they left, Ember heard her giggling with two other young women.

His face caught fire.

"Look at you blush." Tom clapped a hand on his back. "Best get used to being the loveliest man these lasses have ever seen. I imagine there will be a lot of folks who don't quite know what to make of you."

"Great." Ember grimaced.

"One good thing, they don't know you're the earl yet. There's a bit of freedom in anonymity. Enjoy it while you've got it."

Right. Anonymity. Not for long. He was probably the only male omega they'd ever meet, and that would bring him not anonymity but notoriety.

Everywhere they went, breathless, giggling girls stared at him like poleaxed cows. Yet try as he might, he found it almost impossible to imagine himself falling for any of them. They reminded him too much of his sisters. The emotions they engendered in him were the deeply protective ones—all instinct —driven by his wolf.

His wolf, in fact, had risen to the surface, making him more reactive and emotional than he'd ever been in his life. Some of this he credited to deep grief. The last time he'd been to market, he'd been between his father and mother, holding their hands and begging for sweets.

The rest of his unease was purely instinctive. He could feel people's stares. Human and wolf eyes alike measured his progress as he moved between shops. His human side told him it was only natural for people to be curious about a newcomer in their midst. The wolf in him wanted to hide.

Was that normal?

His shyness was made worse by the fact that there was no one he could ask about all his feelings. Victoria and Tom would likely understand, but he'd feel like a fool going to them about something so personal. His omega sisters had never even been in public.

He'd die before he asked Lenore.

At some point, he started getting strange looks from male wolves—alphas and betas alike. Over the course of an hour, their expressions went from disapproval to downright hostility. His wolf felt pursued, as if enemies were closing in on him from all sides. The wolves' curiosity made hair prickle on the nape of his neck.

After one particularly fraught near-confrontation with an alpha in the street, he turned to Tom in hopes of the rescue Victoria had promised.

"What's happening right now?" he asked urgently. "Why are the alphas looking at me like that?"

"They sense what you are." Tom glanced around and leaned toward Ember. He lowered his voice. "Keep your eyes down and try to walk with purpose."

"Wait. Why does it turn them into belligerent—"

"Not here." Tom took his arm. "We need to get the rest of our work done quick as we can now."

Ember took a discreet look back. He spotted two alphas watching him like the predators they were.

As Tom dragged him away, they were joined by a third.

Goddess, has everyone gone mad?

Tom hauled him roughly across the dusty road to the farrier's, where they'd hoped to get an opinion on any tradesmen who might be able to repair the coach. Ember entered the smith's shop through the blast of heat coming off the forge and gasped with awe.

There, standing shirtless and sweaty in the infernal glow of molten metal, was the most enormous man Ember had ever beheld. He seemed not to notice their presence, focused as he was on the metal he was hammering into shape. Each strike of the blacksmith's tool released a shower of sparks, like magic.

Ember's head spun. He had never seen such a man before.

The farrier was obviously alpha. Ember yearned to see his wolf. More than yearned. His cock filled, and he ached in places he was mortified to note were becoming slick with ... something. Goddess, what was happening to him?

His eyes bulged with horror. He grabbed hold of Tom's arm.

"We should go," said Ember.

"Don't be daft. We just got here. What's the matter, lad?"

That caught the alpha's attention, and both of them froze.

Ember remembered to lower his gaze. The farrier's hammer had stopped singing, but the silence seemed equally loud in Ember's ears—as well as in his cock and throbbing balls—when the clamor stopped. He stole a quick peek at the man again. This alpha didn't glare at him though Ember felt his gaze slide over his body.

Ember's spine tingled but not with fear.

That was reassuring, right?

Perhaps this alpha didn't see him as prey?

"A male omega," the man breathed the words with awe. "Now there's something you don't see every day."

"Um." Goddess, had Ember *squeaked*? "Probably not?"

The big man lay down his hammer. "Where did you come from, little one?"

"I—oh. Carlysle. The manor house—"

"I know Carlysle. The earl used to visit often when Pa ran the forge. He was always kind to me."

Ember's heart warmed. "Yes, my—" Tom gave him a hard nudge to remind him he was supposed to remain anonymous. "The earl was known to be a kind man."

Something in the alpha's eyes told him he wasn't fooling

anyone, but Tom had said to play the stable hand because of how it would look if the Carlysle heir rolled into the city with a ruined coach.

Lenore's censure would be swift and merciless.

"What can I do for you?" the blacksmith asked.

"We need the Carlysle coach repaired," Tom took over. "And the horses shod as the Carlysle lasses are to attend the prince's ball. Can't have 'em arriving in a wreck not used since the master passed."

"I see. The ball is set for the next moon, no?"

"Yes sir," said Ember. "It's short notice, but—"

"I know a few people who could help you with that, but others will be after the same workers."

"We can pay." Ember held up his purse. "If that's required to expedite things, we can negotiate."

The man nodded. "I suppose that will help."

"Fair warning," Tom said. "It's a wreck inside and out."

"You'll be wanting an upholsterer, then. You should begin there. I know a man whose work is luxurious yet fairly priced."

"And we'll need the exterior repainted," Ember said. "The Carlysle crest must be replaced on the doors to show that Lord Carlysle values his sisters."

That brought a soft smile to the blacksmith's lips. "Good lad. First, find Theo." He gave Tom directions to a shop on a street off the main road. "He'll undertake the upholstery and help you seek out others for the rest of what you need. If he can't do it, he'll point you to someone who can."

"Thank you. You've been very helpful." Ember wanted very much to shake the blacksmith's huge hand, but that didn't seem prudent. Instead, he turned to leave.

"Wait." The blacksmith beckoned. "It'd be best if your young friend stayed here while you make inquiries, don't you think?"

Tom's gaze narrowed. "The boy comes with me."

"I'm not a *boy*." Ember narrowed his eyes. "I'm—"

"You're out of your depth out there, that much is plain," the farrier said. "It's best the lad stays away from the townsfolk. He's safe with me."

That seemed to Ember like an excellent suggestion and not just because he was drawn to the farrier like a moth to flame. He turned to Tom, hoping he'd agree.

Tom glared at them both. "I wasn't born yesterday, sir, begging your pardon. The lad is my responsibility."

"I can stay here with Mr. ..." Ember hoped to get the stunning man's name.

"Hugh," the farrier said. "Hugh Smith."

"I can stay with Hugh while you find Theo." Ember found a wooden benches and sat.

"Course you can." Tom grabbed him by the sleeve and dragged him to his feet. "Not happening."

"Why not?" Ember pulled back with a frown.

"I said the lad is safe with me, Tom," Hugh repeated.

"Well, you would, wouldn't you?" Tom waved Ember toward the door, but he stood his ground.

"You can find out the truth," Hugh spoke directly to Ember. To Tom, he added, "Let the boy ask his wolf if he's safe with me."

Ember was so confused. "Will my wolf know?"

"Your instincts come from the Goddess herself. He'll know if I mean you harm."

"All right. Go ahead, Ember." Tom looked none too happy, but wolf instinct was something he didn't have.

With Ember's wolf so close to the surface, he was already in danger of overtaxing his emotions. The dizzying scents of fire and alpha and horses filled his nostrils. Asking his wolf if he should be there seemed silly. Of course his wolf would want to stay. His wolf was fascinated.

Ember's head reeled, heavy with feelings he'd never known before, instincts he didn't know he possessed, desire that was wholly new to both his human self and his wolf. Shocking, acute sensory cues assailed him. He could *smell* the people walking past outside. He knew if they carried bread or fruit. He could hear their words without even straining to listen.

All of this was disorienting, to say the least. Hugh understood, though. He knew Ember was new to all this. If he stayed, Ember could probably ask him what it all meant. Dutifully, Ember asked his wolf if he was safe with Hugh, and the truth was right there: Hugh was safety *and* answers. Hugh was alpha, but he was kind. Hugh reassured him and made him feel protected.

When Ember could breathe again, he nodded toward Tom. In control for the first time since they'd arrived, Ember told Tom to leave without him.

"Hugh's right. For whatever reason, my presence was causing trouble on the street. It's best I stay here while you make our bargains with this Theo." He pulled out his purse and took out several coins, but he held back before handing them over. "Mind every penny. You know what this cost me."

"But—"

"Who is master here?" Ember asked quietly though he knew that Hugh would hear him. "It's all right, Tom. You may go."

"Understood." Tom stalked away from the forge, and that suddenly, Ember was alone with Hugh.

"So." Ember was still breathlessly aware of Hugh's bare chest. "I'm safe with you?"

Hugh smirked. "You are."

"Uh ... Must I be?" Ember didn't know where his bold words came from, but he couldn't stop himself from asking. His wolf was shameless. Why not, though? His wolf was apparently an animal filled with instincts and unsatisfied hunger. "Because—"

"Oh, sugarplum." Hugh chuckled. "The Earl of Carlysle isn't for the likes of me."

"You say that now, but—"

"No, sweetheart." Hugh put enough distance between them

that Ember's head cleared. "Simmer down, little wolf. Your time will come."

Ember huffed with disappointment. "Then can you at least answer my questions? Because I don't even know who I am right now. Everything's so bright, and I can smell things I've never …" He took a breath, closed his eyes, and swooned. "I can smell my *arousal*. Can you? Oh, Goddess."

Ember wanted to die.

"Sorry about that." Hugh barked out a laugh. "It's your omega fragrance. It's natural."

Ember's cheeks caught fire. "You smell really good."

"Thank you." Hugh folded his arms across his chest. "But maybe I should slip on a shirt while we talk."

Ember moaned. "Must you?"

"I must." Hugh picked up a smock and raised his arms to pull it on. The falling fabric drew metaphorical curtains over all of Ember's fantasies. Ember sighed. "You're kind of a scamp, aren't you?"

"I don't know about that. Maybe?" Ember answered.

Hugh studied him. "Is this your first time in town since you were a boy?"

"I haven't been here since my mother died."

"So, it's your first time as a mature omega, yeah? How old are you now, sixteen?"

Sixteen? "I'm twenty-one." Ember glanced away, mortified.

"Ah." Hugh nodded. "You're a late bloomer, then. And of course, your stepmother kept you well out of the public eye."

"How do you know that?"

"Servants talk."

Ember frowned at him. "We've barely had any servants for years."

Hugh snorted. "Turned-off servants talk the loudest. It seems to me that your stepmother prepared her girls to take their places in society, but you've been left to run wild. Is that why you're dressed like a groom?"

"That's right. I spend most of my time at the stables anyway. I love horses." The man was too astute by half. "This ball means everything to my sisters. They have the chance to meet alphas from all over Helionne and beyond her shores. I'm determined to do everything I can to see that they shine."

"Of course they'll shine," Hugh said a little bitterly. "It's up to omegas to accept their fate, marry the richest man, and push out noble babies year after year for the sake of their families, destiny be damned."

"Is that a bad thing?" Ember blinked. "It's traditional for noble omega girls to marry titled alphas. Everyone understands that."

"And if their hearts lie elsewhere? What then? I loved an omega once, and she loved me." Hugh glanced at his massive, callused hands. "You see these? They're strong, but even I couldn't hold what was most dear to me in the face of your noble *tradition*."

"Oh, Hugh." Ember realized too late that he'd stepped on Hugh's tender heart. "My stepmother may be ambitious, but I'm the earl. For what it's worth, I would never allow my sisters to marry someone they couldn't love, not even if it left Carlysle in ruins and me working at the livery stable here in town. My sisters are dear to me. I won't let them down."

"I knew you were special." Hugh's smile broke over Ember, as brilliant as the summer sun. "From the moment you walked in, I knew."

"I'm not special, I'm rare. A male omega." Ember sighed. "No one has ever said I'm special."

"The Goddess knows what she's doing. If you believe nothing else, believe that." Hugh patted his arm. Ember's heart gave a lurch. "You want to do right by your sisters? I vow to help you in any way I can."

Ember pictured the carriage in fine form. "The Carlysle crest used to glisten, even in moonlight. I think they must have used real gold in the paint in those days."

"The ball is to take place at the full moon. Your crest will glisten again, I promise." Hugh waited quietly while Ember got his emotions under control. "The Goddess has some plans for you, my one-of-a-kind omega."

"I sincerely hope not." Ember thought of his dead mother, of his stillborn sister. He thought of his father, leaving life all alone on the other side of the world. Those were the kinds of plans that the Goddess had for Ember's life. "Everything in my life has gone terribly wrong so far."

"I suspect that wasn't the Goddess's doing," Hugh said kindly. "You are not a freak of nature. You are the will of the Goddess made flesh. Her plans realign the world."

Ember thought on that for a while. "In the meantime, I don't suppose you could answer some questions?"

Hugh sat up straight. "I'll try."

"Do you know why my wolf exploded to life just now? If I'm overwhelmed in the market closest to Carlysle Manor, how will I take my family all the way to Spindrift Palace? I have to travel through Moonrise Bay. What if I lose control there?"

"Have you no wolves at Carlysle to guide you?"

Ember winced. "Lenore, Geoffrey, and my sisters. I doubt they know what to do with me."

"All right. Let's see if I can answer some of your questions. Shall we go inside?"

After Hugh banked the fire, Ember followed him to his private chambers, where he produced a palatable cup of tea and some stale biscuits. True to his word, he answered all of Ember's questions, offered advice on maintaining his focus.

Hugh also horrified him.

"Me?" Ember asked, aghast. "I could have … I could get … You *lie!*"

"It's true, Ember. All omegas bear children." Hugh offered him a clean handkerchief. "Our lore says male omegas—though they are as rare as sightings of the great comet—bear young the same as females."

"No ..." Ember felt all the blood drain from his head. "I need to lie down."

"Here." Hugh pushed Ember's head between his knees. "Breathe, Ember. And don't be afraid of your nature. Your wolf will know what to do when the time comes."

"I knew it!" The door flew open with a loud crash. Tom took in the scene: the tea, the biscuits, Hugh holding Ember's head down while he desperately tried to maintain consciousness, and frowned. "What's going on here?"

"Wolf business, don't be an idiot," Hugh answered. "Ember will be all right. Give him a minute."

Tom narrowed his eyes. "While you were busy with *wolf business*, I've secured Theo for the work on the coach. He's bringing a wagon to return us to Carlysle. We can come back to check on his progress whenever we like."

"That's wonderful." Ember felt so relieved. He lifted his head and turned to Hugh. "We left the coach and horses at the livery stables. The horses will need to be shod."

"Your wish is my command," Hugh said with a slight bow.

"They're called Jasper and Juniper. Beware because Jasper's a clown. He'll nibble your cap or even your hair if you let him." Ember stood.

"I'll be aware."

"Thank you for answering my questions. It's a lot to take in, though."

"Talk to your stepmother. She may surprise you."

"Thank you, Hugh."

"All in the service of the Goddess, little wolf."

Ember followed Tom outside and winced when the fiery rays of the afternoon sun tried to blind him. At least now he knew his senses would heighten any time his wolf came close to the surface.

Hugh had told him to reassure his wolf that his human side was in control. That seemed to help. His senses and emotions evened out when his wolf felt safe. Thank the Goddess for Hugh, who had answered his questions and bade him treat each part of himself as a separate entity with unique needs.

Now, Ember consciously called his wolf to reassure him that his human side could and would keep them safe, even in town where alphas and betas outnumbered omegas ten to one.

Then he wondered ...

Had his wolf been reassuring *him* all along? Had it been his wolf making him feel strong and capable while he cared for the animals at Carlysle? While he roamed and hunted the woods?

One thing seemed clear. Ember was fully equipped for the life he planned to live. He ought to look forward to the prince's ball instead of dreading it.

A man he assumed was Theo stopped his wagon close to the curb. He held the reins of a bay gelding with a grizzled muzzle. Ember climbed into the wagon, and Tom climbed up after, trapping him between Tom and Theo.

"Tell me the truth," said Tom. "Hugh didn't overstep or try to take advantage?"

"Of course not," Ember said hotly. "Hugh was wonderful. He was patient."

"Fine. Good for him. Wait, what did he need this patience for?"

"Goddess, remember his muscles? He was spectacular, really." Ember turned to Theo. "Don't you think Hugh is spectacular, Theo?"

Tom and Theo exchanged glances.

"Maybe." Theo tried to hide his smile.

"He's kind too." Ember sighed again. "He said I was special."

Tom grunted. "All right. I believe we've heard enough about Hugh."

"Plus he answered all my questions."

Tom shook his head and glanced away but not before saying, "Guess he answered a few of mine too."

CHAPTER 6

*S*even whole days passed before Ember was allowed to travel to Carlysle Crossing again. Seven *long* days, where seamstresses swarmed the manor like indignant pigeons, Lenore drilled Eleanor and Lucy mercilessly in deportment and dance and elocution, and Carlysle's three remaining maids burst into tears with the regularity of clockwork.

Ember and Geoffrey suffered painful fittings for livery. Despite his misgivings, Ember felt rather splendid when the clothes were finished. As "first footman," Geoffrey was to wear a finely embellished cutaway coat over an embroidered waistcoat in the Carlysle colors, forest green and cream, along with black trousers tucked into knee-high boots. As coachman, Ember's forest green coat was longer and plain, with a single row of buttons down the middle. His black trousers were fuller through the thigh and also tucked into tall, shiny boots.

The two of them made a handsome picture, but Lenore openly lamented that the sweet beta Geoffrey was neither handsome enough nor tall enough to be a footman in one of the great houses.

"Never mind her," Ember told him when they were alone again. "Think how Tom would look in that outfit."

That got Ember one of Geoffrey's sunny smiles.

Feeling more like a pincushion than a person over the course of several days took its toll. Ember found himself spending more and more of his time in the stables, out hunting alone, or in his room, contemplating all of the things he'd learned from Hugh.

All omegas could get *pregnant*?

The concept simply wouldn't sink in.

For one thing, Carlysle was a country estate. Ember had spent most of his life around livestock. Admittedly, most of their animals were horses, but he knew how breeding worked. He'd seen mares in heat and stags in rut and countless animal offspring born.

He knew where babies came from, and nowhere in the nature he'd studied all his life did males bear young.

It was unfathomable.

It was obscene.

It had to be some joke Hugh was playing because of Ember's naïveté.

Ruminating on the subject, Ember went so far as to lock the door to his rooms, strip off his trousers and smallclothes, and look at himself—which took some doing, honestly—in the cheval mirror. From the front, from the back, upside down, and with his legs sprawled open like one of Lucy's broken dolls he could see nothing that was not … er … standard equipment for the male of the wolf shifter species. It was impossible.

It *had* to be a joke.

Yet Hugh had been so serious when he spoke of an omega's role in childbearing that Ember found he couldn't be certain.

Once dressed again, Ember headed for the library to see if there was something—anything—in his father's books that might provide a clue.

There were books on animal husbandry, the family's ancestry, their history, wolves in general, omegas specifically, and after what felt like hours of reading, things were no clearer to Ember at all.

After he'd snapped the last volume closed, he realized he'd been so engrossed that he'd missed someone entering to light candles and set a fire in the fireplace. Probably Millie, the overworked tweeny. He'd have to thank her if he saw her, though Lenore would wince and call it unseemly.

Speak of the devil, Lenore's measured footsteps stopped outside in the hall, the knob on the library door turned, and the handsome older woman came inside, head held high.

She brushed some imaginary bit of fluff off her skirts and studied him. "You've been reading?"

He eyed the stacks of books guiltily. "I'll put everything back as it was."

She came farther into the room, stopping beside the table where he'd discarded the books that bore no fruit.

"Hmm." She moved a couple so she could see the titles and eyed him contemplatively. "*The Omega Mystique? The Puissance of the Positive Omega?* What are you looking for, exactly?"

He flushed deeply. "Just some information."

"I understand." She sat opposite him, and he felt his heart sink. "I'm an omega if you have questions."

She must have seen the surprise on his face because her lips quirked uncharacteristically. Judging by other woman, he thought the unfamiliar expression might have been a smile.

"I know I come off as … unsympathetic. I never imagined I'd find myself in this position, alone with children to raise and few resources. I suppose I've let myself become cold."

His gaze travelled to her clasped hands. "I don't see you as—"

"Please, don't humor me." Her laugh sounded rusty. "All of this has been most difficult for you, I'm sure." She relaxed in her chair. "Why don't you pour some brandy, Ember. I believe we could both use a fortifying drink."

Flabbergasted, he did as she asked. He returned with two snifter glasses, a modest pour in each.

She sipped delicately and made a face. "*Swill.*"

He didn't drink.

"Don't get me wrong, I purchased this cheap stuff, but I would honestly kill for a glass of cognac imported from the vineyards in the Lustére River Valley, where I was born."

Her candor was unprecedented. He wouldn't speak and ruin it.

"You can't imagine the light there, it's golden. Picture a wide blue sky, and year-round sunshine falling over fields of lavender and grapevines as far as you can see. Everything is rich with life, the soil so black and fertile it yields the finest wines in the world. We had the rarest liquors, the best perfumes, food so delicious it nourished your soul as well as your body.

"Imagine bringing your little omega daughters from that to this land, which while beautiful, has distinct seasons. Imagine your mate leaves one day on a quest to give you the life he dreamed of for his family, and you wind up virtually penniless, alone in a foreign land."

"I'm so sorry for your losses, Lenore." Ember discovered it was true. He ached for her almost as much as he mourned for his parents.

"Imagine, then, you find yourself the guardian of something uncanny. Something you don't understand. Something—" She stopped herself.

"An abomination."

"I don't think that." She shook her head. "I *never* believed that. But I wondered—"

"What to do with it?" he asked hoarsely. "Me?"

She nodded. Took another sip. "Nobles are no better than livestock traders. We wear fine clothing, but we buy and sell our children for land, for power, for money or prestige. I hope I can be forgiven for placing higher stakes on the assets whose value I understood. My girls might marry princes. Dukes."

"And what can I be but a curiosity?" he asked bitterly. "Should I be glad you didn't sell me to the circus?"

"Cruelty doesn't become you, Ember." She glanced away, swallowing hard.

Ashamed of his outburst, he looked into the fire. He saw the many, many times he'd interpreted this woman's actions as selfish and uncaring.

"I'm sorry," he admitted. "I didn't understand your position."

"I married your father, bringing with me little girls who took his attention away from you, and then he died. It's a wonder you didn't murder us in our beds."

"So neither of us is as horrible as we might have been."

"If this is to be a night of confessions,"—she swallowed the last sip of her brandy and held out her glass—"I believe I'll have a second drink."

He poured them both another. His first glass had already heated his blood, warming his belly and thawing his heart toward this woman he'd never understood.

"Why are you researching omegas?" she asked. "I've found no mention of a male omega in your family ancestry, nor any written account of another like you. Not here anyway. Believe me, I've looked."

"Perhaps it's been so long that any record has been lost."

"Yet a male omega is not unheard of, is it? It's in the spoken lore," she said thoughtfully. "The children's tales. I recall a fairy story my nurse used to tell me about a little boy omega who grew up to be a sorcerer or a king or—"

"Mother told me that one." He had thought she'd made it up. "She said male omegas were always destined for greatness as they embodied all the qualities of our kind."

"Do you believe her?"

"Would you? Given the historical literature never mentions a male omega at all? If there was ever another, he's now nothing more than a story."

"You're frightened," she observed with some surprise.

"Of course, I'm frightened. I have no idea what to expect. And now Hugh Smith says—" He shut his mouth with a snap.

She leaned forward. "What does he say?"

This was unbearable. How could he say it?

He closed his eyes and blurted, "Hugh says all omegas bear young."

"He said that? Really?" Her eyes widened with shock. "He told you that, even though there's nothing *anywhere* in the written records that proves male omegas even exist, much less that a male omega carrying a child is possible?"

"He must have heard it somewhere." Ember shrugged, feeling suddenly foolish. "He believes it, at any rate."

She drew in a breath. "That must be a tall tale, Ember."

"Like the existence of male omegas is a tall tale?" He gripped his glass tightly. "I'm not a myth."

"I can well understand your anxiety. Have you consulted your wolf?"

"I believe he's as in the dark as I am," Ember said dryly.

"What do you want?" she asked. "I mean, if the male omega isn't a fairy tale, how do you see your happily-ever-after?"

Unbidden, the image of an alpha like Hugh came to his mind. The manor restored. Sons and daughters. But those were a female omega's dreams. Impossible for an anomaly, a freak of nature to achieve.

Weren't they?

"Whatever my dreams are, I'm the Earl of Carlysle. Eleanor and Lucy must be settled well. I want them to be happy. I must make sure you're provided for."

Her eyes glittered, and she turned away for a moment. When she turned back, she wore her usual aloof expression. "Once the girls are established in their own homes, I plan to return to my homeland. I have relatives there. You will no longer need to worry about me."

"I see." His throat burned at her words. "You know you're always welcome here, though."

She nodded. "Now you see why this ball is so important to me. Resources aren't endless. If we can make a match for them now, I can't tell you what it will mean for all of us."

"I understand, Lenore. But hear me. My sisters aren't *livestock*. They must both be satisfied with their choices in their hearts and in their minds—not simply in our pocketbook. I hope they find their true mates but at the very least, they must marry alphas they can love. This is my final word on the matter."

"Of course," she said dismissively. "Although a girl must listen to her mother when—"

"That's where you're wrong, Lenore." He put his glass down and leaned forward. "Whether I'm dressed as a poor relation or playing the part of John Coachman, I am twenty-one, which makes me Lord Carlysle by law. And while I might allow you to negotiate their omega marriage contracts, it is *I* who will be signing them."

She frowned, ready to fight. "You—"

"I will not surrender either of my sisters to a man who cannot win their hearts. My sisters are not for sale to the highest bidder but only meant for the finest one."

She slumped limply back into her chair. "I have underestimated you from day one, haven't I?"

"Possibly."

"All this time, despite your grievances, you have been a kind and generous brother to both my girls. They love you." Lenore rose and walked to the door. Before she gripped the knob to exit, she turned back. "I could ask for nothing more."

~

*T*he following day, after the girls rode, and the stable work was finished, Ember bathed the stink off himself then rode to Carlysle Crossing with Old Tom by his side.

Their objective was to check on the coach's progress and make certain the work was moving quickly, as promised. With only six days left before the prince's ball, any potential problems needed to be addressed immediately.

Ember's private mission was to learn as much as he could about how and where Hugh got his information, and what on earth would make him believe this *male omega childbearing* nonsense.

As before, Tom grudgingly left Ember with Hugh Smith while he visited Theo and the other tradesmen. The sight of the brawny blacksmith at work was no less startling, no less ... er ... moving than last time. The alpha was a vision of manhood, a glaring reminder of Ember's slim omega stature and his failure to live up to any masculine ideal.

Oh, but Hugh was distracting. Very distracting. Ember forgot all the questions he'd planned to ask in the face of such a glorious specimen of male beauty.

"You'd better come in and have a cup of tea, Ember," Hugh said fondly. "You're looking overwarm."

Ember checked the corners of his mouth for drool as the alpha partially covered his forge to bank the fire.

Once inside Hugh's pleasant if humble home, Ember took a cup of tea and a couple of biscuits. He managed to gather his thoughts, mainly because Hugh had donned a shirt.

"You'll be gratified to hear your coach is coming along very well." Hugh brought a wooden chair and sat it near Ember's, facing the hearth. "The interior looks rich again, and Marcus Landry is working on the paint. Marcus's sister Lily is painting the Carlysle crest. She's quite the artist, for all she's still barely eighteen. Those two have Fae blood, you know. They're talented."

"How many people are working on the coach?" Ember asked. "Did I provide enough coins?"

"Did you?" Hugh shrugged. "The people of Carlysle Crossing remember your father and mother fondly. Some are throwing their lot in because they know that good marriages mean good trade in the future, but most simply want to see Carlysle Manor thrive again."

"Really?" Ember asked uncertainly. "They should still be paid for their work."

"Gil Glazier wouldn't have a shop if it weren't for your father and mother's help when his pa died. He's grateful for the opportunity to return their kindness. He replaced the coach's lanterns with fine brass fittings for pennies on the dollar."

"He shouldn't—"

"Ember, the people of Carlysle hold your family in high esteem despite the chill that fell over the manor when your father passed."

"I didn't know that," Ember said softly. "That's ... very kind."

"Kindness begets kindness, Ember." The word *begets* fell on Ember like an anvil. What a way to return Ember to his most pressing concerns.

"Goddess, you remind me. Last time you told me all omegas can bear young."

"I did." Hugh failed to smother his laughter "Is that what's got you so anxious?"

"Where are you getting your information? Because I searched the library at Carlysle, and—"

"You wouldn't find anything there, boy. Male omegas are so rare they're barely spoken of in whispers."

"That's my point. How can I believe you? There's no proof. And I looked, you know. I couldn't just take your word for it, so

I read everything about omegas that I could get my hands on, and I looked at my"—he dropped his voice—"*man parts* in a mirror. I looked at everything at length, and I honestly believe you must take me for a fool."

"Man parts—" Hugh sputtered and turned away with his hand over his mouth. A minute later, he turned back, eyes tearing. "Goddess. No, well ... you wouldn't necessarily see anything, I don't think."

"But—"

"What makes us wolves is magic, you numpty." Hugh shook his head. "You don't see my wolf in the mirror when you look either, but he's there when I shift."

"But omegas don't *shift*."

"You are still a *wolf*. You feel your wolf inside you, don't you? Is that not true?"

"Are you saying I have a lady wolf inside me? Because I can assure you, my wolf is as male as I am." He clenched his fists angrily. "That's probably not saying much when compared to an alpha like you but—"

"What do you mean, like me?" Hugh frowned.

"I mean a *quintessential* alpha. You have muscles on your muscles, a forest of chest hair, and do not get me started on how you smell." Ember lost focus as his gaze traveled over Hugh's perfect manly form.

"My eyes are up here," Hugh said fondly.

"Just because I'm not some bulked-up alpha doesn't mean I'm destined to find myself in a family way."

"Ember." Hugh sighed. "Magic is magic. It's inexplicable, occult, and mysterious. Magic makes us what we are. You are an omega because the Goddess wills it, no more and no less. There is a mystical reason for that fact, I'm sure. You must trust the Goddess to know what she's doing."

"I do, but what if there's no reason? What if my mother got

hold of a bad mushroom, and that's why I'm the way I am? What if I'm a mistake, like a lamb born with two heads?"

"A two-headed lamb? Have you seen one of those?"

"No, but—"

"You are not a mistake, Ember." Hugh went on gently, "There is lore surrounding your kind. Just because they're rare—just because no one has written about male omegas in the history books—it doesn't mean there haven't been any. Perhaps there are more male omegas out there, in seclusion or hiding what they are because the people around them don't understand them either."

Now there was a thought Ember had never considered.

"All right. Say I believe I'm not a mistake. What makes you say that male omegas can bear children like females?" he asked again. "That's the thing I want to know. Why are you so certain?"

"My instinct. My senses, maybe." Hugh tapped the side of his nose. "You smell like fertile earth to me, like every other omega. My wolf is certain. And you must bear this in mind when you're around other wolves, especially alphas, do you understand? You will not always be safe around alphas."

Ember did understand, based on his reaction to Hugh.

Hugh's very presence kept him breathless and aroused, his senses overcome by that delicious alpha scent, by Hugh's nearness.

"That's why I'm so drawn to you?" Ember asked.

"I am a *fine* example of an alpha." Hugh preened.

That seemed like a good sign to Ember.

He leaned into Hugh's space. "Then how about we—"

"I told you before"—Hugh backed away—"you are not meant for me."

"But could we not just test your certainty a bit? Maybe—"

"No, Ember." Laughing, Hugh laid his hand flat on Ember's chest and shoved. Though Hugh's stern alpha voice made

Ember want him all the more, Ember fell back into his chair with a laugh.

"Too bad." He gave a full body shiver.

"Cool down, little wolf. This is good training. Just imagine. You'll feel this same pull toward any alpha. That's your omega nature. Your stepmother has probably advised her daughters to resist an alpha's allure in order to hold out for a true mate. It's a shame she didn't give you the same training."

"So I must resist this feeling?"

"You *must*. Otherwise, it will be simple for an unscrupulous alpha to take advantage. That's why female omegas are kept home until they come of age. It takes practice to learn how to discern the difference between your wolf's excitement over any alpha from your wolf's desire for their true mate."

"Perhaps if my mother had lived, she'd have helped me understand my omega nature better."

"No doubt she would have."

"Thank you for explaining things. I'm still not sure I believe you." Ember valued Hugh's advice. He didn't feel like a freak around the alpha. Perhaps it was best that they remain friends rather than confuse things with rogue feelings that could only come from their wolves.

Hugh had already mastered denying his baser instincts. And while Ember might be bursting with curiosity, Hugh was right. Ember was not for him.

Ember's wolf knew: Hugh was not *his* alpha.

Two questions remained: Did he have a true mate? And how would a cash-strapped rustic like Ember ever find him?

CHAPTER 7

*E*ach day of final preparation seemed to last for months at home. The girls spent hours with their maids, trying different hair styles. Lenore moved about the manor with a frozen expression of false calm on her face.

For the first time since they'd met, Ember understood her.

He'd seen her true face, and he knew what she yearned for. Recent events had given him a glimpse of the battles she'd been fighting all alone.

If he wished she'd treated him the same as his sisters, if he wished she'd educated him as an omega, he couldn't blame her for her failures. There was no precedent for him. She'd been as ignorant as he was. It wasn't her fault if he was as much a mystery to her as he was to himself.

Besides. What if Hugh's nose was wrong?

Perhaps all he scented from Ember was *omega*, and he put the idea of fecundity into Ember's head for nothing.

Ember would worry about what it all meant later when he wasn't busy worrying about his sisters and the ball and the coach and the day-to-day care of the horses of Carlysle Manor.

Spending time outdoors seemed to help him with his anxiety

over the wait. He went hunting with Tom, and they came back with several pheasants and a sack of mushrooms. It felt good to do something normal for a change.

After a few such days, Ember noticed how their current common goal drew the people of the manor together. They talked more. They laughed—even Lenore.

They became more like a family through the adversity of a shared burden: the need to hide their lack of resources at all costs, at least at the ball. This turmoil brought the people of Carlysle together as nothing else ever had.

Lenore was ruthlessly practical. While she had nothing inside her that would coddle a heartsick boy, she did reward his acumen when it came to fixing the coach, just as she rewarded the girls when she deemed them acceptable debutantes. They were all under immense pressure to perform at all times. As they worked toward making the best showing at the prince's ball, any residual resentment between them disappeared.

The day finally arrived when Ember was to pick up the coach.

The morning mist clung to the trees, leaving everything glistening with droplets of dew. A spider web caught his eye, empty of its weaver but damp and lovely, casting rainbows as the sun rose higher into the sky.

"Are the girls riding today?" Tom asked as he joined Ember by the stables.

"Not today. We're to pick up the coach, remember?"

"Oh, aye." Tom said. "It's not like I could forget. What's wrong? You look like you had a bad night."

"Lenore is putting so much into this ball. I can't help but worry. What if it's all for nothing?"

"Then the girls will go to the next ball and the next. They're not going to be spinsters. They're far too lovely."

"But we have nothing to provide them with new gowns after this. I can't keep selling our horses."

"So they'll wear their older ones. *Lovely* covers a lot of short-comings, Ember. Also, they're bright and personable. Lucy'd melt in the rain, she's so sweet. Have no fear for your sisters. They'll do just fine."

"Goddess, I hope so."

"What about you?"

Ember jerked in surprise. "What about me?"

"Have you thought about what you want in an alpha?"

"Me?" Ember asked. "Are you mad? I told you Lenore said I'll have to make do with a burger's daughter. I don't believe I want to marry anyway. I think I'll spend my life building the finest stables in the kingdom."

"Come on, boy. I've seen you around Hugh."

"Hugh isn't my alpha."

"Maybe not, but someone is, don't you think? We tell omega girls that there's a special alpha waiting for them. It must be true for boys as well."

"We tell children the moon is made of cheese. That doesn't make it so."

"I guess we'll have to wait and see. Perhaps we should have a bet?"

"All right. If some alpha comes and sweeps me off my feet, I'll build a fine cottage for you and Victoria when you retire."

Tom laughed that off. "And if you end up alone? Will we be tossed out like baggage?"

Ember elbowed him. "In that case, the cottage I build for you won't be nearly as fine. I will take care of what's mine, Tom. Alpha or no."

"Master." The look on Tom's face was one of awe. Perhaps he understood that Ember was determined to care for Carlysle and everyone in it, now more than ever.

"So. Done and done." Ember was just entering the stables when he noticed a disturbance by the front gates. He and Tom turned to see a flock of birds rise into the air.

Was that music?

The two men moved quickly toward the sound even as Lenore opened the manor's fine front door, and the girls peeked out.

"Is it tinkers?" Lucy asked excitedly. "Or mummers?"

"I—" The sight of their coach coming up the drive gave Ember chills. "It's Theo. He's brought the coach to us!"

Ember ran to see what they'd done and then stopped, overcome by the sight. It wasn't just Theo who'd come. Marcus and his sister Lily, Hugh, Gil Glazier, and several other people he hadn't met danced merrily alongside Jasper and Juniper, who moved beautifully in synch.

"Everyone wanted to come and wish you well," Theo shouted as he tied off the reins and stepped down from the coachman's seat. "The people in the village have been abuzz with the news since the prince announced the ball."

"We want to see Carlysle make a name for itself again." Gil removed his hat.

"Thank you." Ember's voice cracked. "Your kindness will be remembered."

"Take a look," Theo prompted. Ember looked to the door where Lenore and his sisters stood.

"Sisters?" At the invitation, the girls left their mother and ran down the steps to join him.

Ember considered all the work they'd done. The coach looked amazing. It had probably never been that shiny or that luxurious before. The paint gleamed in the sunlight. Marcus must have painted it and then covered the surface with beeswax and rubbed until it glowed.

Ember ran his hand lovingly over the Carlysle crest on the door. He gave the lovely Lily a nod of his head, and she flushed with pride.

"Thank you, Lily."

"My pleasure, Lord Carlysle." She curtsied. "May your journey be a safe one."

"Oh, Ember, look," Lucy called from inside. He glanced through the window and saw there were soft leather seats and velvet curtains the girls could close for warmth.

"It's like nothing I've ever seen." Even Nora was taken by the elegance of the thing. "I'm speechless."

"That's got to be a first," Tom muttered fondly.

"Mother, come look! Just imagine how we'll look, all dressed in our ball gowns, arriving at the ball in this!" Lucy leaped from the carriage and hugged him, heedless of their audience. "Thank you, thank you. I have the best brother ever."

"You've done a remarkable job," Lenore told the waiting crowd. "We will cherish this coach. I know"—her voice cracked—"you held my late husband in great esteem. I think if he were here, he would have exactly the right words. I ... am not ... good like he was. But I thank each-and-every single craftsman from my heart. I will never forget the kindness you've shown here."

There was a smattering of applause. A couple of throats cleared.

"There will be refreshments, outside the kitchen." She seemed to surprise even herself with the offer. Equally surprised, Ember bade Tom help Victoria and Geoffrey with preparations. The man scurried off. "Please consider yourselves our guests."

"So, Lord Carlysle." Hugh approached him. "Is it everything you imagined?"

"And so much more. I can't thank you and Theo enough."

"We were all glad to help. The coach gave Theo the opportunity to explore another of his interests. Watch."

Ember turned to see Theo chatting with Lily while Marcus looked on with a wary eye.

"Ah." He understood. "Lily is very lovely."

"And talented and sweet. Theo is besotted. I believe he's

going to ask her to marry him soon. Your project gave him the chance to approach Marcus and soften him up to the idea."

"That's nice to hear." Ember clasped his hands behind his back. "I like to think I'm doing some good in the world."

Hugh's eyes appeared to lose focus when he said, "It might be your destiny to do just that."

Ember shrugged. "*If* I have a destiny, you mean, and I'm not some freak of nature."

Hugh glared at him. "I know you don't see it, but there is something inside you that makes others want to do better and be better. That's your gift, and you don't notice it because you're so busy trying to do better and be better yourself."

"You talk nonsense." Ember nudged him with his shoulder. "But I like you anyway. Help me get the coach inside the coach house, so we can celebrate with our friends."

Hugh and Theo helped him get the carriage put away. Gil led Jasper and Juniper to the stables. Tom set out a long table and opened a barrel of ale. Victoria placed a buffet of cheese and ham and bread before their friends, and though it was simple fare, it was welcome and created a festive atmosphere that lasted the whole afternoon. Ember couldn't remember a more festive event at Carlysle—not since his father and mother had passed.

Lucy and Eleanor partook but only as far as sitting demurely beside their mother while the music lasted. When Lenore went inside the manor house, they left with her.

At one point, Ember saw Lenore in the window of the study, and he wished she would have spent more time outside. His father might have coaxed her to mingle. As she'd pointed out, his father often found the right words. Instead, Ember lifted his mug to her, and she nodded to acknowledge his tribute.

Hugh watched him, so he decided to give in to any self-recriminations at a later date. Perhaps he was growing up, though, because he finally understood that the pain that isolated him from Lenore and his half-sisters was within his power to control.

It was too bad he was learning this on the precipice of change.

"Penny for your thoughts?" Hugh asked.

"I'd owe you change." Ember set his mug aside.

"This is good. Lenore was right to allow a small celebration. These people won't soon forget it, and they'll talk in town. It will go a long way toward cementing your reputation as the gracious earl."

"I'm fairly sure that's why she did it."

"Still. She didn't have to." He stood. "Do you mind coming with me, Ember? I have something to give you."

"Do you?" A frisson of warmth shot down Ember's spine. "What could it be, I wonder?"

Hugh gave him a playful shove as they left the table. "Not that."

"You don't know what I was thinking."

"You keep forgetting my alpha nose."

"Oh, Goddess." Ember wanted the earth to swallow him.

"Don't be shy. It's wasted on me."

"All right. What do you want to give me?"

"It's in the carriage."

Ember followed Hugh to the coach house. The coach still seemed to glow faintly, even in the gloom. Ember thought about lighting its lanterns, but like wearing dress clothes to the stables before church, he was convinced it would ruin things somehow.

"Am I right that this isn't only mundane craftsmanship?"

Hugh grinned. "Possibly."

"So there is magic at work here." He would not waste one second of the coach's magic before they set out on their journey the following night. Instead, opened the carriage doors to the afternoon breeze. "It feels different."

"There's always magic at work, Ember. And as an omega, you're more sensitive to it than most."

"Shouldn't I know what it's doing?"

"It's only a few protection spells, as far as I know. They're not something you need to worry about. This, though ..."

Ember followed Hugh to the back where there were three boxes lashed onto the footman's perch. Hugh held out the first, smaller and flatter. Ember took it from him.

"I had the seamstresses make this for you. You said your stepmother wants to make an impression."

Ember took the box from him and lifted the lid. Inside, he found a cloth festooned with tassels and embroidered at the corners with his family's coat of arms.

"It's beautiful," Ember let the silken tassels fall through his fingers. "The embroidery is so fine."

"It's a hammercloth." Hugh took it from him and spread it over the coachman's seat. "Just for show."

"Thank you." Ember didn't know what else to say. "But you didn't have to get me a gift. Your care of Jasper and Juniper was more than enough. Do you think I didn't notice how beautifully groomed they look?"

"I hoped you would."

"They glow like the coach."

"What can I say? They enjoy being brushed." Hugh gave Ember a second gift. "Here. This one is much more fun."

"Hugh—"

"Don't bore me with your gratitude. Just look."

The second package held a coat but not just any coat: a many-caped great coat such as the royal coachmen wore.

"Oh," Ember breathed. "I love it. The fabric is so soft!"

"Try it on. You're awfully small for the average coachman; I need to make certain it fits."

Ember slipped the beautiful garment over his clothes, and while it hung on him a little, he would never admit it wasn't

perfect. Was there an odor, though? It wasn't a new garment,
but—"

"I love it." The smell was definitely from another wolf. The
sleeves and the length were precisely right—as though the coat
had been measured for him—but the body of the coat was
wrong. Too big by far. He smiled his thanks. "It's brilliant."

Hugh reached out and pulled on it. Obviously, he was
observing its roominess. "It's meant go over your livery. You'll
thank me that it's not too tight after riding around in it for a
while."

"Oh." Ember flushed. "Of course, it's big."

"And that wolf you're scenting? I had a beta wolf wear it, so
it won't be obvious to anyone what you are, understand? Try to
keep it on as much as you can." He held out the third box, this
one square. "This is the best gift. I promise, you'll love it."

"Oh?" He lifted the lid on that one. Inside the tissue, he
found a squat top hat, complete with a jaunty little embellish-
ment with his family's crest. "Oh! I do love it. Hugh, this is the
most wonderful hat in the world." He placed it on his head. "And
see? It fits perfectly."

"Of course, it does."

"How can I ever thank you? You've been such a wonderful
help through all of this."

Hugh adjusted the tilt of the squat top hat on his head. "A
successful journey will be thanks enough. Get your sisters to the
ball and back in one piece."

"I will."

"And since you'll be forced to wait, my cousin Yancy owns a
coaching house I can recommend. It's called the Red Wolf Inn.
Ask for a private dining room."

"The Red Wolf Inn."

"That's it. Once you drop your sisters at the ball, head for the
Red Wolf. You'll find my cousin behind the bar; tell him I sent
you. He'll take good care of you."

"Thanks so much. I don't know what I'd have done without your help."

"You'd have been fine. The Goddess has a plan for you."

"You know what? I think she must since I have friends like you." Ember wished he had a mirror, so he could see himself in his fine coat and hat. "I will never, ever forget your kindness. I hope, as the new Earl of Carlysle, I'll live up to your faith in me."

"You already have, lad. You'll be a powerful man someday. I feel it here." Hugh touched his heart. "Don't let me down."

"I won't." Ember took off his coat and hat and placed them carefully inside the carriage along with the hammercloth Hugh had given him.

"Beware alphas, once you're at the inn," Hugh warned.

Ember turned back to him. "What?"

"Not all alphas will have your best interests at heart. I don't want to frighten you, but there are three rules you must not break. You're leaving Carlysle for the palace, so you'll be stopping in Moonrise Bay. The city will seem massive and impersonal to you. It's a port, so there will be traders and sailors from all over the world."

"I see. That means alphas, I take it."

"Many, many alphas. If the inn is busy, you should stay near the horses, in the stable. Whatever you do, don't engage with alphas."

"All right." Don't engage. He could do that. He held up a finger.

"If you must engage at the bar, leave when it's safe to do so. Don't allow yourself to be *alone* with any alpha."

Ember held up a second finger. "Don't be alone with an alpha. I've got it."

"And if worse comes to worse, and the temptation is impossible to overcome, under no circumstances should you let an alpha knot you."

Ember's jaw dropped. He knew what "knotting" was. Did Hugh imagine Ember would be as easy as a dog in heat?

"Say it, so I know you understand."

"I must not let an alpha knot me." He ought to have died just saying the words. Again, Ember wanted the ground to swallow him. My Goddess. He'd asked for this excruciating plain speech by being a naive ass about omegas. "You have my word, Hugh."

Hugh grunted. "There will be hundreds of coachmen, and they'll start to line up early to collect their charges after the ball. Be in line by midnight unless you want the girls to wait in the night air."

"I will."

"Tell me the rules again, Ember."

"I must not engage with alphas. I must not be alone with an alpha. I must under no circumstances let an alpha knot me. I must be in line to pick up my sisters at midnight."

"Very good." Hugh clapped Ember on the shoulder. "You're ready, lad."

Ember clasped his hands. "Thank you again."

~

*B*y dusk, the tradesmen left Carlysle tired but far merrier than they'd been when they arrived. Ember saw to the horses, especially Jasper and Juniper. He made sure the coach was safe then closed the doors and barred them.

Inside the house, he washed up and met his sisters at the table, where they were eating the same things the villagers had enjoyed—a light supper of bread and ham and cheese with a bit of fruit to liven the meal.

"I don't have to tell you how proud I am that as a family, we've accomplished all our goals," Lenore addressed all of them. "The rest is up to the two of you. I have no doubt you will charm the prince and all the alpha guests present. While we're at the ball, I expect you to take your cues from me. I've made a study of all the nobles who would be a good catch for you, but you must take the measure of each man. You must use your intuition. You must let your wolf tell you whether you should trust an alpha or pass him by."

"Our wolves know whether someone is trustworthy?" Ember asked. "Hugh taught me that."

Three sets of similarly hued eyes started back at him.

Lenore frowned before speaking. "I regret very few things, but the greatest is that I didn't train you as an omega. I was too narrow-minded to see that despite its rarity, your nature should have been my priority, at least as much as I prioritized my girls' omega nature. I fear I failed you."

"That's all in the past," Ember told her. "I understand now."

"Very gracious of you, but I don't absolve myself."

They stared at each other while the girls looked on, almost dazed by their exchange.

"Let me ask you this," Lenore said abruptly. "Did you feel safe with Hugh Smith?"

He nodded. "I did."

"Was your wolf aware of him as an alpha?"

"Very much so." At his admission, the girls giggled helplessly. "But my wolf helped me see he wasn't *my* alpha."

She gave him an approving nod. "Perhaps you learned what you needed without me. Nevertheless. In future, I plan to guide you. I'd like to be a better stepmother to you, Ember, if you'll allow it at this late date?"

"I will. Of course, I will."

Hugh said Ember made people want to do better. Is this what he meant? Could Hugh be right in saying he had a greater destiny than to be the lonely, aberrant Lord Carlysle?

Perhaps after the prince's ball, Ember might see his future clearly at last.

CHAPTER 8

$\mathcal{T}$he big day began with brilliant weather. The sun shone in a cloudless sky. Even though the temperature was moderately chilly when Ember put Jasper and Juniper in the traces, the day warmed quickly. A soft breeze brought with it the fragrance of wildflowers while birdsong crested to drown out the sound of horses' hooves.

Ember proudly drew the vehicle up to the steps of Carlysle Manor to retrieve his stepmother and sisters. Geoffrey, in his role as society's youngest, shortest footman, leapt down from his spot next to Ember to usher the ladies inside. Tom, Victoria and the maids stood by to watch them leave.

Lenore wore the deep purple and jet jewelry of Rhielôme widows in mourning. This surprised Ember though he didn't know why. He'd simply assumed she would want to be seen in a color better suited for a party since his father had been dead for ten years. Her adherence to mourning forced him to reevaluate the woman yet again. Had she actually loved his father?

Perhaps she truly had.

That was something to consider another day.

For their part, his sisters glittered like fairies in a painting.

Velvet cloaks covered them from head to toe, but their pale faces were dewy and pink with happiness. The occasional glimpse he got of their magnificent gowns showed gossamer light fabric sparkling with gemstones that Lenore had gleaned from her own gowns and jewels for the occasion. Nora wore blue to match her eyes. Lucy's violet gown made her eyes sparkle with an ethereal, purple hue.

For the first time since he'd known them, they looked like the princesses they were.

The Carlysle ladies' beauty did strange, prideful things to Ember's heart, despite his incognito capacity as their coachman. He wanted the world to know: Carlysle's daughters were cherished, loved, and worthy of any man at the prince's ball—even the prince himself.

If Ember wiped his eyes as Geoffrey seated his family and closed the coach's doors behind them, he planned to blame it on bees gathering pollen. Geoffrey swung up beside him, and their gazes met. It appeared his eyes were bothered by the activity of bees as well.

"Bye, we're really going!" Nora called to Tom and Victoria.

"Bye, Tom. Bye, Victoria! Bye girls, wish us luck!" said Lucy.

"You don't need luck, you're Carlysles." Victoria waved at them as she walked beside the coach for ten feet or so. "Go and do us all proud!"

"Bye, ladies!" Tom wasn't walking beside the coach, but he probably rubbed a rabbit's foot in his pocket or performed some other superstitious task.

Ember clicked to Jasper and Juniper, and they eased into a trot. Finally, Ember could let out the breath he'd been holding for a fortnight. He could do this. *They* could do this. They had already done the impossible and pulled together gowns and a coach along with a coachman and footman in livery.

He had Hugh's gifts, so he looked proper from his fancy hat

and greatcoat down to his boots. He maintained a steady hand on the whip. He could deliver his family safely.

Then he'd have a drink because by the Goddess, he would have earned it.

He smiled at Geoffrey, who smiled back and then howled to release the joy his beta wolf must have been feeling over their adventure. Ember tried out his own howl, but it came out more like a painful, drawn-out yip.

Red-faced, he decided he'd have to practice that in private.

"It'll come." Geoffrey nudged him. "When your balls drop."

"You're five years younger than me!" The brat. "Shut up."

As they came to Carlysle Crossing, Ember automatically tightened the reins to prepare for the traffic. Something seemed wrong, though. There were people lining the streets.

"Look," Geoffrey said with wonder. "They're waiting for us."

Ember gasped with pleasure. The road took them through the heart of town, and it seemed that every single person who lived there had turned out to bid them farewell. He saw Hugh first, dressed in a coat and breeches, with boots polished to a high shine. The crazy man doffed his cap as they passed as did the others, following his lead.

The ladies shouted, "Good luck," and, "Go get 'em," and, "Give us a Carlysle queen," as they went by, waving and tossing flowers into the street before them.

The girls had to be eating up all this attention. He heard them shouting their thanks at the noisy, cheering crowd of people they'd never even met, but who nevertheless loved them, loved their family, and wished them well.

Nothing had prepared them for this outpouring from the people whose livelihoods and fates were so deeply entwined with Carlysle Manor and the family who lived there. They'd been isolated at Carlysle Manor but not forgotten. The entire town wished them luck.

Ember passed the spectacle in a kind of humble shock until

the coach reached the actual crossing, and he maneuvered the horses onto the road that would take them to the sea. Their route would take them through a long, fairly boring stretch of farmland where mostly small houses dotted the landscape. Wildfire gossip had spread the news that the prince was having a ball, so here and there a curious family had come to the road to watch and wave as carriages passed carrying young omegas dressed in their finery.

Even horses and cows could be curious, and they dotted the pasturelands, lifting their heavy, sleepy heads at the sound of carriage wheels, only to seemingly shrug huge shoulders and go back to their grass as if to say they didn't see what all the fuss could be about.

For Ember, it was his first taste of true freedom. He lifted his sensitive nose to the wind to allow his wolf to scent the air. He detected animals, some he didn't even have names for, so many flowers, and trees, and then the sea—oh, so close—the iron-kissed funk of salt and ozone and some sulfur-laden *something* that was like nothing he'd ever smelled before.

"What's that awful—"

"Seaweed," Geoffrey answered with a wrinkled nose. "Smells rotten, don't it?"

"But also good," Ember said. "Does that make any sense?"

Geoffrey leaned back to inhale deeply. "Everything smells good because it's new and different from what we've had all our lives."

They smiled at each other, after which Ember kept his gaze on the road. He had a job to do. He could gawk when he was a passenger someday.

The light faded as they got closer to Moonrise Bay. Despite the night's promised moon, they needed to light the lanterns if they were to make the rest of their journey safely.

They pulled off at an overlook of sorts. "See if the ladies wish to stretch their legs?"

"Aye." Geoffrey swung down nimbly and let the Carlysle women out under Lenore's strict eye while Ember lit the lamps.

They all walked for a bit and came back ready to go the rest of the way.

"From here, the road will begin to congest as we go," Lenore said. "The streets in Moonrise Bay can be very narrow. Do you have a plan for where you'll pass your time?"

"Aye, ma'am."

She gave an eyeroll. "You're not really a servant, Ember. Call me Lenore."

"Lenore, sorry. Hugh's cousin has an inn. I'm to make myself known to him."

"If we don't get to speak properly before that, be cautious. No one can know what you are. If there are alphas near, which"—she eyed the horizon with some distaste—"there no doubt will be, don't—"

"Engage with alphas. Hugh warned me."

Her brows lifted. "What else?"

He was grateful for the ocean breeze when his cheeks caught fire. "Don't engage with alphas, don't go anywhere alone with alphas, under no circumstances let an alpha knot me—"

"Hugh said that?" Her eyes widened in shock. A smile touched her lips. "Well. I guess that's a good thing."

"And he told me I must get back in the coach line to pick you up by midnight, or you'll end up having to wait for me."

"I see." She shook the hem of her cloak out over her skirts and then stepped back. "Hugh is very wise. Carry on, then."

He tipped his hat. "Ma'am."

"Cheeky, Ember." Lenore winked at him. *Winked.*

Am I even awake?

Geoffrey helped the ladies inside and closed the doors. Ember grinned as he took the seat next to him.

"Ready?"

Geoffrey nodded, and Ember got the horses into motion

again. Jasper and Juniper's well-shod hooves clopped along the road faster and faster. They were making good time.

At the crest of the hill overlooking the aptly named Moonrise Bay, they were in for a stunning sight. The moon looked huge from its position low on the horizon. Seeming to rise from the sea itself, it cast glimmering silver light over the black water —the illusion of a solid walkway a man might take to the moon's very surface, aided by foam on the crest of the waves that broke ashore.

Goddess above, the vista was breathtaking. Dizzying, even, as though the stars wheeled around the moon to dazzle a traveler's eye.

Below, the city of Moonrise Bay was laid out like a carpet of sparkling gems. Golden lights glowed in the windows of ordinary houses, but magical red, blue, green, and purple scintillated from houses of worship and the homes of wealthy city dwellers, most of whom served the king in some capacity.

And on the opposite hill? Their destination: Spindrift Palace, the seat of power in Helionne and the home of the royal family.

Ember took a deep breath and urged the horses on.

Lenore was right. From that point, the road required all his attention. There were other coaches, open carriages, wagons, and riders to watch out for. In the city, he had to keep an eye peeled for pedestrians taking their chances to cross the busy streets.

There were animals too. The city seemed full of dogs that scrounged through the vast rubbish tips to survive. Cats, grown fat chasing rats that darted among the shadows, were visible only because of their light-reflecting eyes.

Despite its lyrical name, Moonrise Bay stank. Ember missed the clean country air as they drove past dank gutters and bins that smelled of foul things: rubbish, rotting meat, and human excrement.

They made their way along High Street and then left it for

Palace Road, which turned perilous at once, seeing as it clung to the curves of the mountain upon which Spindrift Palace was built.

The way was slow going because of the number of carriages lumbering upward, so it fell to Jasper and Juniper to stop and go, stop and go, always with the weight of the heavy coach trying to drag them backward over the best part of an hour.

When at last the palace lay before them, Ember took in the sight in speechless wonder. Spindrift looked like it was made of sea spume and snowfall, caught in a vortex created of white stone and sparkling glass. It stood three stories tall with spindly towers around a glistening rotunda. A thousand brightly lit windows gave the building a lacelike texture.

It was hard to take the place in. To Ember's eye, it looked like stars had been stacked by the Goddess herself, their brilliance undimmed. Only the moon outshone Spindrift, her light a constant and forgiving backdrop against its manmade, shimmery brilliance.

Lines of torches guided them to the front of the line at last. A daunting group of liveried servants escorted one family with lovely omega daughters after another from their carriages and up the stairs to the palace's welcoming foyer. Oil-burning warmers kept the chill from the courtyard. They warmed the air while giving off the fragrance of orange blossoms, black tea, and clove.

Ember soaked everything into his heart, into his memories. This night alone would surely be enough to last him a lifetime of country days and nights at Carlysle.

Now he understood Lenore's urgency.

Now he knew that an opportunity like this could only come once in a lifetime.

Even if they gave the girls an entire, proper season in Moonrise Bay it could not compare with this. Eleanor and Lucy would meet alphas from all of Helionne's aristocratic houses here. They'd meet royalty from home and abroad. Their desperate gamble could pay off on a magical night like this one.

When it was their turn to leave the carriage, Lenore, Eleanor, and Lucy stepped out in silence. Eleanor and Lenore kept their body language calm, but Lucy turned, almost frantically searching Ember out. He met her gaze with his warmest smile and nodded. A tip of his hat seemed like a natural way to wish his youngest sister luck. She took a deep breath and turned back with her head held high.

The two younger Carlysle ladies picked up the hems of their skirts and ascended the stairs of the palace in Lenore's wake as though they still had dictionaries balanced on their heads. The three women drifted serenely, like beautiful new ships under sail to an unknown world.

Were they frightened or excited about the adventure to come?

He hoped they were excited, delighted, aware of how special they were, even in this glittering milieu. They were his sisters, and he loved them dearly.

"As the Goddess wills," Ember spoke for himself, but at his side Geoffrey repeated his prayer.

"As the Goddess wills." Geoffrey shot him a frankly mischievous grin. "I'm due a drink, John Coachman. How about you?"

"And then some." Ember gently nudged the horses forward. The road to the palace was a loop, it seemed. They took the longer, less-scenic half of the route back down the mountain into Moonrise Bay. He and Geoffrey had the entire evening ahead to enjoy the city before them.

In his mind, Ember recited the rules as set forth by Hugh. About alphas. About knotting. About getting back on time. His blood seemed to quicken as his wolf crept closer to the surface of his skin, and not for the first time he had the notion that as the Earl of Carlysle, as the only male omega born in centuries, the rules didn't necessarily have to apply to him.

He was an anomaly. He was an exception to the laws of nature. His very existence broke the rules, and Ember's wolf suddenly wanted out, rules be damned.

Ember's wolf had waited long enough.

Ember winced, but he also agreed in principle.

Despite Hugh's warnings, this time outside the narrow walls of Carlysle seemed as good a time as any to give the wolf his due.

CHAPTER 9

*A*t the Red Wolf Inn, Ember and Geoffrey went inside while the lad who worked the stables saw to their horses. Ember would have forced himself to go without waiting for Geoffrey, even though it terrified him, but he was grateful to have the boy's company as they made their way to the bar.

Though it seemed quite early, the crowd was thick, and most of the patrons were already merry with drink. Ember kept his shoulders back and held his head high, so he wouldn't look like a frightened rabbit. Geoffrey helped him push his way through the throng and catch the barkeep's eye.

Was that Hugh's cousin? He was huge like Hugh but not as brawny. Of course, pulling taps didn't require the muscles forging horseshoes did. They were similar in coloring and had a certain lantern-jawed masculinity in common.

Geoffrey ordered two pints. The barman looked them over. When he saw Ember's hat, he narrowed his eyes.

"You a Carlysle man?"

"I am." Ember dropped coins on the counter for their drinks. "Drove the Carlysle ladies to the prince's ball. Hugh Smith said I should take my rest here."

The big man smiled. "Oh, aye. Little cousin Hugh. Is he still as big as a house?"

"He is and then some." Geoffrey mimed how big. "Like an ox, is Hugh. Glad he counts me among his friends."

"He's helped me a great deal," said Ember. "I'm lucky to know him."

"He's a good man." The barman held out his hand. "Yancy Smith."

"John Coachman. Seems crowded in here."

Again, Yancy's eyes narrowed on him. "It's the full moon, plus the ball, so it's perilously packed tonight. I wonder ..."

"Yes?" Did this man see through him already?

"We keep a private room for the nobs and clergy, but it's not in use right now. It might be best if you drank in there."

Ember glanced around and realized he was attracting attention, either because he and Geoffrey were young compared to the other drinkers or because his beta-scented coat was fooling no one.

"Hugh mentioned I should ask for the private dining room. That would be much appreciated. We'd like food if you're still serving." Ember gave the man a few more coins. "For your kindness."

"I'll send food with Grace." Yancy called the woman over. "See that these two get to the parlor and make sure they don't need anything while they're there."

"Will do." She gave a saucy smile and led them out of the bar. "Yancy must like you. He hardly lets anyone in here 'less they're nobs."

"Thank you." Ember dropped a coin in her waiting hand. "We have a mutual acquaintance."

"Not my business. I'll be back with food. More ale?"

"Yes, please." Geoffrey eyed the woman as she left them. "She was pretty, wasn't she? I'm kind of sorry we can't stay in the bar. Did you see? This place is *full* of women."

"Settle down." Ember removed his hat and hung it on a peg on the wall. He considered whether to remove his coat, especially when Geoffrey frowned and leaned over to whisper in his ear.

"Why do you smell like a beta?"

"Guess," Ember replied.

It took a few seconds, but then Geoffrey's eyes widened. "Tricky. I like it."

"The idea was Hugh's." It was too hot to wear the coat inside, so he removed it but kept it draped over his lap.

"It won't fool anyone for long," Geoffrey cautioned. "Just makes it seem like you and some beta—"

"That's why I plan to stay here and be invisible."

"Good thing all the gents who normally use this room are probably at the ball."

"Lucky for us."

"Here you go, gentleman." Grace returned with bowls of thick stew and bread and two more pints.

"Thank you." Ember kept his eyes on his food while Geoffrey gave her the kind of smile a country boy gives a girl he didn't grow up with.

"I'll check on you in a bit." Out of the corner of his eye, Ember saw Grace send a little wink Geoffrey's way.

"Did you see that?" Geoffrey asked. "I think she likes me."

"She might. Why don't you find out?"

"Hugh told me to stay close and make sure nothing happens to you."

Ember frowned. "I'm safe enough here."

"Honestly, he's right." Geoffrey turned serious. "No one's seen anything like you before. We have no idea how they'll react, but given alphas are always going to be alphas, it's better to be safe than sorry."

"Hugh is an alpha."

"He's a *rare* alpha. Why do you think they parade omega girls before the alphas at all those parties during the season?"

Ember lifted a shoulder. "It's the marriage mart. That's—"

"That's only part of it." Geoffrey lowered his voice further still despite the empty room. "Omegas smell different."

"I'm aware we smell different from betas and alphas."

"Yes, but an omega's scent is meant to draw alphas in and make them"—he lowered his voice to a whisper—*"randy.* An omega's scent is the perfect complement for her true mate, but all alphas will desire her."

"Wait, go back. An omega's scent attracts their true mate? More than other omegas' scents?"

Geoffrey bobbed his head. "It's like a lock and key, once the right omega and alpha find each other. That's where a ball like this one comes in."

"How come I never heard of this? Hugh smells delicious to me, but he says he's not my mate."

"Alphas smell good to you because you're an omega. Your true mate's scent will ruin you for anyone else. It's fate. Your sisters are probably on the hunt for their true mates, but not everyone finds theirs. They might have to pick from the alphas there. Alphas are pretty content to mate anyone, it seems, unless they've found their true mate."

"So I've heard." Ember wasn't looking for a mate. He wouldn't mind finding an alpha, any alpha, to spend some time with. He was a grown omega with needs, after all. "That doesn't sound unreasonable, actually."

"My point is, alphas don't wait for their mates when it comes to sex. And all omegas exude the same alpha-enticing aroma. The younger alphas—or the wicked ones—won't care if you're someone else's true mate or not."

Ember studied Geoffrey's expression "I don't understand."

"Let's hope you never do." Geoffrey shuddered. "But that's why they keep omega girls away from alphas until they reach a marriageable age. And it's why Hugh doesn't want me to leave you alone here."

"Even if someone ... if they wanted that from me ... there's still the fact that I'm a man. I'm not some helpless schoolgirl, whatever you think. Don't you want to meet a girl and have some fun?"

"Yes, but Hugh says the same rules should apply to you as to your sisters. Omegas need chaperones. That's all."

Each time Grace checked on them, Geoffrey's cheeks colored. When he tried to engage her, it was clumsy but charming. Ember felt sorry for him. The lad was only in Moonrise Bay for one evening. He could find himself a girl, but he was stuck babysitting Ember on Hugh's ridiculous orders.

That didn't sit well with Ember at all.

"Geoffrey, honestly." He gestured to the empty room. "I know the rules, and I'm fine here. Go and have a nice time."

"No, I can't—"

"Of course, you can. I don't have to order you to talk to a pretty girl, do I?"

Geoffrey seemed to consider this. "If I go ..."

"You'll be in the bar if I need you, won't you? It's just a shout away."

"Promise you won't leave this room."

"What if I have to piss?"

"Let's go now, together."

Ember recoiled. "I beg your pardon?"

"I'll go to the bar, but let's take care of ... necessary business first. That way I know you'll be inside this room and not wandering around on your own."

"Oh, all right." Ember stood. "Remember we need to leave at midnight."

"Fine." Geoffrey escorted Ember outside to relieve himself, and then they returned to the still-empty private dining room. Geoffrey left after making Ember promise to stay put.

Ember gave a relieved sigh.

The room was warm and well appointed, nothing like the noisy taproom. There were some pastoral paintings on the walls along with farm equipment: a shoulder yoke, a number of horseshoes, and the bellows and tongs of the smith's trade.

Ember felt comfortable and sleepy, warm enough because of the fire. He took a seat in a wingback chair in front of the fireplace to wait the evening out.

While he rested, he contemplated what he'd learned. Being omega was confusing, and Ember was uncertain. Had Geoffrey meant to say that certain alphas made a habit of seducing young omegas who weren't their mates? Was it worse than seduction? Did they force themselves on the girls?

That wasn't much of a worry for his sisters because Lenore kept an eagle eye on them. And of course, he wasn't any alpha's idea of an *omega fatale*.

Or would curiosity be enough to make someone try it on with him?

To that end, Lenore was an omega. Was she in danger simply because she didn't have a husband or son at the ball with her? Oh, Goddess. Ember cursed Lenore for not telling him all these omega-related things. She was surely aware he might someday have a need to know, but thinking furiously about omega problems now wouldn't fix them. He needed to rest up, for the long drive home. Eventually, he let his eyes close.

Three well-dressed young alphas burst drunkenly into the room, and what had been a problem for another day became an urgent matter. Ember startled, still half asleep. He checked the clock on the wall. Still early. Surely these alphas hadn't already abandoned the prince's ball?

"Goddess, what a bore," one of them said as he flung off a forest green cloak. "I'm not looking to marry, but Mother insisted I show my face to raise the family standard, as it were."

"And you went like an obedient hound." A second man

smirked, lifting his bushy, wax-curled mustache. "Such a good son."

"The crop of girls this year was thin, and only a few in the bunch were worth a second look." The third man took the time to remove his peacock-hued cloak and a hat with a large white plume in it. He hung them next to Ember's things *just so*. "Oliver Ehrenpries seems to have found one. He disappeared early, though. Maybe he developed cold feet?"

"Seavane was lovestruck as well. From the way the grand-mothers gushed on about them, those two found their true mates."

Another alpha entered the room wearing a half mask that covered his eyes.

"Who the devil are you?" said Mustache.

The man frowned. "Call me Domino though it's none of your business."

"The prince's ball isn't a masquerade, in case you're going." Green Cloak said helpfully. "Might have been more fun if it was."

"Prince Christopher will want to see his future bride, I'll wager," said Domino.

"Just so, you're probably right," Green Cloak admitted.

Just Ember's luck, there were now four alphas in his suppos-edly private parlor. Ember should have known that some might quit the ball early. None of them seemed to have noticed him yet, but he could watch them easily in the mirror over the mantle. Should he stay hidden or leave and possibly invite trouble?

Ember couldn't tear his gaze away from the alpha named Domino. He was utterly dashing, with a clean-shaven, heart-shaped face and fair skin beneath hair so black it glistened like a raven's wing. Even though Ember couldn't see his eyes, he was mesmerized.

Goddess, who was that?

He stole Ember's breath.

Ember's entire body tingled.

If Hugh was a fine man—and Hugh defined the word fine—this man was majestic. Perfection. Even if Ember hadn't seen him, he would have felt his presence. This was an alpha steeped in magic, his power akin to the sound one heard before glittery fireworks appeared in the sky. Ember felt the concussion of the man's presence inside him. *Boom!* As if all the air was sucked from his body, as if a blast of magic tore through Ember's chest, his very heart, excitement burst within him. *Boom!*

Ember had trouble catching his breath. He must have stared too long, or too openly, because the alpha turned toward him. Domino's scrutiny brought the others' attention to him as well, exactly the thing he'd been trying to avoid.

As discreetly as Ember could, he stood and pulled on his coat. He hoped to leave and locate Geoffrey among the throng in the bar. If that failed, he would return to the stables after letting the innkeeper know where Geoffrey could find him.

When he turned to leave, the first three alphas blocked the door while Domino leaned against the wall, watching.

"What have we here?" Peacock asked in a singsong voice. "Since when do coachmen sit in the private dining room?"

"Have to complain to Smith about it. He mustn't let just anyone in here. Could be a thief."

"I'm no thief," Ember said the word harshly. "I'm leaving. Let me pass."

"Pay a toll,"—Green Cloak wrinkled his nose—"beta."

Ember sighed. "How much?"

Mustache said, "Perhaps we're not short of cash, boy."

"I'm not a boy." Ember gritted his teeth. "Just tell me what you want then I'll go."

"Wait, something's fishy here." Green Cloak stepped into his space, too close, to sniff at him.

"What in the Goddess's name do you think you're doing?" Ember stepped away. "Back off."

Mustache sniffed at Ember's neck from behind. "You're no beta—"

"That's enough of you." Ember reacted by grabbing a handy tankard and smacking the lout across the face with it.

"My dose." Mustache cupped his bleeding face. "You'll pay for that, omega."

The others stared as though their companion was mad.

"Can't be an omega. He's a gent," said Peacock.

"Don't be absurd. It's an omega dressed as a gent. I smell her too, cinnamon and ginger. I like them spicy." Green Cloak rolled his shoulders. "Hold her."

"No!" Ember's heart raced.

"You're going nowhere till we say you are, my little omega spitfire." Peacock grabbed his arms from behind. Ember kicked out, keeping Green Cloak at a distance while Peacock stuck his nose in Ember's neck and breathed in deeply.

"Stop that!" Ember cried out. Where was the other alpha? Was Domino just going to let this happen?

"More like cinnamon and chiles. And something darker, like cacao."

"I want to smell." Mustache got close enough to breathe him in while Ember tried futilely to wrench his arms free. "Gingerbread and clotted cream."

"Let me go! Hey you, Domino, help me!" Ember squirmed and kicked and bit, but while he might have been a match for one man, even an alpha, three were too many. "Don't just stand there like a gaping fish."

"I'm going to enjoy this, girlie." The one whose nose he'd bloodied looked feral and furious.

"I'm not—" Hands cupped his balls.

"What in the black abyss!" Green Cloak stepped back and pointed at him accusingly. "She's got bollocks."

"What?" asked Mustache.

"She has bollocks. She must be some kind of witch."

Ember struggled harder. "I'm not—"

"The devil you say!" Peacock grabbed his balls and felt his way to Ember's flaccid cock. "Goddess. The omega has bollocks and a limp little cock as well."

"Watch what you call little!" Ember wrenched himself away and readied his tankard to bash more heads in. Nearly out of his mind with fury, he held out the heavy pewter cup, moving it toward anyone who tried to get close. "I said get back!"

Mustache and Peacock backed away. Green Cloak wasn't daunted.

"Witches don't tell me what to do, bitch," he sneered.

The alpha lunged for Ember, but the silken hiss of a knife being drawn from its sheath froze everyone in place. Green Cloak didn't give a fraction of a twitch. Perhaps it was the blade at his throat.

"Uh, uh, uh. Three against one is bad form."

The three alphas' gazes locked on Domino's fierce face.

Green Cloak winced. "It's just some omega playing pretend."

"Mind. Your. Manners." Domino didn't lower his blade. "You're in the capitol of a civilized kingdom."

Ember wished he could see the Alpha's eyes just then. He imagined they were dark, and mysterious, and brooding. Perhaps if he gazed into those alpha eyes for too long, he'd swoon.

Hugh was going to lose his mind when he heard about this.

"We're leaving," said Domino. "Coachman, you're with me."

"I am not." Despite Ember's fantasy, he was under orders to stay away from alphas.

Domino's eyebrow rose above his mask. "You want to spend more time with these fine men?"

"Domino. Whoever you are," Green Cloak frowned, "It's me. Perkins. Earl of Belwind."

"I know," Domino growled. "But you're acting the fool. The lad comes with me."

"The *lad*"—Ember sneered—"has a mind of his own, thank you."

"Then you'll be smart enough to know a rescue when you see one."

Ember huffed unhappily. "I know an *alpha* when I see one."

"Move," the alpha growled.

Ember got his tankard ready. "Make me."

"Domino, this is all wrong. You hear that voice?" Mustache pointed at Ember. "The omega *sounds* like a man too."

"A male omega has to be witchcraft," said Perkins. "And he attacked us."

"I want the witch dead." Mustache's nose was definitely not as patrician as it had been when he arrived. "Look at *by dose!*"

"A healer will see to your nose, Graeme. You accosted the fellow first, and you deserved what you got."

"He's not a *fellow*, he's an omega," said Perkins. "Have you ever heard of a male omega?"

"Doesn't mean there aren't any." Domino gave Ember a shove. "Goddess curse you, stubborn fool. We need to leave before anyone else gets wind of this."

Ember's supposed rescuer bent over and hoisted Ember over one shoulder, keeping his blade free to threaten the other three. "Now, I'm going out the back way, and I'm taking the omega with me. If you follow me, I'll fight. I believe we all know how that will go."

"Go, then. Take your prize." Perkins gave the man a shove. "But if I see you again, omega ..."

"Yeah, yeah," Ember said from his awkward position. Goddess, the man's shoulders were so wide that Ember was almost comfortable. "This had better be a rescue and not an out-of-the-fire-and-into-the-pan situation, or so help me I will—"

"Shut up, you." A huge, heavy hand slapped Ember's ass. "I

didn't wish to make my whereabouts known this night. You may have ruined all my plans."

Ember swung to and fro as the man took him from the parlor, down the back hall, and out through the kitchen. Once they were outside, Domino set him on his feet.

Ember dusted himself off and opened his mouth to say thank you, but a shout went up in the taproom—a kind of roar —that shattered the night.

"Run!" said the alpha.

"Wait. What? I don't—"

"Your sore-nosed 'suitor' probably just told everyone in the bar he'd seen a male omega. Welcome to the freak show."

"I'm not a—"

"Freak, I know. I still suggest we run." Domino caught Ember's hand and took off. Dragging behind him, Ember stared at their joined fingers for an annoyed half second before making the decision to sprint away with him.

Somehow, Ember wound up in the lead even though he had no idea where he was going.

CHAPTER 10

"Where to?" Ember called back to the alpha with whom he wasn't supposed to engage under any circumstances. He could just imagine the look on Hugh's face if he ever found out about this.

Hugh truly will kill me.

"Where are you staying?" Domino asked.

"Nowhere. We're here for the duration of the ball."

The alpha swore. "Fine. We'll need to hide you somewhere."

"I was doing just fine until certain alphas ruffians came in."

"Those *ruffians*, as you call them, are a baron and two earls."

It was on the tip of Ember's tongue to tell this bossy alpha that he was an earl too, but he held back. Rank wasn't important, survival was.

"Where's your coach?" Domino asked.

"At the Red Wolf, where else?"

"The stables will have to do, then."

The alpha dragged him to a halt, tugged him into an alley, and then doubled back via the alley behind the coach houses, restaurants, and taverns that lined the street. The air stank of vomit and piss and garbage, but Ember barely noticed. Heat from the hand engulfing his was the center of his world.

They entered the stables with quiet footsteps, ready to run if anyone accosted them there. When nothing happened, they crept further inside.

Every stall was occupied, and the horsey stink made even Ember's eyes water. At least it would be hard to pick out his scent if anyone had followed them.

"This should do." After a glance around, Domino pulled Ember toward a ladder leading to the loft.

Once they'd climbed up, Ember dragged off his coat and draped it over a mound of hay beneath an unglazed window overlooking the courtyard. Noise on the cobbles below should give them plenty of notice if anyone come looking for them. Moonlight filtered in, limning the alpha's masked features like a lover's caress.

"What are you looking at?" Domino asked.

"Nothing, I ... oh—" Ember glanced away unhappily.

No one should be that handsome.

In such a tight space, Ember found it impossible to avoid the alpha's heady masculine scent. His head spun with it. Hugh's scent had been delicious, but Domino's made him salivate. He nearly went mad from the sheer luxurious richness of it. He felt ravenous, desperate to see if Domino tasted as good as he looked.

"You smell amazing," he admitted.

"Do I?" There was humor behind the alpha's question. "As do you, little wolf. Your fragrance is quite ... something else."

"You're making fun." Ember tore his gaze away.

"Never. I just can't fathom it." Domino sat opposite him, knees crossed in a childlike pose. His gaze was almost mesmerizing. "You're a man and an omega. Goddess, what a gift. I can't believe I *found* you. It's as if my most private prayers have been answered."

"I don't understand." Ember had been through too much to answer riddles. "What do you mean?"

"You have several scents on your person. Two betas and three omegas that I can tease apart, but your fragrance is definitely"—he leaned closer and breathed in—"omega. Your scent steals my breath and makes my heart race as though it wants to burst through my chest."

"People need to stop *sniffing* me. It's rude." Ember blushed and looked away. "I suppose I smell like some variation of cinnamon and ginger."

"No. You—" The alpha swallowed hard. "Nothing so mundane. You smell like starlight and destiny and creation itself. It's as though the Goddess made you only for me."

"Right." *Dangerous talk.* The alpha couldn't be serious. Couldn't be trusted, if Hugh's warnings were to be believed. How likely was it that he'd found his true mate tonight? Not very. But the alpha smelled so ... alluring. Enticing. Enchanting. Ember's wolf had grown frantic. His one-word message: *mine, mine, mine, mine.*

"Female omegas don't shift. Can you?" Domino asked.

"I can't." Whether from lust or fear, Ember's hands trembled. He clasped them tightly on his lap to hide the effect the alpha had on him. "Will they still be looking for us, do you think?"

"It appears they've lost interest," Domino said as he checked the courtyard below. "We should be safe enough here."

Safe? Hardly. Not with an alpha who looked like that.

"You should probably go," Ember told him.

"And leave you here alone if I'm wrong, and they're still searching for you?" Domino laid a hand on his arm. Ember's heart fluttered wildly. "I'm not going anywhere."

"You've been very kind." Ember turned away from the man's seductive beauty. "But I don't think—"

"Please don't send me away. Not when I've only just found you. What's your name?"

"John Coachman," Ember replied as he'd been instructed to. Domino smiled ruefully. "You don't trust me."

"I'm cautious," Ember couldn't help acknowledging. "Should I call you Domino?"

"Yes." His lips twisted wryly as he pointed to the mask. "It's the custom, when one is masked."

"I probably shouldn't have gone into the tavern, but Hugh thought I'd be safe as long as I didn't engage with any alphas." Ember leaned against the wall. "I did try not to."

"Who is this Hugh, your mate?" Domino frowned. "Your *mate* let you come to Moonrise Bay by yourself?"

Ember flexed his fists. "Hugh is not my mate, but even if he were, it would not be up to him to 'let' me do anything. Goddess, I begin to see why Lenore is the woman she is."

"Who is Lenore?"

"My"—Ember caught himself just in time—"mistress. Widow of the late Lord Carlysle. I drove her and her daughters to the prince's ball."

Domino raised a brow. "You call your mistress by her first name?"

Oh, bother. "Not in her hearing, I can assure you."

"Carlysle," Domino mused. "I know the name. The heir just came of age, but since the earl's death, funds have been limited. That's a weak position from which to come begging for a royal prince."

Ember gasped as if Domino had impugned his honor. "The Carlysle girls are hereditary princesses of Rhielôme as well as adopted daughters of a Helionne earl. They're intelligent, kind, and lovely. They would be magnificent mates for any alpha, including the prince."

"I'm sorry. Of course, they would." The alpha humored him. "Do you have any idea how adorable you are when you get testy?"

"I—" Ember coughed to hide his shock. "Excuse me?"

"Tonight, the Carlysle ladies will have first crack at every bachelor in the kingdom. If they're as fine as you say, they will meet with wondrous success."

"Wait. Before that. What did you say?"

"I said you're adorable." Domino reached out and cupped his cheek. "You're very pretty."

"Not this again." Ember sighed. "I've been told I'm too small and too pretty to be a real man. Is that what makes me 'adorable'?"

"Who on earth would say such a thing?" Domino asked. "What do you see when you look at me, omega?"

"Someone very ... shiny. It's probably because of the moonlight," he qualified. "You're glowing a little bit if you know what I mean. I—" Ember should have quit while he was ahead, but it was as though his wolf possessed him. "I see an alpha so wondrous I can hardly look at him without being dazzled."

"I want to kiss you, John Coachman." Domino's tender expression made Ember lightheaded. He could barely get enough air into his lungs. "Will you allow it, please?"

Ember felt bold. He felt wicked. He gave plenty of warning as he reached around to untie the mask that hid Domino's gaze from him. Even after he'd accomplished his goal, he hesitated, as if asking if he had permission to end the subterfuge.

"Go ahead," the alpha whispered. "I don't mind."

The silken mask fluttered to the straw between them. Domino's dark-eyed gaze held him as surely as if he'd drawn his blade and pinned Ember to the floor with it.

"Oh ..." Ensnared, Ember's human side worried that kissing the alpha might be a bad idea while Ember's wolf hurled at his boundaries as if trying to burst free. His wolf had never been as determined to win control. Common sense told Ember to slow things down while his wolf was ready to tackle Domino to the floor and roll in his mouthwatering scent.

"All right. Kiss me." Ember couldn't resist. Were all alphas this ... compelling? With Hugh, Ember had been curious and attracted; he'd never felt as though he'd die if he couldn't taste him.

Domino moved slowly. He laid his hand on Ember's shoulder first and then slid his palm up until his warm touch wrapped around the nape of Ember's neck. Everything about the glide of Domino's hand over Ember's skin was hot and enervating. His touch seemed imbued with magic, leaving waves of sensation that shivered down Ember's spine and pooled in his belly.

Ember's cock nudged against his tight trousers, aching. Domino's touch liquified his insides, and the dampness he now knew was a normal part of an omega's arousal, thanks to Hugh, left him slick and sticky.

Goddess. Even before Domino's lips pressed softly to his, he was out of his mind with need. He welcomed Domino's first kiss, and the next, and the next, until he found himself kissing back, until Domino slipped his tongue between Ember's untried lips and—shockingly—coaxed his tongue into an intimate dance.

Ember feared he'd burst into flames from the heat of Domino's hand, the sweetness of his musk, the way their scents seemed to mingle together to make something altogether different, and perfect, and theirs.

"John," Domino whispered against his lips. "John, I can't believe that all this time you've been out there, and I—"

"Waiting," Ember gasped. "I think I was waiting for you."

"Beautiful boy." Domino pressed him to his back. "Can I show you what you were waiting for?"

"I—" Hugh's warnings seemed faint now, drowned out by mad desire. Why would anyone warn him off this intense exhilaration? Ember wanted Domino, wanted whatever Domino would give him. "Yes, please. Please show me."

The alpha unbuttoned his coat and slid a hot hand beneath

his shirt. Ember felt branded. Fingers lightly caressed his chest. They tugged his nipples, shooting more fire straight to his cock and balls. They slipped over his abs and down, and down, until they were making their way under the waistband of his trousers.

"Goddess, Domino. I feel ..."

"Give me permission, sweetling. Let me touch you." Domino kissed his nose. "Or tell me to stop if I go too far."

Stop? If Domino stopped what he was doing, Ember would surely die.

"Anything." Ember barely whispered the word. "Do anything you like with me because I don't know. I'm not"—he swallowed—"I want everything."

"Goddess, I want to taste you." Domino kissed his jaw, his throat, his collar bone. He bared Ember as he kissed each part of him, and everywhere his mouth had touched, cool air chilled his damp skin, driving Ember mindless with desire.

Domino's touch seared him, but Ember was happy to burn. He'd been made for this moment. He was as certain of that as he was of anything. Domino parted Ember's trouser placket, and his cock sprang free beneath his small clothes.

"Oh, Goddess." Ember writhed beneath Domino's questing hands. "Please. I need—"

Domino mouthed the fabric covering him. His hot breath and kisses blazed through the last barrier between them and brought Ember to a fever pitch of yearning.

"Oh. Goddess, Domino," Ember cried out softly. "Please, please, *please.*"

If Domino kept this up, Ember would combust, he'd explode. He had no idea what to expect but his heartbeat thudded alarmingly in his ears and his wolf howled for more.

He gasped in despair when Domino dragged his mouth away.

"So perfect." Domino glanced up through dark lashes. "You

were made for me, coachman. Do you understand what I'm saying? You are the granting of a wish I've been making since I first knew what my cock was for. You're an unspoken prayer. I want to see all of you, John. Everything."

"I want to see you too. It's only fair." Ember's cheeks caught fire. "I want to feel your heartbeat and taste your skin."

"My omega," Domino gave a cheeky smile. "Fierce little wolf. Look your fill. Touch. Taste. I'm all yours."

Ember's wolf thrilled to hear the words. To his surprise, human Ember rejoiced as well. Both of them wanted this man, this *alpha*, with every fiber of their being, almost as if he were Ember's ...

Was it true? Could Domino be his mate?

Coincidences happened, and if—as Domino had said—he'd been hoping for a male omega, then perhaps it wasn't a coincidence at all. Perhaps it was the Goddess's will.

Clumsily, Ember picked at Domino's buttons and the fastening of his trousers. With each garment he peeled away, he saw more of Domino's lean muscles. His fit, inspiring body. The breadth of his shoulders awed Ember as did the thick cock that sprang from a nest of black curls.

Ember reached for it without asking. He simply wrapped his hand around the velvet skin-clad steel and realized how forward he must seem.

"I'm sorry." He opened his hand as if it burned. "I don't know what's come over me. That was rude. I beg your pardon."

"You'll beg, all right, but not for my pardon." Domino nuzzled into his neck. "You have my permission to touch me anywhere, darling. Everywhere. Satisfy your curiosity with my body while I gorge myself with yours."

Domino gripped his buttocks and brought their hips together so he could wrap his hand around both their cocks at once.

Ember had never known what he should want, what he

ought to feel. Domino knew what Ember needed without asking. Long strokes. Gentle, twisting strokes. Teasing strokes that were not enough to satisfy, Domino played him expertly, he cupped Ember's balls, and rubbed his taint, and nudged a finger into Ember's slick channel.

Ember arched. *"Umf."*

"Do you like that?" he asked. "You're so wet for me, sweetling."

Heat flooded Ember's cheeks. "I know, but—"

"That's your beautiful omega body getting ready for me. Do you want my cock inside you? Do you want me to stuff you and fill you? Do you want my knot?"

"Kn-knot?" Ember gasped. He wasn't supposed to want that, but deep inside he wanted Domino's knot. He'd beg for it if he had to. Ember wanted Domino deep inside him, piercing his core, filling him with his seed and knotting him. Domino's cock was everything. It was the only thing. He'd never ask for more in this life.

"When I take you, my knot will bind us together for a time. Our bodies will belong to each other forever."

"I—" Hugh had made him promise to avoid alphas. He had exhorted him not to let an alpha knot him. But Hugh hadn't known Domino might be—had to be—Ember's true mate, and Ember didn't want to listen to his counsel anymore.

Ember doubted he could say no to anything Domino wanted anyway.

"Do you want me?" Domino asked. "You must say the words."

"Oh, yes. I want you."

"Good answer." Domino sighed as if Ember's answer relieved a great worry. "I need to make you only mine. Do you … Is there anyone else, little wolf?"

"No one." Ember lifted his hand to brush a dark curl from Domino's sweaty forehead. He didn't see how there could be anyone else after meeting Domino. The passion that consumed them might be sudden, but no one would ever measure up to Domino in Ember's eyes. "There's no one else."

Domino was *theirs*. His wolf and he were certain.

"What about you?" Ember asked. "Do you have someone?"

"There's no one." Domino met his lips for a ferocious, possessive kiss. "Only you, now and forever. Do you believe me?"

Ember nodded.

"Do you trust me?"

"I do." Hugh told him to trust his wolf. Ember's wolf knew this man was his alpha. Ember reached for him. When they touched, their mystical connection seemed both impossible and inevitable.

Domino's fingers quested inside him. They found a spot so sensitive, so jarring, that Ember grew faint when he rubbed it. They continued playing, kissing, exploring, until Domino declared Ember was ready for him. He bade Ember open his legs and his heart to an invasion so intimate, so breathtaking, Ember nearly lost his nerve.

Domino's cock felt huge. It stretched Ember to an enervating state of pain and pleasure. He wrapped both arms around the alpha's neck and clung to him. Domino nudged so deep inside him his balls met Ember's flesh. Then he withdrew and shoved in again, over and over. Ember lost himself as each wave of rapture swept over him, so sweet, so piercing that he had to fight the desire to shout with joy.

When Ember's body had drawn so tautly with heat and yearning he couldn't bear anymore, something like the stomach-dropping excitement of taking a good horse over a tall fence held him suspended for a moment's time. His body dissolved into ecstasy, pleasurable spasms racked him, shivers of joy began in his balls and took over his entire being. Ember clung to Domino as his every new strike electrified him again and it seemed to go on forever.

"Will you be mine, omega?" asked Domino. "I want—need—to knot you. To *claim* you."

"Yes, Domino." Hugh's warnings had receded to a corner of Ember's lust-drunk mind along with time and responsibility and any other mundane thing. "The answer is yes. To anything. Yes."

"Thank the Goddess." Domino's controlled movements seemed to go haywire. He gave a shout and bit the juncture of Ember's neck and shoulder hard as he flooded Ember's channel with the warmth of his seed.

Ember's eyes teared from pain and pleasure, from the joy of their coming together. Everything, from penetration to the endless, languid bliss and bite was perfect. Domino was perfect. His cock thickened inside Ember, holding him pinioned. Ember's wolf surrendered, body and soul, to his alpha. He'd never felt so alive, so complete, so *happy*.

Can it be so easy to fall in love?

"Mm. Mine." Domino shifted his weight off Ember, though they were still locked together. He held Ember close and whispered into his hair. "My beautiful omega. Mine."

Domino's triumph was a palpable force between them. He was pleased.

Ember had pleased his alpha.

"The Goddess is merciful." Domino kissed each of Ember's eyes. His nose. His lips. "I'm so lucky I met you. I very nearly didn't stop here tonight. I only meant to avoid the ball and my friends and family's well-meaning matchmaking."

"Why?"

"I seem to be wired to want men, but my parents have been destined for me to mate an omega." Domino stroked his hair. "Until you, I never met an omega I could love."

"I see." Ember had assumed he'd mate with a woman. He'd never thought he'd get what he wanted. Except for Hugh, he'd never been attracted to anyone. Of course he barely knew anyone.

"I wanted to tell my parents, but they were so convinced. None but a noble female omega would do. I must have heirs."

"I'm told—" Ember coughed. "Goddess, I can barely say the words out loud. I'm told that all omegas can bear children."

"You?" He tilted Ember's chin to look into his eyes. Whatever he saw there must have convinced him. "A male omega with child. How does that work, I wonder?"

Ember lifted a shoulder. "I am as in the dark as you are."

"Doesn't matter if you can or can't," Domino assured him. "My wolf says you're my true mate. No one can deny the Goddess's will."

Ember had never been that certain about anything, but he wanted to be.

Chance meeting with his true mate aside, he still had all the problems he'd woken with that morning. He was a penniless earl from the rural interior of the kingdom. Even if his sisters married well, there was little to recommend Ember besides his status as the only male omega around. What could he offer a man like Domino, who was so obviously a noble, whose parents would be properly appalled if he brought home a male omega mate?

Ember had learned another thing from Hugh: the higher up the social ladder one climbed, the less even *true* mates were guaranteed to end up happily ever after.

At least they had this moment. He could comb his fingers through Domino's moon-frosted hair, watch the way his lashes cast crescent shadows beneath his beautiful dark eyes. But he was also very tired. He couldn't seem to keep his eyes open. While they talked he drifted off, still tied to Domino in the most intimate way imaginable.

He didn't wake until he heard Geoffrey's whistle from the courtyard below.

"Oi, John Coachman," came Geoffrey's whisper shout.

"*Goddess.*" Ember took a quick accounting. Domino's knot had gone and his cock had slipped out. Ember was free to move. He felt sore and tired but happy. His body spoke a new language —one that made leaving Domino akin to tearing off a limb. He would have to think about that later. After he took care of his family.

"Domino? Wake up. I have to leave. It's midnight."

"No, you don't." Domino didn't wake, precisely. He tightened his arms around Ember's waist.

"I'm sorry." It took some doing, but Ember extricated himself from Domino's arms. "I can't be late to pick up my—that is, *the* —Carlysle ladies."

He dressed quickly and pulled on his boots. Goddess, how could he have fallen asleep on the most important night of his sisters' lives?

He had to go despite the nearly crushing desire to stay at Domino's side.

Domino slept on, oblivious to Ember's distress.

"Domino," Ember whispered. "Take care of yourself. Remember me."

"If you must wake me, bring me coffee." Domino lifted an eyelid, though he was still clearly half asleep. "I'll come for you soon, John Coachman of Carlysle Manor. I *will* find you and bring you home to my parents."

Ember didn't know whether to be happy that Domino knew where to find him or terrified what he'd say when he discovered Ember had lied to him about everything.

Both, he thought.

He dropped a brief kiss on Domino's lips and said, "Thank you for the most wonderful night of my life, my alpha."

Domino's lips twitched into a smile. "My alpha. I like hearing ... that, omega mate."

Then he rolled over and gave a loud snore.

Ember took one last look then sprinted down the ladder and out the stable door. He was frantically searching for Jasper and Juniper when he heard Geoffrey again.

"Ember," Geoffrey whispered. "There you are, I looked everywhere."

"I was in the loft, hiding. Then I fell asleep."

"Thank heavens you're here now. I hitched up the horses and brought the coach around. We're supposed to be in line to pick up the ladies right now. We're going to be so late."

"I'm sorry. We'll get there in plenty of time if we hurry." Ember matched his stride to Geoffrey's more frantic one despite his protesting body. He didn't look forward to sitting in the coachman's box for the long ride home.

Almost desperate to run back to the loft, Ember took the reins and climbed up to his seat. As soon as he and Geoffrey were settled, he urged the horses forward. Hooves clattered over the dewy cobblestones. Geoffrey talked about the waitress, Grace, and all the people he'd met in the bar. Ember finally flicked a last glance back toward the Red Wolf.

"What are you looking for?" Geoffrey asked. "Are we being followed or—"

"Nothing like that." At least not now, he thought.

Perhaps Domino would seek him out later.

Perhaps he wouldn't.

Ember hadn't taken Hugh's warning to heart. He'd shattered every single rule Hugh had laid out for him. At the time, his wolf had been sure they were doing the right thing, but now? The farther they got from the inn and the alpha, Ember found he could think rationally.

He'd slept with an alpha.

He'd allowed an alpha to knot him. To *claim* him. There might be ... consequences.

How was he going to tell Hugh what he'd done?

What would he say to Lenore if circumstances forced him to confess his transgression?

"Something the matter?" Geoffrey asked after a long silence. "You were gone for quite a while. Do I smell alpha?"

"Of course. We were just at an inn filled with alphas. Everything's fine. We're here for my sisters, and that's what we should be focusing on. Their happiness."

"I get the feeling you're not telling me everything."

Ember winced. "No one tells anybody *everything*, Geoffrey."

Geoffrey eyed him. Did he appear ... debauched? Did he have straw in his hair?

When they finally reached Spindrift Palace, Ember took a place in the long line of carriages waiting to pick up ball-goers. He hoped he didn't live to regret the things he'd done this night. He certainly didn't regret them now, except ...

How was he going to tell Domino he'd lied about everything?

What if Ember never had to tell him the truth because Domino had been lying to him as well?

It took a long time for Geoffrey to collect the girls. Long enough for Ember to keep his promise to Victoria and spy the other ball-goers leaving the party in their finery. There were women of just about every age, but the preponderance seemed to fall between seventeen and twenty-five years old—just the right age for a twenty-seven-year-old prince looking for his omega bride.

There were plenty of men, as well. Most were alphas and highly ranked military betas, dressed in their finest clothing and most heroic uniforms. Perhaps some were rich second sons, looking for titled wives. Perhaps his sisters had been able to attract their attention.

It was highly unlikely they'd capture the prince himself, or any of the wealthy dukes, even though the title of "princess" could level the field, maybe even tilt it in their favor.

What Ember was actually hoping for wasn't clear until he saw Lenore and his sisters sweep down the stone stairs with Geoffrey. Despite the crush of people at the ball, they still looked exquisite. Their cloaks and gowns made them look like delicious confections. Their carriage was elegant, their cheeks flushed with excitement, and their smiles radiated joy. Even Lenore, who had few facial expressions, looked pleased.

The girls must have been a success.

That was what Ember wanted most.

His sisters looked proud and deliriously happy.

Maybe proposals would come of this night. Probably they would. Now that he knew what it meant to fall in love, he hoped, prayed with all his heart, that his sisters had found their true mates.

Geoffrey settled the girls comfortably and leaped up onto the bench beside Ember. "They said it went very well."

"I'm so glad."

"Apparently, a royal duke was quite smitten with Nora."

"Really?" Royalty. She deserved no less.

"Must be why the mistress looks so smug. Lucy said they danced three times. And Nora said Lucy was pursued by no less than three alphas, and the one she liked was also a duke but not a royal. They're all agog and won't get a wink tonight, I'll wager."

Ember sighed. "Wish I'd been there to see it." He didn't wish that, really. If he'd been at the ball, he'd never have met Domino, and he wouldn't give up the time spent with his alpha for anything. He glanced up at the moon and said a silent prayer of gratitude to the Goddess.

Thank you for the happiness I found tonight. Please, let my heart and my wolf be right about the alpha Domino. If not, help me to accept my misguided decision and live with the consequences.

Ember could accept that he'd taken a chance.

He acknowledged that he'd gone against everyone's advice.

He only hoped he could handle the results if it all went terribly wrong.

CHAPTER 11

it, Prince Christopher Albert Charles Ehrenpries, crept into the palace before dawn cracked the horizon over the sea.

There was no reason for him to employ stealth. No reason for him to stick to the shadows, except maybe he was still walking on air, and he wanted to keep his happiness to himself for a time.

John Coachman was on his mind, the omega's fragrance still clinging to his skin. If he closed his eyes, he could picture the lovely, delicately boned face of his true mate as if he'd painted it and hung it in the family gallery.

Hair like sable, soft curls, pale skin, doe eyes. His slim body was strong from work, his hands rough. He was perfect.

Kit already longed to have him again.

He wanted John's sweet body beneath his.

The Goddess is good, he thought as he made his way to the family's private living area. *The Goddess is wise and kind. She did not doom me to the lonely life I feared but gave me the greatest gift of all.*

I will never doubt Her love for me, for all Her children, again.

Kit almost made it to his chamber before his father stepped from the royal suite, hands clenched in fists on his hips.

"Christopher, come with me this instant."

"I just came in. I should get washed up—"

"You will come *now*." His father scowled at him as he turned and walked inside. "Close the door behind you."

With a shudder of apprehension, Kit did as his father bade him. "Did something happen to Mother?"

"I'm fine for now, darling," his mother answered from her lavender chair. She didn't look fine at all.

"She would be better"—the king glowered at him—"did she not know of your deception."

"What?" *His parents knew? How?*

"Did you think I wouldn't know that your cousin took your place?" she asked, aggrieved. "It's not even the first time. I'm your mother. It took me all of sixty seconds to see through the ruse."

"I'm sorry." He hung his head.

Blast. With the charm they'd purchased, Oliver was supposed to look exactly like him. It had worked in the past, so Kit guessed their mannerisms had given away the lie. He'd reminded Oliver not to spend any time with his parents, but sometimes Kit's father could be incredibly persistent. Like now.

"What did he do?" Kit asked.

"He was his charming and polite self. He found a girl he liked very much and then abandoned her to play your part. I allowed it because there was nothing else for it but to play along." The king grunted. "It was humiliating. A farce."

"Your father's right. It was ill done of you," his mother said quietly.

Did she look paler than usual? Maybe his conscience bothered him. She did not look well. "I'm sorry, Mother. I never meant to hurt you."

"Why would you do such a thing when you knew I wanted so badly to see you settled before—"

"I'm sorry, I am." He knelt at her feet. "But I knew that I'd never find my mate among the noble omegas you brought here, and I didn't have the heart to tell you."

"Why?" she asked. "Why couldn't you find an omega mate? We invited every suitable girl in the kingdom."

He lowered his head. "Omegas are invariably female, and—"

"Ah. You don't want to marry a—an omega? A woman?" she asked carefully. "Goddess, it would have been much easier if you'd said something before now."

"Bella—" The king narrowed his eyes. "Does this mean—"

"Hush, beloved, let him say the words."

"I want a consort, not a queen." Kit laid his head on his mother's lap. "I'm sorry. I know that it's highly irregular, and there's the question of heirs—"

The king gaped at him. "Let's see if I have this right, Kit. I invited every single noble omega in four kingdoms to attend a ball in your honor, and you couldn't be bothered to say, *oh, by the way, Father, I want a consort?*"

The queen gave a dry chuckle. "Think about your blood pressure, my darling."

"Mine? What about yours?" He studied her with such concern that even Kit felt frightened for her. "This was your mother's wish, Kit. She asks nothing of us, and you could have at least—"

"I don't want your guilt, darling. I need to know that the young man I've raised will be good, and honorable, and happy with the mate of his choosing."

"Then it's all right, Mother. Last night, I met someone."

"Whom?" his father asked.

"Er—" Kit hesitated. He'd not slept much the night before, and he had a bad feeling he wasn't going to be able to make them see how amazing his night had been. After all, as far as he knew, he'd found the only male omega in existence and it was his true mate.

This was going to take some explaining.

"Is High Priestess Yanlain available to discuss this? I'd feel better if she were here."

"You need a priestess?" his mother asked.

"Yes, if she's here, could you please ask her to come? And maybe Lothaire as well?"

"You want the high priestess and a court historian in attendance while we discuss the person you met last night." The king eyed him warily. "Will you need a solicitor as well? You'd better not be playing another one of your games, Christopher."

"If it's feasible"—Kit twisted his hands nervously—"I would like to hear what they have to say about things before I tell you the rest."

"So mysterious." His mother asked her maid to order tea for when the two counselors arrived. "I hope you have a good reason for all this."

"I do," he assured her.

The king rose and gave the bellpull by the door a tug. He asked the runner who arrived to bring the individuals Kit had asked for to the council room.

The small reception area was still cold when they arrived. Maids lit the fire and candles while the king's steward found a more comfortable chair for Her Majesty. Yanlain was the first to arrive. The king invited her to sit at his conference table. Yanlain's silken robes rustled as she took the chair he offered.

"What is this about, Your Majesty?"

"My son wishes to speak with you. He asked for Lothaire as well."

They had to wait a bit longer for the historian as he'd had to be retrieved from nearby Ehrenpries University. The man was old, but he was known to be an early riser. He had no doubt been dressed by the time he was summoned. Kit waited anxiously while the king, queen, and Yanlain made small talk, mostly about the weather. Lothaire entered the room wearing scholarly robes and the funny, high hat that marked him as a counselor to the king.

"I came as soon as I could, Your Majesty." He made his way to the table and sat across from Kit. "Good morning, Your Majesty, My Queen. How do you do, Your Highness? Yanlain, I hope I find you well this morning?"

"We shall see about that," she said enigmatically, "after we find out why we're here."

"Go on, Kit." The king—at this point not his father but his head of state—glared at him. "Explain why you wish to speak with us."

"Well, as you know, I found a way to avoid the ball." He glanced at Yanlain and Lothaire. "It wasn't well done of me, but I had my reasons. I knew I could never be happy with any of the omegas you invited, Sire."

The king flushed. "You—"

"Please, I beg of you, listen. I should have said this long ago, but I put it off because I thought you wouldn't understand. My whole life, I've watched your love grow stronger. I know what it means to have a true mate. Maybe I'm selfish, but I want that kind of love for myself someday and"—he bit his lip until he tasted blood—"I believed it was impossible because I could never truly love an omega. Or any woman, for that matter."

"All right," said Lothaire. "You cannot love a woman. But you'll be king someday, and you'll need heirs. What will we do then?"

"He's right, Kit," his father agreed. "Will you have our line die out because you'd rather be with a man? Selfish boy."

"We should hear him out, my love," said the queen. "He says he's found someone."

"I found my true mate," Kit told them. "A male omega."

Yanlain's eyes bored into Kit's very soul. "Is this true?"

"It is, yes," Kit admitted. "I didn't even know male omegas existed until last night. But I met a man who is unmistakably omega."

The king made an unhappy sound and leaned back with his arms crossed. He didn't look very open-minded at all. Kit's mouth went dry.

"Carry on." The king waved a beringed hand. "Say what you have asked us all here to listen to."

"You don't know what it's like to imagine going through the motions with a girl I don't love, don't want … that way. Being with her day in and day out, creating heirs instead of bringing children into the world out of love." Before his father could give him further grief, he held up his hand. "I was prepared to choose a name out of a hat, though I wasn't keen to do it. I want to be a proper heir, Father, to do what's right."

"Then why couldn't you attend the ball?" asked the queen.

"Because it felt like a spectacle. Like everyone would watch my every move and wager who I'd choose and make bawdy jokes about me, and I—I just couldn't bear the thought of that."

"Oh, Kit." The queen placed her hand over his.

"I want to be what you want."

"You're my boy, and you're perfect in my eyes." She shook his hand. "Even if you don't want what I want for you. Understand?"

Eyes burning, Kit nodded.

"This is, if I may say, the dilemma of many noble-born offspring," said Lothaire. "One is exceedingly lucky if one finds one's true mate. It isn't the norm. Yet many happy marriages are made from friendship and respect."

"I know, and I was almost ready to accept that fate," Kit offered. "But I've found the man my wolf and my heart tell me is my true mate. I understand why you're angry, but I'm certain a great many other people found their mates last night, and that's a wonderful thing, isn't it? The Goddess surely smiles on all of us."

"All right." The king muttered. "Tell us about his paragon of yours."

"As I said, he's a *male* omega. He works for the Saeger family. You know the Earl of Carlysle? He's their coachman." He held up his hand as the four of them began talking all at once. "Is it not true that the wolf knows its mate? If so, then that man is my true mate. He brought Carlysle's omega sisters to the ball, but of course he had to spend the rest of the evening hiding his nature from everyone in Moonrise Bay."

"Yanlain? Lothaire? Enlighten my son about omegas. My son is an alpha. He is royalty. His true mate must be an omega of breeding, and omegas are *women*."

"Hm ..." Yanlain had grown contemplative after her initial shock. "Who is to say the Goddess couldn't create a male omega?"

"Who indeed?" Lothaire gave Kit a nod. "There have been male omegas in Helionne lore, but they're very rare. It's been hundreds of years since one has come to light. Your own line, Your Highness, has had such a mating. King Philgrave Ehrenpries had an omega consort—what, eight hundred years ago? My colleagues and I postulate that because a fever decimated the omega population, your ancestor found no eligible woman to wed. Or perhaps there were political reasons? No one knows."

"What if it was a Goddess blessed mating?" Kit asked. "Are there diaries? What did you learn from the records of their personal lives?"

Lothaire stroked his beard. "We have no first-person source material from the time. It's possible there was some natural disaster, such as a flood or a fire, that caused the loss of those records, but I believe it more likely that someone who came along later didn't want their king's male coupling to be known."

"That's right." Yanlain nodded. "There was a time when alliances between same-gender couples were forbidden. Our sect has always supported true matings regardless of status or gender. Many priestesses of our faith were kept under scrutiny, jailed, and faced banishment before King Esidron decreed that wolves must mate as the Goddess wills. He believed the wolf knows its mate, and those unions are blessed."

"That's excellent news for me." Kit's mood lightened quite a bit. "Because my wolf is certain John is his mate."

"You would bring a coachman here to rule the kingdom as your consort? A member of the serving class?" His father tapped the table with his fingers. "That's impossible."

"I think we should at least meet this man," Yanlain said tentatively. "You have nothing to lose, Your Majesty. You might ask the court physician to perform a medical test to ascertain whether this man is a true omega, or—"

"He is an omega. I can assure you," said Kit.

"Kit." The king sighed. "Any beta whore can pass herself off as an omega for a limited time."

"My dear!" The queen's shocked words gave him pause.

"I beg your pardon, darling, but it's true."

"Not to a healthy alpha wolf," said Lothaire. "The nose doesn't lie."

"He's right. Don't be offensive, Father. I know an omega when I scent one. I was as skeptical as you, but I swear by the Goddess it's nothing but the truth."

"Son—"

"It's a simple enough matter to find out unless you have a reason you don't want it to be true ..." Lothaire practically dared the king to act.

"Lothaire, don't think that because we're old friends I won't lock you in a dungeon and throw away the key."

Lothaire's lips quirked. "Who would you play cards with, then?"

Yanlain turned to Kit. "It seems to me that you believe you've found your true mate. I will support you as long as there's no unwholesome plan at work. You must bring your young man to me. I wish to speak with him."

"You can't be serious, Yanlain." The king shook his head. "Even if a male omega birth occurred in the past, there's no reason to believe one has been born in this generation. Female omegas are thick on the ground. Why would the Goddess create a male omega, and how is it that he's set his sights on my son, the future king? I fear a sorcerer might be manipulating you, Kit."

Kit's hands fisted. "And maybe the Goddess wants me to have a consort I can love."

"Oh, Kit. I will pray that it's true," said the queen. She stood shakily and braced both hands on the table. "Now I fear I'm very tired. Let me speak with Kit alone, please."

"Of course, my dear." The king rose. "Let us all adjourn to my study while they talk, shall we?"

The others left the room empty but for Kit and his mother.

"Mother, can I get you anything?" He went to the tea cart and prepared a cup. "Here, this will warm you up."

"Thank you, darling." She accepted the tea from him and held it with both hands. They looked positively bloodless. "Tell me about your young man."

So he told her. How he'd donned a mask and let Oliver take his place using an illusion charm. How he'd gone into Moonlight Bay to bide his time, found his coachman, and saved him from those louts Perkins and Graeme. How he'd known fairly quickly that it wasn't a chance encounter, that he'd found his mate.

117

"He told me to call him John Coachman, but that can't be his real name. He seemed wary of exposing his true identity so I played along."

"Of course, he was, if he'd just been accosted."

"He wore Carlysle Manor's livery, so that part of his story is true. I must ask the current earl to speak with him if I want to get to the bottom of things."

"The Saegers family. Let's see …" She seemed to search her memory. "The mother died, and the father remarried a foreign princess with two little girls if I recall correctly. By now, the boy will have taken on his father's title. I'll write as soon as possible. Perhaps we can find out more about this coachman before we take further steps in this matter."

"It doesn't matter what anyone finds out. He's my mate." He tapped his chest. "I felt it here."

"Perhaps," she said, frowning. "But protocol demands we investigate his background. We must meet him and get to know his family as we would any omega you'd met at the ball. You must take the time to court him and then if all is well, make an offer for his hand."

"But—" Kit's face caught fire. "He's mine, I know he is. I—I've already claimed him."

"What?" She raised a shaking hand to her heart. "After a single encounter?"

"Doesn't it happen that way sometimes?" He wanted a hole to crawl into. "Emotions run high, and—"

"It doesn't happen that way in a royal family." She coughed and couldn't seem to catch her breath. "Have you lost your mind?"

"Mother, please. Sip your tea." Her sudden outrage worried him. "Breathe slowly. I don't understand. I thought you'd be happy for me."

"Kit, you've been trained in protocol. You're the royal heir—"

"He doesn't know that. I wore a mask in the tavern, and we were in the—it was dark—when he took it off me. I swear to you, there wasn't a hint of recognition."

"Maybe not, but you're obviously of the ruling class. A young man of the serving class might not feel he has the right to refuse your advances."

"Mother! I didn't take advantage of him."

"But you know better. I *taught* you better. And you would never have treated any other omega—any girl—with that same sort of abandon, be she noble born or not."

"Well, of course not, but it's different with girls, isn't it?" He wouldn't have done anything with a girl.

"It shouldn't be!" His mother's skin took on a grayish hue. "You must never use instinct as an excuse. You must court your omega. Offer the protection of your name. What ... what must he think of you?"

Aghast, all he could say was, "I didn't think of it that way. Let me call someone for you, Mother, you look unwell—"

"If you care about someone, you place their needs first. Your mate must feel very alone right now. You must find him ... make up for your rash actions. Protect him if you've already claimed him. Do you understand me?"

"Mother, I'm so sorry, my shock was so great on finding him that I just—"

"You're not the first boy to lose his head." She patted his cheek lovingly, but her hand felt like ice. She was so weak she dropped it back to her lap with a sigh. "Court your coachman, woo him, win him. He deserves to be more to you than a tumble, yes?"

"Of course."

"You wouldn't stand for it if *we* made your mate feel less." She leaned back in her chair. "Can you call my maid for me?"

"Of course, Mother." He left to find the woman and send her

to aid his mother. On the way back, he stopped in at his father's study.

His father, Lothaire, and Yanlain were still arguing about the existence of male omegas, and what it might mean to the kingdom if he took a consort instead of a queen. To his relief, his father didn't seem angry anymore.

"Did you have a nice talk with your mother?" asked the king.

"Yes, we did." Kit couldn't help worrying over the state he'd left her in. "I left her with her maid, but she didn't seem well."

"That's because she's not well, Kit." The king blinked his eyes. "Did she advise you about all this?"

"She reminded me that I must treat my mate like any other omega. I must woo him, win him. Offer for his hand with all the pomp expected of the royal heir."

"We don't know a thing about this coachman." The king narrowed his eyes. "He is a young man, right? Not some widower twice your age with a passel of children?"

"We can all hope—" Yanlain's words were cut off by a sudden, dreadful scream.

"Bella!" The king shot to his feet and started running.

"Was that Mother's maid?" Kit tore after him. The sounds of several women wailing drew them to the royal suite.

"Goddess help me, I'm not ready. Bella!" the king gave his own anguished cry. Kit entered the royal chamber behind him, They found the queen lying on the floor in front of her altar. A finger of sun caressed her pale face; her wide blue eyes lay open and staring blankly.

It was clear the queen—Kit's mother—was gone.

Kit's heart shattered. Grief rolled over him like a terrible storm.

"She asked me to bring her more candles," one of her attendants sobbed. "I left for only a moment. When I returned, she was there at her altar."

"Damn it," the king cursed. "She wasn't strong enough for

your shenanigans, Kit. I should have spared her this mess you've gotten yourself into."

"Your Majesty, the queen's time was at hand. This is not your son's doing," Yanlain said softly, having followed them. "She probably wanted to commune with the Goddess one last time."

"Oh, my darling girl." The king lifted his beloved onto his lap and cupped her face between his palms. Grief etched every line in his body. He rose to his knees with her in his arms and howled as though his heart was breaking.

The sound was visceral, primal.

It called Kit's wolf to battle despite there being no foe he could vanquish and nothing he could do to right this dreadful wrong. The power of his father's voice began the change in him. His wolf took over and transformed seamlessly. It was good. Being wolf was easier. His human grief abated, his anguish seeming to lie just out of reach. Kit's father called his name, but he shook off his clothing and tore out of the room.

"Catch him," his father ordered. "Don't let him leave the palace grounds."

With servants giving chase, Kit ran past his bedchamber, past his father's study, and down the stairs. On instinct, he headed out through the kitchens, He passed startled cooks and several maids before bursting through the open service door.

Like his sire, Kit howled his misery. He howled with grief and pain and fear of things he could not name. Others took up his cry as he made his way past the grazing lands and into the woods. He couldn't put enough distance between himself and the palace. There was no place far enough away to escape the loss of his beloved mother.

Goddess. He'd let his mother down, and now she was dead. His wolf wanted her to meet his mate, and it was too late. Too late for the queen to get to know John. Too late for her to attend their wedding. Too late for children of their union to know how good his mother was, how kind, how wise. She would have been so happy, and he'd ruined everything.

How could he live with himself now?

Did anything even matter anymore?

Content to have four legs to help him flee as fast and as far as he could get, Kit ran and ran and ran.

CHAPTER 12

*D*espite being up most of the night, the morning after the ball was like any other to Ember. The horses didn't care if he was too tired to think or too sore to move; they needed feeding, to be turned loose, and to have their stalls mucked out, same as usual. Tom helped where he could, but the cold and damp made him stiff in the mornings. Ember didn't hold it against him.

The girls slept in, so after Ember's chores he found a cozy spot in the barn for a nap. Three hours later a fly, curious about the man lying in the barn where he normally only found horses to annoy, awoke Ember from a deep, dream-filled sleep.

He opened his eyes, looked around, and wished he could stay in the dream where his maybe-mate, Domino, held him tenderly. Where Domino found ways to excite and arouse and astound Ember with his careful, gentle hands and fascinating male body.

Goddess, how was Ember supposed to focus on work with the memories of last night banging on the door of his mind, loosening the restraints he had tried to bind them with, confusing him and causing predictable, embarrassing reactions?

He was just like his sisters, swooning over a man he'd met the night before; but unlike them, he'd begun to have serious doubts about the wisdom of his actions.

Men like Domino, worldly men, sophisticated, beautiful men, didn't chase after servants. Despite what Domino had said about them being mates, Ember didn't know whether he'd hear from the alpha again.

To make matters worse, in the cold light of day all of Hugh's warnings had come back to haunt him. Now that he wasn't caught up in the moment, he blushed at the things he'd done, the liberties he'd allowed Domino to take.

Last night might have been a terrible mistake.

It was absurd to dream of something a man like him probably couldn't have. He'd started out very practical, but his naive wolf and his stupid, gullible heart fought so hard to believe in fairy tales.

Ember went inside to find that Geoffrey had already heated water for his bath. Despite his caution, when Ember undressed, Geoffrey saw all the marks and bruises on Ember's skin. Ember slapped a hand over the bite where Domino had claimed him, but there were several other embarrassing marks on his body, beard burn and love bites on his neck and chest from Domino's eager mouth, and visible fingerprints on his hips.

Eyebrows raised, Geoffrey shot him a shocked look. "I *knew* I shouldn't have left you alone! What happened?"

"By all that you hold dear, keep what you see to yourself," Ember begged. "Can you imagine Lenore's face if she found out?"

"I swear no one will hear it from me. But"—Geoffrey searched his face—"are you all right? No one ... forced you ... did they?"

Ember sighed. "No, of course not. I met someone and things happened rather quickly, after that."

"I'll say. You weren't gone for more than two hours."

Ember sank into the water with a shrug. He wasn't ashamed, precisely. He'd done nothing people hadn't been doing since the dawn of time. But keeping his tryst to himself was for the best. He made Geoffrey promise not to say a word.

"I promise, your secret's safe with me." Geoffrey looked at him differently, though. He wasn't contemptuous, only sad. Ember felt his pity like a blast of icy snow. Was that how people might look at him from now on?

After he'd bathed and dressed respectably, Ember went to the library, where he found Lenore doing needlework. Her smile was serene for a change, which reinforced the notion that things had gone well the night before. The girls had draped themselves dramatically on the divan.

"Good afternoon," he greeted them. "Tell me, how do you feel about the ball now?"

Lenore lifted her gaze from her work. "You'll be pleased to know that the girls were a tremendous success."

"Truly?" he asked brightly. "I knew they'd have every man there hopelessly in love. Was there anyone special?"

"I fear it's my destiny to break every heart except for the one that won mine," said Nora pertly. "He was an omega's dream alpha."

"Then by week's end, Moonrise Bay will be littered with the bones of your languishing admirers," he teased. "Tell us all about this paragon."

"I promised him I wouldn't jinx things by talking about him, but we danced three dances together. One was a waltz. Being in his arms was heavenly. There's sure to be a scandal, especially since he had to leave before the prince even made his appearance! My dance card was full for the rest of the night, but no one was nearly as wonderful." She laid her hand over Lucy's mouth. "Don't you dare say his name, Lu. I forbid it."

Lucy shoved her hand away. "I won't, for heaven's sake. You

don't need to smother me. What do you think, Ember? I developed a tendre for someone too."

"Did you?" Ember asked. "What is your lucky young man like?"

"He's amazing." She sighed. "And I'm not jinxing anything when I say he's a *duke*."

"A duke? Good heavens, is he handsome?" Ember took a wing chair by the fire as his father used to do. Given his sacrifice and the girls' success the night before, he believed his father would be proud of him. "Did he offer you pretty words?"

"Oh, he was so lovely and kind. He likes animals. He told me all about his hunting dogs, *and* he keeps a cat as a pet. Isn't that strange for an alpha? You'd think a cat would have better sense, though apparently the opposite is true. His cat adores cuddles, though his valet despises the fur it leaves on his clothing." Lucy closed her eyes and giggled. "It was as if we'd known each other forever."

"Tell us how your wolf reacted, dear." Lenore must know already; perhaps she wanted Ember to hear about it.

"My wolf adores him." Lucy flushed deeply. "I believe he's my true mate. He didn't say anything so forward, but I just felt something different with him. He smelled so impossibly delicious. I nearly swooned."

"My secret sweetheart was my true mate for certain," Nora proclaimed proudly. "He even said so. He told me he'd waited for me all his life."

"All right, girls." Lenore put aside her needlework. "I feel duty bound to remind you that alphas say sweet things to naive young omegas even if they have no intention of pursuing them. It's best to see if they back up their pretty words with actions before letting your heart become involved."

Ember's eyes shot toward her. He felt hot all of a sudden.

"Something the matter, Ember?" Lenore asked. "You look flushed, dear."

"Er, no. Nothing. I think my bath was a bit warmer this morning."

"You need to remind Geoffrey that he's heating bathwater, not soup."

"Noted." He tried to smile, but the result was half-hearted.

"Are you certain you're all right?" Lenore studied him closely.

"Of course." He felt laid bare, stripped to his very bones. Lenore wasn't a stupid woman. Did she sense he'd done more while they were at the ball than wait with the carriage? For once he didn't appreciate her sharp attention to detail.

"If there's anything you'd like to talk about," she said carefully, "my door is always open."

"Thank you. I did my morning chores on little sleep, but other than that I'm fine." He couldn't look away. She'd never been so kind to him, but along with that came her forthright gaze. It was as if they'd turned some kind of corner when they'd teamed up to give the girls the advantage of the prince's ball. They were allies now, and he must never forget how intelligent and intuitive she could be.

"All right. If that's the case, I insist you spend the afternoon at rest. Your sisters and I will tiptoe to make sure you're not disturbed after supper. Perhaps we might consider hiring a groom. I'm aware of how hard you work in the stables—"

"I enjoy being with the animals, but it sounds nice to have help."

"The next time you're in Carlysle Crossing, ask Hugh Smith if he knows an able lad looking for work, will you? I fear we've taken terrible advantage all these years. Now, though, you'll be responsible for the stewardship of your inheritance, and—"

"Such as it is," he interrupted dryly. "I would greatly appreciate your help while I learn what's needed to take my place as the earl."

"Of course." She had the grace to blush. "I have neglected your education, though you seemed very happy running wild."

"I was happy. And now I'll pay for it unless I undertake a great deal of hard study to catch up."

Lenore nodded. It seemed they truly did have an understanding.

Why now? he wondered. Perhaps she knew that he had resented her and his sisters for a time. Perhaps she was aware that he'd childishly blamed her for his father's death. Now, with maturity, he knew the Goddess took her servants home when it was their time. These days, it was only regret that held Ember in the past. He missed his parents. He wished they'd had more time.

Ember glanced toward the girls. "My father would have loved to present you at court. He'd be so proud and pleased that his girls made such a sensation."

"He would," Lenore agreed.

"But what do we do now?" Nora asked. "Must we simply sit around sewing until our alphas come to call? Why are omegas not allowed to have a say in their lives? How will I bear waiting until he offers for me? Oh, Goddess, what if he never does?"

She rolled dramatically, hiding her face in the cushions.

"I'm afraid waiting is an old and very worn pastime for omegas." Lenore smiled fondly as she picked up her needlework. "Alphas spend an awful lot of time making decisions we know are inevitable."

"Was it that way with our Father?" Nora asked. "When you met, did you know he was the one?"

Lenore glanced at Ember before answering. "Your father, Nora, was a lovely man, but ours was a marriage arranged for reasons of property. While I cared for him, I did not love him. I cared for Ember's father too, but we never got the chance to let anything like love blossom between us. Some omegas don't find true mates, and we still live accomplished, happy lives."

Lenore had *never* married for love? How unfair he'd been to her. She was ambitious, yes. She was cold as well. Exacting. But to never experience loving and being loved by one's true mate …

Ember felt sorry for her because one night with Domino had been enough to show him what love could be, even if he never got another.

"I'm sorry if I made things worse after my father died." Meeting her gaze was difficult.

"Life goes on." Lenore pulled a bright yellow thread through the hoop of the tapestry she was working on. "Endings are painful, but new lives are always beginning, young people marry whether or not they find true mates. Babies come into the world. Nothing lasts forever."

"Oh, Mother." Lucy walked over to curl up next to Lenore. She laid her head on her shoulder.

Lenore patted Lucy's hair. "It's fine, Lu. I'm fine."

"I wish the earl had lived to meet my mate," said Nora.

"The earl will meet him," Ember reminded her. "And I'll chase him away with Old Tom's shotgun if he isn't kind to you."

"You know I was talking about your father."

He winked. "I know."

She dropped her head against the cushion behind her. "How long do you think we'll have to wait to hear from our alphas?"

"It could be months," Lenore answered honestly. "You've set your caps for men whose families may want to challenge their decision. They might need convincing that a rustic earl's sisters —be they royal princesses in a foreign land or no—are worthy mates for men with titles and fortunes such as theirs."

Nora gasped. "But we're true mates. How could anyone deny us?"

"Some families put more faith in property than the Goddess's wisdom."

"Do you think our dreams are hopeless, then?"

"No, my dear." Lenore frowned. "Of course not. I simply want you to understand that there is much to think about when it comes to marriage between noble families. Many things will affect your future husband's choices. All of this takes time."

Nora pouted. "I can't bear it. Why couldn't I have been born an alpha? *I'd* know what to do with someone who tries to tell me I can't marry my true mate."

"I wouldn't mind being an alpha," Ember said dryly. "Things would be much easier around here."

"Oh." Lucy's eyes widened. "I'm certain Nora didn't mean to imply—"

"Everyone has something they wish they could change," he admitted. "But things have a way of working out for the best."

"In the meantime," said Lenore, "perhaps we should talk about what it takes to run a large household? You will need such skills if your alphas offer for you."

"Oh, yes." Lucy's eyes shone. "Let's have lessons."

"This makes a change," said Ember. "You used to find any excuse to leave the schoolroom."

"It's strange, but now that I know what I want, it seems much more exciting to learn everything I'll need to know if I get it," said Nora.

Ember laughed. "Excellent observation. Very true."

"And what do you want, brother?" Nora asked. "You're an earl and an omega. Mother, if an omega's a man, must he wait for an offer, or can he make his own offer preemptively?"

"That is a good question, is it not?" Lucy teased. "When will you begin looking for a mate, Ember?"

"How do you know I haven't? Perhaps I've already found my alpha," he teased. "In answer to your question, I would wait until they offered for me." Ember's words dropped into the room like a boulder launched from a trebuchet. Lenore narrowed her eyes in thought.

"Alphas are always men," Lucy stated, wide-eyed with shock. "Aren't they?"

"I'm a male omega. There's an exception to every rule."

Nora's eyes widened. "You'd let a lady alpha offer for you? How droll would that be, if she bent her knee and dirtied her skirt?"

"Oh, Ember." Lucy came to sit on the arm of his chair. "You'll find someone who would love to be Lady Carlysle, and she'll be perfect."

"Thank you." He reached up and gave her hand a squeeze. "Right now, I'm saving all my wishes for you and Nora. After that, we'll see, won't we?"

"Oh, my goodness. I'm so excited I can hardly stand it." Lucy twirled across the room.

"Grrr." Nora tossed a throw pillow at her. "I want my future resolved now. I want my alpha."

"Have patience for once in your life, Nora," Lenore said. "The future is in the hands of the Goddess, and She loves us all. Take heart."

"May we be worthy," all three omegas intoned out of habit.

CHAPTER 13

Through his grief and pain, Kit lost all track of time. He stayed in the royal forest evading humans and predators alike. He hunted when necessary, ate whatever he could catch, and slept on the thick carpet of leaves that made up the forest floor only when he could go no farther.

An entire moon cycle passed while he stayed in wolf form to escape his despair. Eventually, fewer parties came looking for him, even though there were more people on the palace grounds than he'd ever seen.

One day, church bells clanged in the towers of the Moonrise Cathedral for what seemed like an eternity. People from every city in Helionne clogged the roads leading to the palace itself. Kit hid as close to the road as possible, unable to stay away while the procession he recognized as his mother's final journey passed by.

Summer turned to autumn, and the weather changed.

There was rain but nothing that worried him until one day a mountain of ominous dark clouds scudded in from the sea. Lightning arced across the roiling sky, followed by thunder that made even his wolf tremble. Without a conscious decision, Kit sped along the road from the palace grounds, down the sharply inclined road, and into the city of Moonrise Bay.

The long, fraught journey eventually took him to his cousin Oliver's townhouse; the one place he might find safety and shelter without being sent back home in disgrace.

Since he arrived at night, he slept in the muddy bushes behind the row house until after dawn. Rain continued to come down by the bucketful while wind howled overhead. It was hard to tell from the sky if the hour was decent for visiting until the barest change of light indicated the night was over.

He took a chance and scratched at the tradesman's entrance. A kitchen maid answered but immediately ran screaming to the butler about the strange wolf at the door. Kit waited on the porch until Oliver finally arrived, still wrapping a velvet dressing gown around his half-naked body.

"Christopher?" He gaped at Kit. No doubt he looked like the veriest stray mongrel alive. "Goddess, where have you been? The whole kingdom has been frantically searching for you. You missed your mother's *funeral*. Shift and explain yourself. Your father's out of his mind with worry."

Kit's wolf shrank, trying to make way for his human to take over, but ... he couldn't seem to shift.

That's odd.

He shook water off his coat and tried again but nothing happened. His heart raced as he glanced up at Oliver, who stared at him expectantly.

"Well, come on," said Oliver. "I haven't got all morning."

Shifting into human form had always been a simple matter of will. A manifestation of the magic Kit wielded as an alpha. He was spoiled, that was all. Things came too easily to him. He hadn't tried shifting for weeks, so naturally it wasn't going to be a snap.

He relaxed and tried again and again. Nothing.

Kit simply *couldn't* shift.

He stood in Oliver's service porch, quivering with damp and cold. All he could think about was a hot bath and a cup of tea. He would enjoy neither unless he could shift. Goddess, what was wrong with him?

"All right, old man? Are you too cold to shift? It's no wonder." Oliver ushered him inside and ordered one of the maids to draw a bath. "Obviously, you're still in a mood. You know, Kit, if I were your father, I'd have you flogged. Maybe a bath will help you realize the dire situation you're in."

Kit couldn't say no to a bath. He couldn't say anything. Blast!

There were stories of wolves turning feral after a great personal loss or family tragedy. Kit had always believed they did it on purpose, but now he wondered if it happened because they went too long without shifting.

How long did it take?

Goddess, was he doomed to stay wolf forever?

He growled, then whimpered over his inability to communicate with his cousin. Being around Oliver should make things easier, shouldn't it? And being around Oliver's human staff as well. If everyone else was in human form, Kit was sure he'd shift eventually if only because he hated being odd man out.

"Shh." Oliver put a hand on his neck and guided him toward the stairs. "Grief does funny things to people. Don't worry. We'll have you fixed up in no time."

Oliver was right. Grief gnawed at Kit but so did guilt. His mother's dying wish was to see him mated, and what did he do? He'd refused to attend the ball she'd given for him. Not only that, but she'd taught him to be honorable with omegas, yet he'd met a perfectly innocent omega, told him they were true mates, violated him, claimed him, and then had barely woken up long enough to reassure him that they'd see each other again soon.

He'd been in wolf form for ages. Left his omega without a word.

No wonder he couldn't shift back; he was a cur.

"Your mother wouldn't want you punishing yourself." Oliver gave his neck a squeeze. "You wouldn't have found a mate that night even if you'd gone through with her plans for you. We both know that."

I did find my mate! Kit wanted to scream the words, but the only thing that came out was a pitiful yip.

"As it happens, I found my omega mate," Oliver informed him.

Kit stilled.

"I met her before I left and changed to make my appearance as 'the prince.'" Oliver tested the water with his hand before practically shoving Kit into the bath. "I saw this lovely girl and knew right away she was mine. She's titled, but has absolutely nothing. Thankfully true mates are a blessing from the Goddess, even in the eyes of my mercenary mother."

Despite his own unhappiness, Kit was delighted for his cousin. He gave a wolfish grin and nipped at him playfully. At this, Oliver broke into a smile.

"My girl's a bit of a handful, though. Very outspoken. Wait until you meet her."

Kit lifted his brows, lowered to his haunches, and splashed Oliver with his tail.

"You beast. What was that for?"

Kit growled and nudged the soap with his nose.

"You don't expect me to wash you." Oliver's jaw dropped. "You do. Goddess, you're a nuisance."

Someone had to wash him; Kit was utterly filthy.

He made to splash Oliver again.

"All right, all right." Oliver picked up the soap and began to lather Kit's fur. "It's not just me that got lucky. Seavane found his mate as well. She's the sister of my girl. Lucky that we're nearly neighbors in town because separating the two would be against our best interests. I've always liked Seavane. His hunting dogs are truly exceptional."

Kit liked Seavane too. He was a decent sort of man, a little shy, but fun to go larking about with.

"So the ball was successful in terms of how many matches were made. I don't suppose that helps, though."

Kit's enthusiasm wilted. He ducked underwater and stayed there for as long as he could hold his breath. When he surfaced, Oliver appeared worried.

"Don't drown yourself, Kit. I'm certain your mother passed believing you were trying to do what she asked of you. That something, isn't it?"

Kit shook his head. At least he could do that much.

"She didn't? How do you know? Wait." Oliver drew himself upright. "Your parents didn't catch on, did they?"

Kit gave a nod.

"Blast." Oliver paled. "Will the king punish me, do you think? He hasn't yet."

Kit leapt from the water and shook.

"Stop, no!" Oliver grabbed a towel and held it like a shield. "You bastard, what has gotten into you?"

Kit glared at him.

"This would be so much easier if we didn't have to play charades. Just shift, old man. We'll get drunk and formulate a plan of action. The king can't stay mad at you forever, you're the heir."

Kit didn't move. He continued to glare.

"Unless … you can't shift." Oliver narrowed his eyes. "But that's nonsense because—"

Kit yipped and yipped until Oliver finally caught on.

"You can't shift? How awful for you. I can't imagine how you must feel." Oliver opened the door to his bedchamber. "Here, let me get you a blanket. Stay on the floor, I won't want my bed soaked."

Kit let Oliver wrap the blanket around him and curled up in its warmth gratefully.

"Oh, cousin." Oliver patted his back. "What are we going to do now?"

When Kit didn't answer, Oliver smiled sadly.

"I've been your partner in crime since we were in leading strings. I'm not about to give up on you now. Rest a while here while I research to see if there's anything in the books about getting stuck in one's wolf form."

Oliver closed the door between them.

Goddess, Kit was exhausted. He hurt everywhere. Between the weather and miles of four-footed travel, he felt spent in ways he couldn't have imagined. How long had he been in that dazed state? More than a moon cycle. Besides that, he didn't have any real way to know.

Now, with his head clearer than it had been since he'd shifted, his human's agitation was a splinter beneath his skin. He and his wolf wanted their mate with a longing so ferocious that when Kit closed his eyes, John was all he could see.

The Carlysle coachman. He could find the omega easily enough if he traveled to Carlysle Manor. He couldn't ask around if he couldn't shift, but he could search out his scent. His wolf could find him. And say what? That he'd gone wolf and failed to get back?

If his father saw John with his own eyes he would eventually forgive Kit. John was unmistakably omega. He was real. What they'd shared was the beginning of a mate bond like his parents had experienced. The king's council might stand against a consort, but they would not deny Kit his true mate any more than Oliver's family would deny his.

In the meantime, though, Kit might die from rage or grief or worse, given there were bigger predators and outlaw shifters who hunted their own kind for sport. Winter was coming.

His mother was dead.

Even as a wolf, Kit had his memories. Images from his childhood, the many times his parents had visited him at school, and the holidays they'd enjoyed. Now he excoriated himself for the aloof and secretive son he'd been as he'd grown older.

How hard would it have been to show more patience with his mother? To be more forthcoming about his nature and what he wanted from a mate? How hard would it have been to spend more time beside her while she recuperated from her many illnesses, chatting or reading to her or simply carrying her out to the balcony while the sun was warm?

How hard would it have been to say, "I love you," more often?

Kit tucked his tail between his legs in shame.

It was all impossible now.

The old saying was true. No one knew what he had until it was gone.

～

Oliver knocked on the door. "Are you all right in there?" Kit blinked awake. He was still a wolf. The light had changed. Long golden bars stretched across his cousin's fancy rug. He growled when Oliver opened the door.

"Come get some food in you, Kit. I'll bet you've been living on rats and drinking filthy runoff for days. With rest and decent meals your human will be back in no time."

Kit followed him down the stairs

In the kitchen, Oliver pointed out a large dish of rich stew and another of water laid out in the corner of the room before taking a seat at his table, lifting his teacup, and blowing to cool its contents. Kit gulped down his food and lapped up all the water. When he was finished, he cleaned his muzzle with his paws as best he could.

"Oh, perhaps you can clear up a mystery for me," Oliver took a flour sack off a peg in the kitchen wall. "I went to the Red Wolf Inn to look for you after you disappeared, and the oddest thing happened. Yancy the innkeeper told me if I found you, I should give you this."

He opened the bag and showed Kit a coachman's hat with the Carlysle crest.

Kit's heart burst with excitement. He lurched forward, hardly daring to believe his coachman had left something behind. Kit snatched it from Oliver's hands and buried his nose in it. He drank in the scent of his mate.

Maybe that was the key to his problem. Maybe all he needed was to find his mate!

Practically dancing, Kit gave an enthusiastic yowl.

"All right, then. Mystery solved, I guess." Oliver went back to drinking his tea. "Wait. Do you know the Carlysle coachman, because—"

Kit leapt on him, dancing and nipping at him. If Kit was lucky, it would only be a matter of showing himself with the hat at Carlysle Manor. But would his omega acknowledge a wolf? He whined miserably.

"What is it? What does the hat mean?" Oliver stared into his eyes. Kit tried not to take it as a challenge, but it was hard to fight his instinct. Oliver glanced away first. "Sorry, Kit, but you should know that my intended is—"

A loud knock sounded on Oliver's front door.

"What on earth could that be?" Lacking his butler nearby, Oliver went to answer himself, and Kit followed, peeking from the kitchen door. There was a troop of royal guardsmen on Oliver's doorstep.

"We're looking for the prince," said the captain. Oliver gave Kit a sharp look. Kit crept backward, out of sight. Oliver sighed heavily. "And like the last time and the time before that, you'll not find him here."

"We've been instructed to search your residence this time, Your Grace."

"Wait. What?" The soldiers pushed their way inside. "You have no right to shove your way in here like this."

The captain held up a rolled parchment. "From the king himself. Do you need to read it?"

"Oh, for the Goddess's sake, it's fine. Look your fill, but please have a care with my staff. I don't wish to have to remunerate anyone you break."

Kit took one last look toward the living room where Oliver shouted random orders. It sounded as if the soldiers wanted him badly enough to tear Oliver's house apart. Another thing to regret.

Kit picked up the coachman's hat and bolted out the back door.

He was too afraid to be taken for a feral wolf to look back.

CHAPTER 14

*N*ora and Lucy had sparkled with excitement in the wake of the ball, but now they positively moped, particularly when the post arrived and there were no invitations and no messages from the men they'd set their hearts upon.

Lenore remained quiet and steadfast. She turned out several lovely pillows, embroidered with wildflowers and butterflies and shy rabbits. Ember had never seen this softer side of her. Rhielôme was famed for its tapestries of battle, not its more whimsical works.

Apparently, Lenore had the ability to surprise him.

Still, the weight of the girls' anticipation was a burden he carried along with his own. He hadn't received a message from Domino, nor did the man show up at Carlysle for a visit. It was too soon, probably. That's what Ember told himself. That, or as Hugh and Lenore had warned him, he'd been seduced by a nobleman who had no intention of following through.

That thought was too disheartening to bear.

They were all in this darkened mood when they received news that their beloved queen had passed. Everyone in the kingdom mourned her loss. Even busy Carlysle Crossing seemed subdued when Ember went to visit Hugh.

He'd planned to pass along the news that the girls had met their mates, but it seemed a frivolous thing in the face of a realm in mourning.

Everyone in Helionne knew the king and queen were true mates and that they'd loved each other deeply. They grieved with him, with their country, with the prince who had only the night before been dancing at the largest ball the kingdom had ever seen.

The funerals of royalty took time and much preparation. There was to be a month of mourning to allow the royal families of foreign countries to make the journey. Anyone who could turn out for the procession marking the queen's final journey through Moonrise Bay would be there. The much-loved Queen Bella Maria Filomena would be laid to rest with the kind of pomp and ceremony their realm hadn't seen since the death of the former king, forty years before.

Ember's own unhappy bewilderment was such that the moment he laid eyes on Hugh, he burst into tears.

"I'm sorry." He wiped his eyes with his sleeve and gave a disgusted sniff. "Goddess spare me, I don't understand myself. It isn't as if I ever met the queen. It's only that the girls believe they met their mates at the prince's ball, and of course they were waiting to hear from them when the news came. They're beside themselves because while they loved the queen, the period of mourning might stretch out the time before they hear from their beaux."

"Thirty days' mourning period," Hugh noted. "Depending on how high up their lads are, the girls might not hear until after the funeral itself."

"I have reminded them, but of course, they're anxious to begin new lives. The coming winter will put things on hold for longer still. I hate to see their happiness postponed this way, to say nothing of the royal family's grief. It's all too much."

"It's all right." Hugh banked the fire and invited Ember inside. "You've been through a lot in the last few weeks. The queen's death has saddened us all."

"The atmosphere at Carlysle Manor is all gloom and doom now." He chuckled wetly. "When I'm overwrought, I escape to the stables. Lenore does needlework, and the girls spend their time learning all they can about running a household, which they refused to pay attention to before now. Apparently, household management wasn't as riveting as watercolors or the language of the fan before they saw marriage on the horizon."

Hugh gave him tea and biscuits without asking.

"Tell me about your adventure?"

"What adventure?" Ember asked.

"Did you go to the Red Wolf Inn as I suggested?"

Ember flushed. "I did. Yancy was very kind."

"Were you able to dine comfortably?"

Ember's cheeks heated. "I ate supper in the private dining room and rested by the fire until some thoughtless lordlings arrived with trouble on their minds."

Hugh frowned. "What happened?"

"They wanted the room." Ember shrugged as though what had happened was nothing. "It took no time for them to figure me out, and they pushed me around a bit."

"They caused trouble?" Hugh scowled. "The louts."

"They might spread the tale of a male omega, but they were drunk and couldn't know who I am. I doubt I'll be hunted, but I can't hide forever."

"This is still troublesome. Do you think they know where you came from?"

"One of the men knew the Carlysle livery, but I don't believe he'll tell the others where they can find me."

Hugh lifted a brow. "Why not?"

"He, um … he assisted me when they accosted me." Ember let his gaze fall. "He helped me hide from anyone who wished to satisfy their curiosity. We talked for a bit."

Surprise and then suspicion crossed Hugh's expressive features. "Was this man who assisted you an alpha?"

"Yes."

Hugh studied him. "Is there anything else you want to tell me about that night?"

"No."

"No, nothing happened? Or no, you don't want to talk about it?"

Ember decided to avoid the question. "Right now, my only wish is to see the girls settled happily. I'm as anxious about their future as they are."

Hugh didn't miss Ember's obfuscation. His gaze lingered on Ember's face as if to spot the lie. "I hope for your sake that's all you need to worry about," Hugh said darkly. "I'm your friend, Ember. Remember that. You can come to me for anything."

"Thank you," Ember said with feeling. "Likewise, you know that while I'm a pathetic specimen, I'm still an earl. If you ever have need, please call on me."

Hugh nodded. "Thank you."

"I should probably go."

They clasped hands briefly, and then Ember left.

On the way back to Carlysle Manor, he sank deep into his private thoughts, primarily about Domino. As easy as it was to sink into the memories, of the night they'd shared, the passage of time made Ember question what he'd done.

Had his alpha gotten caught up in the events that marked the queen's death? Would he wait and send a note or stop by when the mourning period was over, or was he a bounder who had his way with a willing omega and had left without a second thought?

Ember didn't even know his real name.

Goddess, what if Ember never saw him again?

Now that he was clear-headed and a bit morose, Ember saw the many rationalizations he'd used in the moment. He was so lost in the magnitude of his fear, Geoffrey startled him when he arrived at the Carlysle gates.

"Lord Carlysle! Come quick," the boy called loudly.

"Oh, my heart." Ember stiffened with shock. "Where did you come from?"

"Right here. You must have been daydreaming. The mistress has news. She bade me retrieve you the moment you got back."

"All right, give me a minute."

"Are you so old you can't catch your breath?" Geoffrey gave him a playful shove. Ember stumbled slightly, but Geoffrey steadied him. "Sorry, Lord Carlysle. I forget myself sometimes."

"It's fine."

"Did you drink up all Hugh's ale? You're wobbly if I may point it out."

"I had tea, but I'm feeling a bit light-headed. Perhaps I should have eaten the biscuits Hugh gave me, but they were like rocks." They walked to the kitchen entrance together. "Do you have any idea what the news is about?"

"Oh—" The lad's eyes widened. "Two thick letters came today. Do you reckon they're from the misses' suitors?"

"I pray they are." Ember picked up his pace. "The girls have waited long enough."

"But two! On the same day." Geoffrey's eyes widened at the idea.

"Lenore is in the study?"

"Yes, my lord. She's forcing the girls to stew while they wait for you to come home. Best go up right away."

"I'll do that." He was none too fresh, but he hung his cloak on a hook in the kitchen and ran up the stairs. He knocked at the study door, and Lenore called for him to enter. She appeared to

145

be creating more embroidered flowers. The girls looked as if they sat on pincushions.

"I hear there's news?" he asked.

"Letters," Nora shouted. "Mother wouldn't let us look until you got home."

"You're not to look now either." Lenore laid down her needlework. "Your brother and I will discuss whatever we find, and then we will call you. Off you go."

"Mother!" Nora stood with her fists clenched. "Must we leave? After all, the letters concern us. I want to know what they say."

"Me too." Stalwart Lucy backed her sister up. "I want to *see*."

"The letters aren't addressed to you. They're for the earl. Do as you're told. Off you go," Lenore repeated.

"Ember—"

"Nora." Ember clasped his hands behind his back in order to look more like an earl than a street urchin. "Do as your mother bids."

Nora cast her gaze down. "Yes, brother."

The two girls left, but he had no doubt they would be listening at the keyhole.

"So what do the letters say?"

"I wouldn't know. " Lenore hid a smile. "As I said, they're addressed to Lord Carlysle."

"Oh." Her courtesy surprised him as previously she'd opened all letters addressed to Lord Carlysle and only apprised him of those that concerned the stables and horses specifically. "Yes. Of course. Thank you."

He went to the desk where they lay unopened. "Is it all right if I sit here?"

"Of course, Ember. I've moved my things to the room adjoining mine. As you are now the earl, the study is yours."

"Lenore. I'm not sure I can—"

She held up her hand. "I'm not abandoning you to the work

of running Carlysle Manor. You may ask for help if you need it. But this is the Earl of Carlyle's study. The title and Carlysle Manor are yours. I merely kept everything warm."

"Thank you." In the past, he'd have said the *last* adjective one might use for Lenore was *warm*. He bit his lip to keep from laughing. He didn't know what to say except he hoped he'd be as good an earl as his father had been. That felt like fishing for praise, so he swallowed the words.

"But ... er ... warm?" he teased gently.

Her lips twitched. "Warmish. Your father was the warm one."

"I hope to be like him." Ember rearranged the blotter and pen. "I need to say ... er ... I appreciate everything you've done to keep our family going in Father's absence."

She glanced away. "Ember, if you don't open those letters, I'll poison the next cup of tea you drink."

"All right, then. Here goes." With a silent prayer that they'd make someone happy, he opened the letters with his father's little dagger and spread the pages out on his desk.

"This one is from the Duke of Seavane," he informed her. "His Grace inquires after the health of Lady Lucy Saeger, youngest sister of Lord Carlysle, etcetera. It seems the duke was enchanted with her. He invites her and Lady Eleanor Saeger to visit during the winter holidays."

Lenore made a satisfied sound. "That's promising."

"He invites us as well, of course. You should go." He glanced up to find Lenore nodding. "I can't leave the place given that we've only got a skeleton staff at present, but I'll make arrangements for the three of you to travel."

"That sounds delightful, though we'll have to order more gowns. I will endeavor to squeeze each coin until it bleeds."

"Much appreciated. About the other missive." He narrowed his eyes as he read. "Ehrenpries? Cousin to the Prince. Goddess. Is she reaching too high, do you think?"

Lenore pulled a handkerchief from her pocket and sobbed

into it. If Ember didn't know her better, he would think the news had overwhelmed her, but he wasn't normally prone to excesses of emotion either, and he'd cried in the marketplace. They were all on edge.

"This is good news, isn't it?" he asked.

"The very best news." Lenore wiped her eyes. "I'm so gratified by their success. If these alphas are really their true mates, they'll be deliriously happy in life. The Goddess has answered all my prayers, and I have you to thank for it, Ember."

"No—"

"Yes, truly. Though we haven't always been close, I hope to rectify that in future." She lowered her gaze and tilted her head slightly, a submissive gesture he had never imagined she'd make, let alone to him. "I underestimated you, Ember. You are going to be a wonderful earl, just like your father."

As if Lenore hadn't uttered the words Ember had most longed to hear, he simply cleared his throat. But he had difficulty holding back tears.

"It appears Seavane and the prince's cousin are neighbors and friends, so a visit to Seavane will bring the girls into contact with the Ehrenpries family as well. They'll be holding a Winter's Eve ball in Moonrise Bay. The girls should love that."

"If everything goes well, perhaps the engagement will be announced thereafter. The Goddess is good."

"May we be worthy." Ember barely raised his voice to say, "You can come in now, ladies."

Nora and Lucy spilled into the room. They were so excited that they fluttered about his desk like butterflies.

Ember left them to their talk of beaux and balls. He headed for the kitchen if only to spare his ears the noise.

Victoria stopped him before he could get a foot inside.

"Were the letters what the mistress thought they were?" she asked. "Are the girls to be married?"

"They were invitations. We believe, if all goes well over the holidays, there's every likelihood their beaux will make offers."

"Oh, what excellent news." Cook whirled and grabbed Geoffrey's hands. The two of them danced a funny little jig. Everyone in the household was losing their minds over the news.

"Sit, Lord Carlysle. I've prepared a nice meal. There's beef pie and fresh bread and cheese."

As soon as she set the plate before him, Ember knew he couldn't eat.

He blamed his queasy stomach on everything he'd been through that day: mourning the queen, those letters, his sisters' excitement, and his new responsibilities as earl. So much had changed, seemingly overnight. The emotional highs and lows that he'd experienced in the previous weeks made his stomach lurch and his head spin.

"Gracious, this does look delicious." He swallowed convulsively. "I fear I could only put down a cup of tea at present."

"No! Are you feeling unwell?" The cook took his plate away with one hand while she touched the other to his clammy forehead.

He shook her hand off. "Must be all the excitement."

"Oh, poor lad. All right. I'll warm supper whenever you feel like eating, shall I? In the meanwhile, drink some tea."

"Thank you, Victoria. Chamomile, I think. Perhaps with some mint as my stomach's undecided about things just now."

"As you wish." She made the tea and placed the cup in front of him.

He drank the fragrant herbal brew slowly and waited to see if his body would settle down. He couldn't afford to be sick. Fall normally arrived with a spectacular storm or two. He needed to make all necessary repairs and prepare the manor for winter. Because the ball had taken so much time and money, resources were thin. Ember and Tom were already behind.

After tea, Ember fled to the stables. It gave him comfort to greet each horse by name. He treated each one to apples and carrots according to their preferences. He'd been there for a while when Nora came looking for him.

"I thought I'd find you out here," she said. "Are you hiding from being an earl, or do you have work to do?"

"A little of both, I think, plus I feel a bit under the weather," he admitted. "What about you? Are you excited about your winter plans?"

"Oh yes." She clasped her hands and twirled. "But I'm sad that you won't be going with us. Mother says you have too much to do here."

"I must take care of the estate, don't you think? Otherwise, who would feed Velvet and Biscuit their treats?"

"That's not really the reason, is it? It's because you're an omega," she said. "And a man."

"Did your mother tell you that's why I don't want to go?"

"She didn't have to. You've hidden what you are forever." She bit her lower lip. "Are you ashamed to be an omega?"

"Oh no, sweetheart." He invited her to sit on a bench in the tack room. "It's simply more complicated for me. I'm bitter because society expects men to be bigger and stronger than I'll ever be, but that can't be helped. There isn't anyone like me that we know of. That makes me feel strange. I'd rather not be seen as an oddity."

"But you aren't just an oddity. You're the very best brother any girl could have. And you'll be an amazing earl." She leaned against his arm. "So it isn't that you mind being an omega, or that omegas are bad? You just wish you weren't so different from other men?"

"I do wish that, yes."

"It must be hard to be the only one." She glanced down, dejected. "Do people actually treat you differently, or are you afraid they will? I haven't noticed if they do."

"That's because I'm Lord Carlysle. Around here that means something. But when I took you to the ball incognito, there were those who weren't so kind."

"Oh no! I thought you visited with Hugh's cousin?"

"I visited his inn," he explained. "While I was there, a couple of lordlings decided to put me in my place. First, it was because I was in livery. They thought me a servant occupying the private dining room."

"I never thought of that." She winced. "I'm so sorry."

"It was nothing until they tried to scent me. I had several scents on my person, meant to confuse anyone who got curious. Hugh hoped I'd pass for a beta."

"And it didn't work? Did someone bother you?" She twisted a lock of her dark hair—a habit from childhood that usually meant she'd done something wrong. "We should never have made you act as coachman. You're the earl. What were we thinking?"

"It turned out fine, but even if it hadn't, you aren't to blame. I knew it might be dangerous for me in a city like Moonrise Bay. It was just my luck that the young idiots left the ball early for a drink in the very place I was hiding out."

"The swine." She frowned. "Where was Geoffrey when this happened?"

"He went to the main room while I stayed in the private dining room."

"Why?" she asked. "What good was that if he wasn't there to protect you?"

"There were several very pretty young ladies there, and I had no wish to ruin his evening. As soon as the idiots began jostling me around, another alpha took my part. He helped me flee, and we talked for a bit."

"Oh, how heroic." Her eyes widened. "Did you get this alpha's name?"

He kept his face neutral. "We only talked briefly, but I know he was a kind and noble man."

"I want to marry a man just like that."

"I shan't let you go to anyone less, I promise."

"I thought I'd find you two here." Lucy sauntered into the tack room. "Mother says she'll have Geoffrey deliver a note to the seamstress tomorrow. Oh, think of it, Nora! New gowns."

"I can't wait!" Nora leapt to her feet, her conversation with Ember already forgotten. "Let's head inside and make a list of things we must pack."

Ember walked back to the house with them. Cook offered him food again, but his stomach warned him not to eat it.

"I can't. I'm sorry. My belly—"

"You look pale." She narrowed her gaze. "You should be in bed. I'll have Geoffrey bring broth up for you. You need something, or your stomach will only feel worse."

"Thank you."

Nora bade him rest, and Lucy fussed over him. When he refused to let them into his rooms to do even more, they finally left him alone.

"Men are so frustrating," exclaimed Lucy.

"Mother says they're the worst patients," Nora agreed.

"They're positively babies."

"Tell your mother I'll see her in her—*my*—office later." He needed to change the way he thought of Carlysle Manor before he made the same sort of gaffe in public. Not that he ever went out in public.

Nora turned back. "Brother, I'm counting on you to come down and try to eat if you can."

"I will," he promised.

In the meantime, he was so tired. When he made it to his bed, he fell into the covers fully clothed and drifted off in a matter of seconds.

CHAPTER 15

*D*ays later, Ember slept through yet another supper. He briefly opened his eyes when Lenore peeked in to check on him. He assured her he was tired from all the repairs he'd been trying to finish before the weather turned foul, and she left him alone after that.

The following morning, he made it to the stables before his stomach rebelled. Though he had eaten nothing, he retched for several unpleasant minutes, feeling as if the Goddess herself was squeezing him dry.

He went to Victoria to beg a cup of herbal tea and returned to finish his chores though he felt sluggish and limp while he did them and exhausted when he finished.

Lenore caught him before he could seek his bed.

"I think we should talk." She blocked the way to his room.

"Certainly. In the study?" He wanted to tell her no, but he didn't want to appear unqualified for the responsibilities she'd given him.

"Can I have Cook send up anything? Eggs? Toast?"

"No, thank you." The thought made his stomach roil. "Perhaps some more herbal tea? I must have eaten something bad because my stomach rebels if I even think about food."

She nodded and called to Millie. "Go to the kitchens and bring dry toast, herbal tea, and some of the ginger candy Victoria makes if she has any put by."

After Millie left, Ember led Lenore into the study and took his seat at the desk. Silence between them had gradually grown comfortable since they'd become allies. For a while, neither of them spoke. He riffled through papers on his desk without purpose, and she gathered the materials for her latest project—a small piece with a charming hummingbird design that he thought might be meant for a reticule.

After a few minutes, Millie came back with a tray. Lenore bade her place it on his desk between them. After the girl left, Lenore poured his tea and handed him the cup.

"Eat some toast. That should help with the nausea."

"How do you—"

"Victoria says you've not eaten in two days." She eyed him with no small amount of pity. "It's not like you to miss meals."

"I couldn't eat," he admitted. "My stomach churns. Perhaps it's all the excitement of the past few weeks."

She was quiet for a moment before speaking. "I do not like to ask, but did anything happen while we were in the palace that you failed to mention?"

"What do you mean?" he stalled, hoping to find a good answer.

"Ember, did you meet someone?" she asked gently. When he didn't answer, she sighed. "I'm sorry to pry, but you've been pale, lacking in energy. You don't eat. Have your senses changed in any way?"

He started to shake his head and then realized: yes, they had.

"My nose is clogged. This toast tastes of nothing. In town I was so overwhelmed by all the activity, I felt faint. It's probably a fever or late summer cold."

"Or ..." She pressed her lips together.

"What?"

"Whether or not you want to share with me what happened on the night of the ball, my intuition tells me you're in the family way."

"No." *Impossible.* "No, no, *no.* That ... can't be."

"Were you with an alpha?" she asked. "Did you allow an alpha to knot you?"

As blood seemed to drain from Ember's face, his senses swam.

"Oh dear. That's answer enough." Lenore sighed. "I take it you didn't listen to Hugh or me when we told you not to—"

"I found my true mate."

"You—you what?" she asked.

"I met someone. He was dazzling and perfect and my wolf knew him. He said I was his true mate. He said he'd been waiting—"

"Oh, Ember." She rubbed her temples with the fingers of both hands. "Alphas will say anything if the opportunity to knot an omega presents itself."

"That doesn't explain how sure my wolf was. I can't describe the feeling, except to say that we were waiting for him. If the Goddess blessed me with a true mate, even a surprise pregnancy would be cause for celebration."

"But why hasn't he come calling? Made an offer?"

"Perhaps he couldn't. Maybe the queen's death—"

"Any worthy alpha would know it's very much in your best interests that he waste no time. A gentleman alpha would have sent a note at least."

"He said he'd find me, but—"

"But what?" she asked.

With a sigh, he told her about lying to Domino. How the dashing alpha had rescued Ember when the men attacked him.

How they'd hidden in the stable. How he'd left at midnight so he could pick up Lenore and the girls on time.

"It sounds to me as though your Domino was a decent, kind alpha." Her words carried caution. "And I have no doubt that you were sincere ..."

"But I lied to him. I told him I was coachman here. What if afterward, he considered me an unworthy match?" Ember dreaded the answer, but inside he already knew what she thought. He'd been a fool, and now he would pay the price.

"If he's an aristocrat of a certain status, say a royal duke, his family might force him to marry an omega of title and breeding despite finding his mate. And before you say that you're an earl, and worthy, of course you are. But his family doesn't have any way of knowing that. After all, won't a duke's family expect him to choose an omega of a close rank? Especially since they've probably never considered the possibility of a male omega."

Ember let his hands fall to the table. "He called me the answer to his prayers."

"And I have no doubt you were *in that moment*. To an alpha who prefers men, yet who has a duty to marry an omega and sire heirs, you certainly would be a gift from the Goddess. But Ember, words spoken in the heat of the moment might seem rash the following morning, or maybe his desires don't matter to his family as much as appearances do."

"So you think he changed his mind in order to satisfy the norm?"

"If he doesn't offer for you? He might have changed his plans to satisfy his parents. His ancestors. Many an alpha has given up his dreams in order to do his duty to his house."

Ember acknowledged this. As in Hugh's case, love didn't conquer all. "What will I do then?"

"Then you will suffer," she said flatly. "It will be the loneliest, most heartbreaking time of your life, and since your night of love seems to have led to consequences, you must make a plan to deal with them."

Ember frowned. "I don't understand."

"If you bear a child, you must decide how to explain it."

"How can I? I'll be a laughingstock. No, it's—impossible."

"Not at all, I'm afraid."

"All right. How likely is it that I'm with child?"

"Very likely if he knotted you, even though it was your first time. You could be having your alpha's baby. What will you do with the child?"

Taken aback, he said, "I'll keep the babe and raise it as mine, of course. No matter what anyone says, the child was conceived in love, and loved it shall be."

She settled into her chair with a smile that Kit thought might be approval.

"Then we must begin to circulate a story. Perhaps one of the servants we let go died, and we took in her child. Perhaps the baby was born in Rhielôme of a distant cousin who died in childbirth ..."

"That's right. I suppose I can pretend to adopt."

"Yes, but you'll need to stay hidden until the baby's born. Not here. You could say you're allowing yourself a much-needed visit to the coast."

"Why can't I stay here?" he asked.

She glanced toward the door. "Even the best servants talk."

"Honestly?" Ember hated lying. He'd lied to Domino, unforgivably. "People already think me a freak, why should we care what they say?"

"We care because once they know you're with child, there will be a scandal of epic proportions. It will not end with you but will also follow the babe for the whole of his or her life."

"Sexual exploits don't cost men as they do women."

"You won't be considered a man because you're an omega. The rules are the same for all omegas whether we like it or not.

A noble omega isn't a person, she's property. An asset. A child born out of wedlock is practically cursed." She stabbed her needle ruthlessly into the fabric. "I know this is hard. Believe me when I say I wish I could have prevented what seems likely to be a painful experience—"

"It isn't your fault," he pointed out. "You tried very hard to make me toe the line."

"I should have tried harder, I think."

"Let's not rehash what's past. Domino is my true mate. Nothing you said could have kept us apart once we were alone."

"I understand." She gave an exasperated sniff. "*Alphas.* One can't live with them, and one can't drop them all into a fiery pit and say good riddance."

He gasped. "Lenore, you have a rather dark side ..."

"Surely since omegas create life, we should have a say in how things are done."

"Here, here." He wanted a brandy. "I know it's early, but do you want a drink?"

"I would love a brandy." When he went to pour, she admonished, "None for you, Papa."

He hesitated. "I thought it might settle my nerves."

"And the baby?" She lowered her gaze to his belly.

"Oh, right." He handed her a drink and plopped back into his chair with a sigh. "I suppose there's a list of things I shouldn't eat or drink, although the Goddess knows, I won't be eating. Anything I eat now will fly back out with my organs attached."

She chuckled. "I'll prepare a list. In the meantime, try the ginger."

He eyed it suspiciously. "I'm not fond of candy."

"Just eat one. It will help, just like the tea helps."

"Do you promise?"

She narrowed her eyes. "Are you a child to refuse medicine when it's necessary? Must I pinch your nose and make you eat it?"

He popped a bit of candied ginger into his mouth and chewed. "It's ... spicy. Not bad."

"When you feel unwell, try eating that before taking toast and tea."

"Lenore," he said suddenly. "Will you be my ally in this new adventure?"

"I'm sorry you have to ask, Ember. That's my fault, I'm afraid. Rest assured I will be right here whatever you need from me."

～

*T*hat afternoon, all Ember had accomplished was a nap, and still he felt exhausted when he startled awake.

What had woken him?

He went to the top of the stairs for answers.

Geoffrey and Hugh stood below, out of breath. "Get ... your master."

Ember started down the stairs. "What is it?"

"The king's soldiers," he gasped. "Looking for you."

"Me?" Ember asked incredulously.

Hugh shook his head. "The coachman from Carlysle Manor."

"Goddess. Did they say what they want?"

"Doesn't matter." Lenore appeared and hurried him back upstairs. "If they're looking for you, it must have something to do with the night of the ball. Didn't you say that men harassed you?"

"Yes ... You think they've come because I'm a male omega?"

"Why else?"

"Couldn't it be"—he glanced around—*"you know who* looking for me?"

"With the king's men?" She took him by the hand and hauled him to his room.

Hugh followed. "Who is you-know-who?"

"It's not important." With his eyes, he begged Lenore not to tell.

"Ember ..." Hugh's nose twitched. "You smell different."

"Never mind that," Lenore said. "You need to find a place to hide for a while anyway. Go now."

"How can I?" he asked. "I have responsibilities. Who will take care of the horses if I'm not here? Who will look after the estate? Who will arrange your travel?"

"I will take responsibility for the staff and the estate while you're gone. We talked about hiring a groom. I'll see to our plans."

"But—"

"If the soldiers find you, they'll find more than a male omega. Do you understand? Word will spread, and you will quickly become the subject of gossip and possibly an object of ridicule. In my country, you and your child would be considered suitable for an exhibit in a private menagerie."

"Wait, what child?" Hugh asked.

Ember took his blanket and laid it flat on the bed. "This can't be happening. Lenore—"

"I will take care of things here. Once the babe is born—"

"Do you mean to say Ember's *with child*?" Hugh broke into their conversation.

"Technically, we're not certain of that fact," Ember clarified.

Hugh glared at him. "I gave you strict instructions: you were to avoid alphas, you were not to—"

"I'm sorry." Ember shrugged. "I ignored them. My fault entirely."

"Where will you go?" Hugh asked. "Have you made arrangements?"

Lenore pulled tunics and trousers from his wardrobe and tossed them on the blanket. "I thought maybe he could go to the Temple of the Moon."

"You want him to hide with rogue omegas?" Hugh asked.

"They're not rogues," Lenore scoffed. "They're independent."

"If you say so." Hugh retrieved smallclothes, handkerchiefs, and stockings.

"Isn't that a place for women?" Ember asked.

"The Temple of the Moon is a refuge for omegas who either don't want to marry or cannot for some reason. Some are fragile physically. Some mentally. But most simply wish to be to choose their fate. They will not turn you away."

"I see." Ember saw perfectly. "I'm to hide out with a gaggle of outcast omegas."

"They're not outcasts." Lenore held up the coachman's coat. "This won't fit in a few months. Best you take my warmest cloak as well."

"Then how will you endure the winter holiday at Seavane?"

"You're going to Seavane?" Hugh asked. "Did one of the girls catch the eye of someone so well situated? Well-done."

"Both girls have been invited because the man that Nora set her cap after lives nearby."

"Who?"

"Oliver Ehrenpries. He's cousin to Prince Christopher."

"No." Hugh's eyes widened. "Congratulations. Your daughters will make a match with the cream of the cream."

Lenore flushed. "I'd hoped for a good match, and this looks to be Goddess blessed."

"May we be worthy." Hugh nodded. "I'm very happy for you."

"Millie," Lenore called to the tweeny. "Bring my winter cloak and scarf."

"Yes, ma'am." A minute later she scurried into Ember's room with the items draped over her arms.

"All right." Lenore rolled Ember's clothing carefully into his blanket, folding the sides in and tying it into a perfect cylinder with her scarf. "That will be all, Millie, thank you."

They waited for Millie to leave before she spoke again.

"It's not far to the Temple of the Moon, but it's inaccessible from land. You must ride to Moonrise Bay and find a boatman to take you."

"I have the coins left from the night of the ball." Ember picked his purse up off the table next to his bed and handed it over. "Will it be enough?"

She frowned. "You should take more in case finding a boat proves difficult. If the weather changes—"

"I have coins enough to see him safely there," said Hugh. "Never fear. I'll accompany him myself to make sure he arrives at the temple safely."

"Thank you." Lenore seemed much gratified by the news. "You have proven to be a true friend, Hugh. I will remember you in my prayers to the Goddess."

"Thank you, ma'am." Hugh tugged his forelock in a gesture that seemed so antiquated that Ember stared at him.

"Soldiers," Geoffrey shouted. Ember went to the window. "They're coming up the lane."

Tom came into view from the direction of the carriageway. "I've closed the gates, lad. That will buy you time."

"Come." Hugh took the bundle of clothing while Ember wrapped Lenore's cloak around him. "Keep your hood on and your head down. They'll think you're my omega wife."

"Oh, goody," Ember muttered from within the fabric.

"Ember." Lenore took both his hands. "I was no substitute for your mother, I know."

"I forgive you," Ember absolved her once and for all. "As well as grief, you had many responsibilities you never asked for."

She nodded. "That said, I do wish you luck, and joy, and happiness, and love. All the things a mother wishes for her child. Do you believe me?"

"Yes, thank you." Ember then did a thing he'd never done before. A thing he'd believed he would never, ever do. He hugged Lenore to him as if she was the mother that he'd missed all those years.

"Bless you," Lenore said. "Go with the Goddess."

Ember ran downstairs after Hugh, who left through the kitchen. He'd tied his horse just outside the door.

To Geoffrey, he said, "Tell Lenore I said she should look for a kitchen helper, not a stable hand. You'll make an excellent groom. Tom, take care of my family for me."

"I will, Lord Carlysle." The old man must know that Ember meant both humans and horses. "You can depend on me, Lord Carlysle."

CHAPTER 16

*K*it ran from Oliver's townhouse, down one dank alley after another, deep in the shadows so he wouldn't cause alarm to either wolves or humans. Both would be alarmed at the sight of a fully shifted wolf in Moonlight Bay. Kit needed to find his mate. That might be the key to his inability to shift. But would his mate even recognize him?

Despite the inconvenience, he carried the coachman's hat in his mouth since it might help John recognize him despite never having seen Kit's wolf.

Carrying a hat, it seemed unlikely his mate would think him a feral or a rogue.

Wait—wasn't he exactly that?

Kit had always assumed that wolves went feral on purpose, either because they'd done something wrong or lost someone precious. He'd assumed they couldn't bear to wear a human face anymore. But what if they shifted and lost time in grief as he had, and then they *couldn't* shift back to human even if they wanted to? Or what if they'd done something so awful that even the all-wise, omnipotent Goddess turned her back on them?

Kit winced at the memory of his last moments with his mother. She'd been so disappointed in him, and she'd died before he could make things right. Now the palace guards were after him as if he was a criminal, beating on doors, searching his cousin's home, and running him down like a thief or a murderer.

It couldn't end like this. The coachman was Kit's longed-for mate. Kit was as certain of that as he was that the sun would rise again each morning. Was he to lose him now because he couldn't shift back?

Kit set out for Carlysle Crossing, aware of its proximity to Carlysle Manor, where his coachman probably lived. He used every trick he knew to keep hidden and exhausted himself trying to stay one step ahead of his pursuers.

When he'd first shifted, he'd gone fully wolf to avoid the crushing grief of his mother's death. Now he was split in two, his wolf was in charge but barely. His most pressing need was *Mate,* but Kit still had access to his human cunning, the ability to understand speech, and the ability to plan ahead.

Kit knew exactly what was in store for him if he couldn't shift back. He'd lose his human again, bit by bit, until there was nothing left of him but the wolf. He would forgot his human life, his human family, his mate. All of it. He would live and die exactly like a natural wolf. Alone.

Though Kit risked attracting the wrong kind of attention by keeping the hat with him, John's scent in the felted wool soothed both sides of his nature and kept him hopeful. It drove him onward even when he was so tired that he wanted nothing but sleep.

By day, he followed the coastal road at a distance; by night, he found out-of-the-way spots in the woods nearby. He slept curled around his mate's hat and awoke at sunrise only to start out again. Three nights passed. Despite his human capacity for time, he had trouble measuring its passing. He had a destination, a purpose, and eventually that was all that mattered to him.

At last, he found Carlysle Crossing. It was almost a miracle he'd made it that far on foot. He skirted the buildings, stealing through the streets by night, trying to decide if this was a place he should explore, or if he should search the surrounding area for Carlysle Manor. He was exhausted and far too thin from eating only the few small animals he'd hunted. His body ached from travel. Perhaps it was best to rest a while and watch and wait.

Humans could be dangerous and tricky.

As desperate as he was to see John again, he concentrated on studying the town folk, eating his fill, and resting. He would seek out John when he was stronger just in case he was met with hostility from the other Carlysle residents.

Mind made up, Kit made his way into the trees beyond the marketplace before getting comfortable and settling down for the night.

He could be smart.

He was close to his goal, close to the answers he needed, and he would be patient like the wolf was patient.

That night, he had human dreams. He saw his mate's face clearly. Remembered the sweetness of his omega scent. His mate's body was so familiar, so warm and comforting and *mine* and *home,* that when he awoke the following morning, he could almost scent his mate on the air around him.

It was not quite dawn when he slunk through empty market stalls, looking in rubbish tips for something to eat. There was no bread behind the bakery, but he gorged himself on rats so fat they didn't have the sense to move when they saw him.

Later, in the distance, he heard the thunder of hoofbeats.

Soldiers—the very same palace guards he'd been running from—rode down the center of Market Street in the blue morning light as if they meant to sack the place. *Blast.*

Kit gripped John's hat tightly between his teeth and hid downwind behind a nearby shed, ready to run again should the soldiers come near him. He watched from that safe distance as they went from door to door, shouting, searching, bullying their way inside shops and homes, always moving to the next and the next.

One resident of Carlysle Crossing behaved suspiciously to Kit's eyes. As the soldiers came closer to his shop, the tall, brawny smith banked his forge, got on his horse, and rode hard to the south.

There was almost something familiar about him, some scent that teased Kit's wolf's nose and told him … something he didn't quite understand. Kit didn't know the man, but he recognized the scent from somewhere, so he followed the horse.

Kit wished he knew where he'd scented the man before. He was curious and a little confused. The scent didn't say "enemy," but it didn't say "friend" either. It was simply an enigma, a wolfy puzzle his human felt urged to solve.

Kit stayed well out of the soldiers' reach, yet to his horror, they seemed to be following the smith too. Could they be chasing the man because he left before they could question him?

Kit's wolf grew more uneasy. Should he continue to follow and possibly be noticed by his family's men or hide and wait until all this human business was over? Getting in in the way of humans could be time-consuming and dangerous for a wolf who couldn't shift. If they caught him, before he found John it could be disastrous.

A new scent made him freeze in his tracks.

Was it the aftereffects of his dream or did his mate's sweet omega fragrance hang on the breeze, ever so softly, to tease him?

Did this mean his mate was somewhere close?

Those faint, precious molecules guided Kit over a fence and into a pasture that held fine horses. He located the smith's horse, as well. The smith's mount was tied near a door from which came the delicious aroma of baking bread.

Kit lowered himself onto his belly to creep closer. He peered around a corner, where he frightened chickens in their pen. Laundry flapped in the breeze as a slightly built girl in an apron looked around, startled.

Was this Carlysle Manor at last? Kit carefully looked into the outbuildings. In one of them, he discovered a coach that smelled like his mate though there was no sign of John's living quarters. Only his lover's drool-worthy scent scattered all over the grounds.

He had to wait. The wolf was good at waiting, but Kit was awful at it.

Suddenly, two men burst from the back door.

Mate. Mate. *Mate!*

The scent of the smaller man drove Kit from where he was hiding at a dead run, hat clenched between his teeth. He wouldn't let anything stand between his mate and him.

The smith leaped atop his horse and pulled the smaller man —*Mate!*—up behind him. Kit gathered every shred of his humanity and tried to shift, so he could call out, so he could make himself known to the man to whom his entire heart belonged. He couldn't do it.

His magic was gone as if it had never existed. Nooooooooooo. Kit wanted to howl but didn't dare call attention to himself. Crushed, he watched the big alpha wheel his horse around. He sped away with Kit's mate behind him.

As one, the soldiers wheeled their horses and went after them.

Kit couldn't catch up; even at his top speed he didn't have a horse's stamina. Getting caught by soldiers was to be avoided at all costs. No, if he wanted his mate, he had to track him by stealth.

Kit begged the Goddess for help as he left the Carlysle lands.

He chased his quarry, more certain than ever that finding his mate, being back with his beloved coachman, was the only thing that might save him from a lifetime without magic.

Mate! Mate. Please don't lose hope.

I will find you, even if I have to travel to the stars and back.

CHAPTER 17

*H*ugh raced with Ember behind him. As there was only one road, they were forced to make a wild, jarring escape through the woods. They took off over the countryside, well ahead of the soldiers, but twice Ember was forced to dismount in order to be sick.

Once, when he believed he could go no farther, they let the horses rest while Ember napped for an hour or so in the shade of a tree that dropped dry leaves on him like a crackling benediction.

The sun stayed warm during the day, but the temperature fell quickly at night. By the time they made it to Moonrise Bay, Ember was grateful for the winter cloak, scarf, and gloves that Lenore had sent with him. Strange how it could feel so cold when only a few weeks before, it had been warm enough inside the stables to lie naked with Domino.

"We'll head for the Red Wolf," Hugh told him. "Yancy will give us a room for the night. In the morning, I'll head for the docks. Best I look for a boatman alone, don't you think?"

"All right."

"You look dead on your feet, lad. Just try to stay mounted until we get there. You've earned a rest."

Ember chuckled against his back. "No rest for the wicked."

"Now you mention it, what the hell happened the night of the prince's ball? It's as if you took my warnings and twisted them into an itinerary."

"Sorry, Hugh."

Hugh sighed as they pulled up to the livery stable. "No need. Sometimes the Goddess has secret plans for us."

"Domino was my mate," Ember said sleepily. "My wolf knew."

When the lad came to take their horses, instead of dismounting, Ember simply fell into Hugh's arms as everything faded to black around him.

CHAPTER 18

*K*it ran as fast as he could, but keeping pace with the horse carrying the alpha and Kit's mate was impossible. His top speed was good in times of need but wasn't sustainable over miles and miles of woods and farm country.

He lost his quarry halfway to the coastal road, and after that he had to use his nose to find them. *North.* They'd gone north toward Moonrise Bay. Right back where he'd come from after fleeing soldiers and city-dwellers alike.

Goddess, it was a risk to rush back into one of the largest cities in the kingdom as a wolf. And if he went back to Oliver's, he'd have to hide right under his father's nose. He could perhaps go to his father … but then what? He couldn't explain himself. His father would recognize his wolf, but Kit would have to find a way to tell his father that he *couldn't* shift before someone decided he'd gone feral and the decision was made to put him down. Even his father had to follow the laws drawn up to protect his subjects.

Evening brought with it the light patter of rain. It wasn't wise to enter the city while it was still light enough to be seen, but his wolf would not be deterred. Kit kept to the shadowed alleys he'd used the last time and made it to Oliver's townhouse undetected.

He scratched at the door, weary and furious. The same kitchen maid who'd opened before said, "Oh, Goddess, you're back?"

Kit sat miserably, unable to answer. He dropped his mate's hat with immense gratitude, panting hard with every breath he took.

"Wait here, I'll get the master."

Oliver came to the door dressed impeccably. He jerked his head, and Kit followed him into the kitchen.

"The soldiers have been back daily. I'm guessing you still can't shift?" Oliver placed a bowl of water on the floor.

Kit drank eagerly.

"What are you going to do? Your father's searching every-where. If you can't shift, you'll be hunted as a feral. What can I do? I want to help you but I don't know how."

Kit nudged at the coachman's hat toward his cousin with more force than necessary.

"All right. This hat obviously means something to you. It's the Carlysle crest. Is that who this hat belongs to? The Carlysle coachman?"

Kit danced and nodded wildly. It was the only way he knew to answer.

"So you want to find the Carlysle coachman." Oliver stared at the hat. "Wait. Is he your mate? Bless me. Did you find your mate on the night of the prince's ball, despite our charade?"

Kit yipped happily. Danced wildly. If he ever got his human form back, he'd never play parlor games again.

"*Shh.* Don't." Oliver admonished. "Best if the neighbors don't hear a wolf in here."

Kit settled back on his haunches and waited anxiously for Oliver to speak.

"The Goddess must truly have a plan for all of us, then,

because Seagraves and I are courting the Carlysle girls. Did you know that?" Oliver picked up the hat. "I was going to tell you last time you were here, but the soldiers came and you ran off. This is wonderful. I can take you to Carlysle if you think it could help. We could find this coachman of yours. I could talk to him for you and see my lovely Nora at the same time."

Kit flopped onto his back with a huff. Wouldn't that have been extra nice to know *before* he'd run all the way there, himself? Before he'd wasted days ... nearly a week, going by himself.

"What? I honestly don't know what you want, Kit. You need to shift so you can find your mate, and you're anxious because you can't shift. Have I got it?"

Kit let out a soft yip.

"Then let's go. I'll have my carriage brought around—"

Kit whined and shook his head and ran circles around his cousin because no, he most certainly didn't want that. His coachman was here, in Moonrise Bay.

"Why not? We could explain that you aren't able to shift, but that you're worried about him. I'm sure he'd like to hear that."

Kit gave a low growl. How could he make Oliver understand? What he needed was someone who could ask around Moonrise Bay. He needed to find out where his mate and the alpha had gone.

He thought of something and ran, hoping Oliver would follow.

"Wait, where are you going? You're tracking mud all over my floors—"

"Don't worry, sir." The tiny maid called after them. "I'll clean it."

"You shouldn't have to," Oliver called back as he took the stairs two at a time. "Blast you, Kit, what the hell are you up to?"

By the time Oliver found him, Kit had what he was looking

for. He held the rolled parchment with his mouth and waited for Oliver to take it from him.

"What do you expect me to do with this? Scry for him?" Oliver asked as he spread the map on the floor. "I don't have the talent for that sort of thing. Do you need me to find a magic user? The girl who sells us our charms, maybe?"

Kit placed his oversized paw on Moonrise Bay. He had to stomp twice before Oliver reacted.

"All right. Yes, good. That's where we are right now. Moonrise Bay."

Kit couldn't help glancing upwards in frustration.

"Don't look at me like that. I don't know what you want!"

Kit stomped his foot on Moonrise Bay again, then dragged it along the coast road and out along the trade road that led to Carlysle Crossing.

"You ..." Oliver frowned in concentration. "You went already. Wait, your omega wasn't there?"

Relived, Kit shook his head. Then he did the opposite, dragging his paw in reverse over the trader's road, up the coast to Moonrise Bay.

"You went all that way and back on foot?" Oliver asked. "Goddess, Kit. You must be exhausted."

If a wolf could be said to shrug, he shrugged.

"You can't keep going on this way. You'll end up making some careless mistake and get yourself killed."

Kit glared at him.

"All right. Tell me how you think I can help."

Kit nosed his omega's hat toward Oliver, then stamped on the mapmaker's rendering of Moonrise Bay again and again, going back and forth from the hat to the map.

"Wait. Is your mate in Moonrise Bay?"

Kit nodded and yipped and danced happily around Oliver's legs.

"All right. Mind the map. You're going to put holes in it."

Kit sat, trying not to run out of patience.

"Moonrise Bay is a big area to search. I suppose there's nothing for it but to ask around at inns and taverns and the like? I should see if anyone's seen him? How am I to do that? I don't know what he looks like or—"

Again, Kit pushed the hat forward. Oliver picked it up and gave it a sniff.

"Ah, I see. I should find his scent from"— he grimaced—"this. Did you eat nothing but rodents on your journey? This hat smells worse than a charnel house."

Kit growled. He had, in fact, eaten a rabbit or two when he realized he could go no farther without food. And a few rats. More than a few. It was none of Oliver's business.

"I've got his scent now. I don't know what you think I'm going to do about it. No human could track him through a city this size, and unlike you, I can't simply run around in wolf form."

Kit ran to Oliver's bedroom, grabbed a cap, and took it back to the study.

"What's this? No!" Oliver wailed when Kit dropped it next to his lover's hat. "That's my best cap, Kit. Now it smells like your slobber. Thanks ever so much."

Kit growled, pushing the hats together.

"What?" Oliver complained. "I don't understand."

Kit once again shoved the hats toward him together. He yipped twice, and when that didn't sink in, he stamped his paw twice.

Goddess, what he wouldn't give for fingers right now.

"Two. Two hats," Oliver mused. "Either you're saying I should get someone to go after him with me ..."

Exasperated, Kit shook his head.

"Or someone is traveling with *him*."

Kit gave a little yip and danced around Oliver again. He'd

have to revise his opinion of his cousin. He was decent at charades.

"You're saying I should be looking for two men traveling together, check if anyone saw them, that sort of thing? One of them is your mate. Who's the other?"

Kit puffed up his fur and lifted out his shoulders to look bigger.

"A big man?" Kit yipped.

Perhaps the man was a friend of the coachman's or a family member. Perhaps the coachman had played Kit false, and he had a new lover already. Kit's heart filled with grief at the idea that his mate might walk away once they found each other, but he had to keep looking. He owed it to his mate to do the right thing. His mother wouldn't rest if he didn't.

"So, your mate and a brawny fellow." Oliver picked up his cap. "All right. All I can do is try."

Kit threw himself at Oliver in gratitude.

"Hey now, this is very unseemly behavior for a mated wolf. Take your paws off me. No!"

Kit knocked him down and slobbered all over his face.

"Think this is funny, don't you?" he sighed. "If you must know, I do too. Now you wait here and rest. I'll see if I can find any trail of your lost omega."

Kit sighed with relief as exhaustion washed over him. Every one of his muscles was screaming from traveling all that distance, his paws were bruised, and his eyes felt gritty. A small amount of rest was a necessity if he wanted to keep going. A few hours of sleep would be pure pleasure.

Plus, he had Oliver searching on his behalf.

"Sleep in here. If the soldiers should come back, run. I'll look for you behind the Crow's Nest, on the docks. The alley there is always full of shipping crates, and it's a good place to hide yourself in the shadows."

Kit's eyes widened. How often, he wondered, had his cousin found it necessary to hide in back alleys near the docks?

"Don't look at me like that. I've done nothing unsavory. Cook has asked me to help locate her son—our wayward groom —more than once."

That made sense. Kit could see Oliver taking his cook's part. He'd barely laid his head down before his eyes closed. He dreamed of John, or whatever his mate's name was. Finding him. Kissing him again. Taking him to his father and begging everyone's forgiveness.

It wouldn't be an easy thing to do. But it was the right thing.

It was what his mother would have wanted.

If his omega still belonged to him, he would never let him go again.

If only.

CHAPTER 19

*E*mber awoke to find Hugh sleeping in a chair beside the fire. Hugh's eyes opened at the slight noise of Ember rustling the bedclothes as he rose and placed his feet on the floor.

"What time is it?" he asked.

"Late," Hugh answered. "Midnight, maybe one? There's food if you're hungry. It's cold, though."

For once Ember's stomach wasn't complaining, and suddenly he was ravenous. It took a minute for him to realize the depth of his hunger then it was all he could do not to inhale his meal. He plowed through what was left of their bread and soup, a small wedge of tasty cheese, and some apples, which seemed to disappear while he wasn't looking. It was all delicious.

When he was sated, he slumped in the hard-backed chair.

"Tired?" Hugh asked. Half his face was shadowed, half limned by firelight. He was the handsomest alpha Ember knew —besides Domino, who in Ember's mind was peerless. But thinking about Domino only made him sad.

"It has been a long day," Ember admitted. "Been a long, few

weeks what with the ball and the aftermath. My sisters aren't very patient."

"But you are." Hugh studied him. "Patient. Persevering. Long-suffering."

Ember growled. "I'm not that pathetic, surely."

"Tell me what happened the night of the ball, Ember. I think that the last time we talked, you might have left out some important details."

After studying his hands for a solid minute, Ember did as Hugh asked. He recounted the whole story from the minute he entered the Red Wolf Inn until the clock stuck midnight.

"Well, you're a dark horse." Hugh's brows lifted.

Kit breathed in a sigh of relief at finally having told Hugh the truth. "It felt right at the time."

"What do you plan to do? Will you find your alpha and tell him you're with child?"

That's when Ember had to share the news that he didn't know how to find him as he only him by the name, Domino. "That can't be his real name, can it?"

"Probably not. You didn't get any farther than first names?"

"We got far enough." Ember indicated his tiny but growing belly.

"I mean were there no other clues?" Hugh asked. Ember shook his head. "All right. I'm more worried about why the soldiers were looking for the Carlysle coachman."

"Me too." Ember went to the window and looked down on the quiet street. He could see the livery stable where he and Oliver had made love. His heart hurt. He felt utterly bereft, having met his mate and losing him in the same night. "Hugh, you once talked about your mate."

"Aye."

"What happened to her?" Ember turned and leaned against the window frame.

"She was a lady." Hugh shrugged. "Her parents didn't

consider me suitable for their girl, true mate or not, so she made them a condition: she would marry an aristocrat, but one from Rhielôme because she couldn't bear the possibility of meeting me by chance. They found her a baron or something."

"Do you ever hear news of her?"

"No." Hugh gave a sad shake of his head. "But I don't wish to either. She was right. It's better this way."

"I'm not sure I could bear that."

"It's not as if I have a choice in the matter. Besides, we're all tougher than we think we are when we need to be."

"Goddess, that shows what you know." Ember laughed. "I'm used to going without, Hugh. I've grown accustomed to preparing for the worst. So much so that having something wonderful in my grasp terrifies me."

"You can change, Ember. You can expect better. Demand it."

"Right."

"Really. Male omegas are rare. They bring change. You're destined for more than hiding out in Carlysle Manor." Hugh poured a glass of wine for himself and watered some down for Ember. "Come sit. The future won't arrive any sooner if you stand guard."

"You must think me a fool." Ember took the cup Hugh offered.

"I think you're growing up. It was wonderful of you to sell your horses and act as coachman for your sisters. By giving so freely, you've changed their destiny as well. All of the Carlysle omegas are bound to do great things."

"I thought you might be right, until I ran into those smug bastards and they showed me what was what. Thank heavens Domino was there."

"It isn't what happens to a man that shapes him, it's what he does about it. How you see yourself will frame your future. You're an earl. Next time, you can order Yancy to throw them out."

"You're right. I should believe in myself, even if no one else does."

"I believe in you." Hugh lifted his glass. "Who knows what the Goddess has planned?"

Ember studied Hugh's expression. The alpha wasn't just a farrier. He seemed too wise, too unflappable. Since the invitation to the prince's ball had arrived at Carlysle, Hugh had been Johnny-on-the-spot every time Ember had needed him.

It was almost as if he knew something Ember didn't.

Ember wanted to question him further, but lethargy draped itself over him as he listened to the fire crackle behind the grate. Occasionally, horses clip-clopped over the cobblestones outside.

Believe in yourself.

Ember's eyes drooped. "I'd better sleep now."

"Indeed," Hugh agreed. "I found a boatman willing to take us to the Temple of the Moon in the morning. He says there's a storm brewing, and the seas will be too rough for a small craft like his to leave later in the day. We'll be leaving at first light."

"All right. Wake me when it's time to get ready."

"Will do."

"You don't have to sleep in the chair." Ember rose and stretched.

"I'll feel better if I'm ready in case anything happens."

"What could happen?" Ember asked as he slipped beneath the cot's well-worn blankets.

"Soldiers? Thieves? Ladies intent on stealing what's left of my virtue? Whatever may be, there are times I like to be prepared. Go to sleep. Let me worry."

"Thank you, Hugh. I don't know how I'll ever repay your kindness."

"No need." Hugh covered Ember with his coat. "I'll keep watch."

◇

*J*ust before dawn, the streets were clotted with a thick, smoky mist. The air felt heavy. Damp cold kissed Hugh and Ember's faces as they made their way past silent pubs and abandoned bawdy houses. Hugh led Ember to the docks where the boatman he'd hired waited for them.

"All right?" The man peered at Ember. "I'm Jem."

He had olive skin and warm black eyes with lighter lines crinkling the corners, indicating he spent his time in the sun. His tiny fishing boat was called the Fisherman's Pride.

"Make yourselves comfortable on the deck," Jem said. "Should be smooth until we get to Wolf's Head Point. Rocks around there tend to make for choppy seas. Once we round the head, you'll see the temple on the cliffs in the distance. If the sun's out, it's a sight, the way light hits the copper roof. Don't know if we'll get that today."

"Thank you," Ember said as Jem helped him aboard.

"I've nothing to feed passengers. Hope you brought rations and some water."

"I did." Hugh showed him a gunny sack and a water skin. "Thank you for reminding me last night, Jem."

"Nothing to thank me for. Just hate to see hungry folks when there's nothing can be done about it. Find a place and sit down. Mind the lines, there."

"Understood." Hugh led Ember to a place near the prow where he could make a nest of sorts for the two of them. He leaned over to whisper, "Don't think he exactly likes ferrying people, but he was willing enough for the right price."

"I hope you're keeping a ledger." Hugh's expenses must be adding up. "You've paid for the inn, the food, the boat—"

"You're good for it," Hugh grinned. "I know where you live and all."

"I will be good for it, someday, when I've filled the stables with horses like Beauty and Beau again."

Hugh settled in with a small smile. "You will."

Ember regretted taking the boat as soon as they met the open sea. The little craft bobbed like a cork over the cold, dark water. Despite feeling better the night before, he lost his breakfast over the side within mere minutes. At some later point, Hugh came to the railing and pried his hands loose. Since he had nothing left to lose, Ember allowed Hugh to assist him back to their spot on the deck, where he slept fitfully for a while.

Impossibly—but just as Jem had warned—when they neared Wolf's Head Point, the tiny boat seemed to rise and crash over white-capped waves. Hugh held Ember tightly while he kept his eyes closed and his thoughts on his baby.

What if being thrown about like this was harmful for the child?

What if his inability to eat and this vicious churning sea drained its tiny life force before Ember could even welcome it into the world?

He placed both hands on his mostly flat abdomen, over the place he imagined his babe might be growing, and prayed to the Goddess for the baby's safety.

"Don't worry." Hugh must have read his panic. "She's probably the size of grain of barley now. I should think she's well-protected inside you."

"She?"

Hugh shrugged. "Odds are fifty-fifty."

Despite Hugh's words, Ember kept his hands protectively over his belly.

When he'd first learned he might be carrying, he'd been in such shock it hadn't seemed real. But now, when he was sick and in peril, the babe seemed very real indeed. She ... Was he to bear an omega? Please Goddess, he wouldn't repeat history and bear a male omega like himself.

What if the child was a beta?

What would Domino say?

There were those among the nobles who treated their beta sons as less than their alphas. Somehow, Ember didn't see warm, kind Domino—who had blithely accepted Ember's status —as the type of father to raise his children with unspoken prejudices. But a girl ... Ember didn't have to wonder how Domino would raise a daughter. They would both cherish her, dress her in the finest clothing, and educate her equally with their sons. They'd prepare her for her future with the utmost care because the world had to change for omegas. He understood that now.

He thought of Lenore, who had worked to stave off poverty for ten bleak years after her husband's death, only to turn the estate over to Ember when he came of age. He thought of his omega sisters, whose futures—whose very lives—lay in the hands of rich, spoiled men.

As the only male omega born in hundreds of years, Ember was proof that things could change. He would give his children the freedom to make their own choices, despite their status.

"Are you thinking about your baby?" Hugh asked.

My baby.

The wonder of it took Ember's breath. "I was imagining what kind of a father Domino will be."

"She'll have two fathers, you know. Bearing a child won't make you a woman any more than swinging a battle axe made my Aunt Gillian a man."

"A battle axe?"

"Oh aye, she fought during the Snow Wolf Uprising in the northern territories. She was so lovely that the enemy invariably dropped their guard long enough for her to cleave them in twain. She married my Uncle Andrew, and they had six sons— all alphas—but not a one of them was ever the soldier she'd been."

"I'd like to meet her."

"Perhaps someday. She lives in Lyrienne now. It's a long journey, so I don't see her but every other year or so."

"Do you know anything about the Temple of the Moon? Seems I'm to be there for a while, so anything you can tell me will be helpful."

"All I know is the temple complex has been an omega sanctuary for centuries. The priestesses there harried our king's grandfather until he eliminated any law identifying omegas as chattel."

"I didn't know that."

"Things have always been hard for omegas, but if the laws hadn't changed, omegas would have no rights at all."

"Seems like we still have a ways to go," Ember grumbled.

"That's true. Cultural traditions haven't changed much. After the age of majority, any omega is legally free to choose her path in life, but in reality, the choice comes too late because she's already wed, or her freedom comes at the cost of her family's approval."

"Or his."

Hugh chuckled. "Noted."

"Do you think there might be other male omegas out there?" Ember asked. "Men like me who feel rare and isolated and hide what they are because they're afraid the world will treat them like freaks?"

Hugh shrugged. "If the Goddess wills it."

"I can't be the only male omega alive. It's too strange."

"I admit I've been curious about that as well. Perhaps if it's known there's one male omega, others will feel safer to come out of hiding?"

A particularly fierce wave caught the little boat. It lurched to one side, and Ember hit the wall behind his back.

"Ouch." He grimaced.

"Are you all right?"

"I'm going to be sick again." He started crawling to the railing. "I—"

"Let me help you." Hugh got him to the railing in time for him to retch, over and over. He produced nothing but spit. "You've got no sea legs."

Ember shuddered. "That's fine, because I'm never getting on boat again."

"Until you come back with the child," Hugh reminded him.

"Goddess, no. I'm staying at the Temple with the omega sisters. I'll take orders if I have to."

Hugh cuffed his arm. "And go through all this trouble for nothing?"

Ember simply held his gurgling belly and tried to sleep. Once they passed Wolf's Head Point, the trip was easier to bear. Hugh forced a bit of water him.

With the sun peeking through clouds directly overhead at noon, the temple came into view. Jem had spoken nothing but the truth; the copper roof reflected the sun's rays brilliantly. It looked as if the whole temple complex was on fire. Ember took interest in the many copper sculptures mounted on the roof. Each one represented a phase of the moon, and all shone brightly as they approached.

Welcome to the start of our new life, Ember told the baby silently. *I promise that from this day forward, I will focus every waking moment on bringing you safely into the world. The Goddess is good. May I be worthy.*

While the temple complex had been built along the cliffs above them, on the shore it had a wooden dock suitable for smaller boats like Jem's. A woman wearing a gray woolen robe and a headdress that marked her as servant of the Goddess waited for them on the beach. Despite his good intentions, Ember required Hugh's aid to walk the short distance to solid ground.

"I saw your sails," she greeted. "We weren't expecting anyone this morning. As High Priestess of the Temple of the Moon I bid you welcome. Call me Iris."

"Thank you, High—" Ember went to bow and acknowledge her status, but instead he retched ungracefully onto the sand, which he wished would swallow him. He wanted to die. "I'm so sorry about that."

"You wouldn't be the first person to lose his breakfast after crossing the waters at Wolf's Head Point." Her laughter was light and pleasant; like the song of the temple's many chains of tiny chimes, it carried on the wind.

"I'm Hugh, and this is Ember." Hugh helped Ember to stand. "I've only come as an escort, so I'll be leaving him in your care, Iris."

Ember turned widened eyes his way. "You can't stay at all?"

"Jem wants to get ahead of weather." Hugh swept Ember's curls behind his ear "You'll be fine here. I promise."

"But—"

"What did I say? Believe in yourself." Hugh pulled a long, slim parcel from the bag he carried. "I made these for you. Keep the knife on your belt and the dagger in your boot, just in case."

Ember unwrapped the cloth. Hugh had fashioned these himself? The knife was double-edged and sharp. It fit Ember's grip perfectly. The wicked little dagger was slim, straight, and deadly as a serpent's fang. "Oh, Hugh. These are exquisite."

"Use them if you need them. I hope you won't."

Ember caught a breath. "Now I'm worried."

"You'll be fine." Hugh's expression softened. "You and your babe. I promise you."

They clasped each other's wrists in farewell.

Ember watched Hugh's back all the way to Jem's boat, where he helped Jem unmoor the fishing boat. Ember barely had the chance to wave before the little craft shifted to catch the wind, and she was off again, growing smaller and smaller against the blue sky.

Ember turned back to the woman. She stared at him in wonder.

"You're an omega?" she breathed the words. "How?"

That answered one question. "I guess there aren't any other male omegas here?"

She shook her head. "Not in my lifetime."

Great news. I am a freak of nature here as well. "I'm with child."

"Truly?" She took a deep breath. "The Goddess is good."

"May I be worthy." He bit his lip. "I could use a nap."

She beamed at him. "Then we'll start with that. Can you walk? I can bring help if you're too weak to follow the path. It's quite steep."

"I'd like to walk after my journey at sea." He studied the distance. "I might be slow."

"Then we'll go at your pace, step by step. We'll take good care of you."

"Thank you." She led him up a path cut from the rocks and lined with the sea grass that grew abundantly all around. When he faced the final stairs, the angle of ascent was enough to dampen any enthusiasm he had.

Oh, Domino. I'm doing what's right for our babe, but I'm alone, and I'm afraid.

How I wish you were here. I believe I could face anything with my mate beside me.

Only the gulls and the sea answered.

Still, Ember climbed.

CHAPTER 20

From where he dozed by the fire, Kit picked out the sound of Oliver's return. He leapt to his feet, heart racing. What must the staff think about a wolf scrambling down the expensively carpeted stairs to greet his cousin? They seemed to take it in stride though Oliver pushed him back.

"Settle down, you hairy devil." Oliver took off his coat and hat. "I bring news, but I'm not sure what we can do about it. My first destination was the tavern where you met your mysterious omega."

Kit bounced. *Exactly what he'd have done.*

"It stood to reason that if he used that inn before, he might use it again. It turns out he did spend the night. Apparently, the man he's with is the innkeeper's cousin. They left for the docks before dawn."

Kit's enthusiasm died. He knew what that must mean. Where would his coachman go? Why would he go by sea? Was he running away from something? *From him?* It couldn't be. Kit had been so certain they'd forged an unbreakable bond. A once-in-a-lifetime love …

"Don't get your fur in a twist," Oliver chided. "I meandered down to the docks with the idea of asking after them. The two men were conspicuous from their disparity in height, and a couple of the old salts sensed your coachman's omega status. Apparently, they paid a boatman to take them to the Temple of the Moon."

Kit gaped in disbelief. The Temple of the Moon was a refuge for omegas who wanted to escape from a world that wasn't kind to them. Women who had fled abusive husbands or girls whose parents treated them like chattel ended up there to lead simpler lives devoted to the Goddess. Why, *why,* had John left his job and his life behind for a life of solitude and piety? It could only mean one thing. His coachman wanted nothing more to do with him.

Kit's heart rejected the thought. *No!* It wasn't true. There was no way his lover would run after what they'd shared. Wouldn't his coachman at least try to find him first?

Oh, no. Perhaps he had somehow learned who "Domino" really was and didn't dare.

"Oh, don't look so glum." Oliver stood. "I found a cargo ship leaving later this afternoon for the Temple of the Moon. If we hurry, we can try to sneak you aboard."

Oliver laughed at Kit's look of disbelief.

"It's not as if I can buy passage for a wolf." Oliver ushered Kit out the back. "I have a plan to get you aboard, but it will require a great deal of luck."

Luck? Kit didn't dare count on his luck right now. He glared at his cousin.

"It will be easy, I promise. I'll distract the tars while you sneak aboard."

Was that all? That was a terrible plan. Kit gave an unhappy yowl.

"What? No. It's foolproof. Once you're under way, what can they do?"

Kit could think of a lot of things, most of them painful or life ending. Oliver didn't know the meaning of the word foolproof, but Kit followed him anyway. If there was a slim chance of finding his coachman—if there was any chance at all—Kit would take it.

He tried again to shift into human form. He put his whole heart and mind to the task, yet he was still stuck. Now, it was as if his courage failed him.

Kit had taken the advantages his life gave him for granted too many times. Had the Goddess finally turned her back? Shifters lost themselves to their wolf forms, turning away from the human world and forgetting the men they once were. How long would it take for him to go feral?

Maybe it wouldn't be so bad. Forgetting might be a kinder fate than remaining as he was, wholly human but trapped inside his wolf. It was with these dark thoughts that he followed Oliver to the docks via the slums and filthy alleys where empty bars and bawdy houses lurked like rat traps for sailors with a little cash.

At the waterfront, a forest of masts stood black against the sky beyond.

"That's her there." Oliver pointed out a racy-looking schooner, its unfurling sails reflecting the gray of clouds overhead.

"I'm not sold on this plan," Oliver admitted. "Looks like bad weather, coming on fast."

The clouds were ominous, which meant danger, but Kit was determined to go. The ship that Oliver had chosen was large enough. She looked seaworthy. The journey would be a short one. Kit started forward, but Oliver blocked the way.

"Are you certain you won't wait? It might be safer tomorrow."

There was no way to know for certain there'd be a ship heading for the Temple of the Moon the following day. His wolf wouldn't stand for waiting. Kit's instincts were taking over, driving him with a force beyond his human will. He yipped quietly.

"Well, if you're certain." Oliver sighed. "If you die out there, your father will put me to the lash."

Kit shook his head.

If the king was to take up a whip, he'd use it on Kit's flesh, not Oliver's.

"All right then, here goes. Traffic is high; the boats are practically locked together out there. Try boarding from the deck of a different craft. Look for any opportunity to do so without being seen, and for the Goddess's sake, don't maul anyone if you get caught. Good sailing, cousin. Be well."

Kit had no way to thank him, so he simply bobbed his head.

Oliver drew himself to his full height and ambled away wearing a mask of polite curiosity. Kit heard him ask one of the dock workers where he could get a skiff. He said something about wanting to buy a cargo hauler. Since Oliver carried himself as though the world owed him, he managed to make quite a scene, stepping into a row boat, and directing the lad aboard to take him to the ship he'd pointed out.

The captain might gnash his teeth, but he'd comply with a royal duke's request for a tour. The young tars were putty in Oliver's hands. Several sailors snapped to do Oliver's bidding, and in no time he stood on the bow of the ship looking out to sea. A leap from the deck of one smelly fishing vessel to the rail of a smaller cargo ship took all of Kit's concentration. He balanced on the rail, grateful the patchy fog, while he waited for the right time to make his final leap.

He made it, thank the Goddess. Once aboard, he slipped into the hold and crawled between some barrels covered by a canvas tarp. He wished he could say goodbye to Oliver—wished he could say "thank you" out loud. When Oliver left the ship, he very clearly heard him cry out.

"Thank you for the tour. Bon voyage!"

Kit stayed hidden and waited. A tug in his belly told him the sails had caught wind. The ship went underway over calm seas at first. To be expected, as they were still within the sheltered harbor. As soon as they passed into open waters, the captain order his men to trim her sails and corrected course. The ship shot off with sharp snap, knocking Kit off his feet.

The seas had some chop. From Kit's experience, things would be far worse when they closed in on Wolf's Head Point. The water there was treacherous; many ships had foundered in the rocky jaws of the wolf landmark.

Kit was grateful for the crates around him, but if the seas got rough, he didn't necessarily trust the ropes to keep them from shifting. They could still come unmoored and crush him or shove him from his hiding place.

As far as Kit could tell, they'd been underway for about two hours when the ship started lurching into the point's turbulent waters.

The captain shouted orders for someone to double-check the cargo.

Kit didn't dare move a muscle. He prayed he could remain hidden; that the sailor wouldn't check beneath the tarp, but the lad found it necessary to check his knots and came face to face with a wolf.

The cry immediately went out that they had a stowaway.

Kit bounded up the ladder and ran. He had no plan except to evade capture. Could he find another hiding place? He darted around men and between their legs, claws skidding over the damp deck. He avoided capture for a few minutes, but they cornered him on the prow.

"What have we here?" the captain asked.

"I found him hiding behind the barrels, sir." The lad's voice hadn't even dropped yet, but he sounded pleased with himself.

"Shift, you lazy bastard." The captain loosed his whip, its tail long and knotted. "You'll pay what you owe like any other man or face the consequences."

Helpless to comply, Kit held his ground. There was nothing but the railing and the water behind him. He gave a couple sharp yips, but that only made the captain angrier. The crew wanted blood. The lash came down on Kit's back, blinding him with pain.

"I said shift, cur. I'll not abide a freeloader."

Kit tried to dart away. The captain gave him another taste of the whip. His wolf instinct got the upper hand. Kit charged under the whip and straight for the captain, who barely avoided getting his throat ripped out and now wielded his cutlass, prepared to kill. The circle of hard men closed in on him. Kit slipped, his claws no good at gripping the deck's smooth surface. The waves had gotten so rough even the sailors holding Kit at bay could barely keep their feet.

When one was felled, Kit saw his opportunity to escape. He raced over the prone man's body even though he could think of nowhere to hide. As he skidded away, he took a painful blow to the head from behind.

"Take that." A man with a belaying pin backed him against the rail. "Cap'n don't want no stowaways, see?"

Still dizzy from the first blow, Oliver didn't see the second one coming.

The tar brought the improvised cudgel down on Kit's head. Blood trickled into his eyes as pain exploded between his eyes. He slumped to the deck, rough hands picked him up, and then he was falling, falling …

Kit hit the cold sea like a boulder launched from a trebuchet.

He hurt everywhere. Waves tossed him. Foamy water got in his eyes, his ears, it went up his nose and down his throat. When he could clear the surface, he saw two Wolf's Head Points, one overlapping the other. He couldn't make sense of it, but he paddled toward that jagged, rocky shore with everything he had.

It wasn't easy.

He swallowed twice his weight in sea water.

The waves were taller than a man, and to top it off, the clouds overhead began dumping rain. Lightning flashed in the sky. Thunder concussed the world around him.

He prayed to the Goddess though she'd stripped him of his magic.

Please, Goddess, You didn't bring my true mate into my life only to take him away again. I'm sorry I tricked people. I'm sorry I took my human form for granted. I'm sorry I didn't respect my parents enough.

I'm spoiled.

I'm obstinate.

I thought I had all the time in the world, and now You have to believe me; if I could go back and change everything, I would, starting with telling Mother the truth about me.

Please. Please, divine Goddess.

I've done enough wrong in my life. Let me begin to do right.

Let me find my coachman and make amends.

I love him. I love him. I love him ...

Rain sheeted down so relentlessly, Kit lost sight of shore again and again. In his human form, he'd have wept with frustration, but in these circumstances he bore his grief while frantically paddling toward the place where he'd last seen land.

He'd begun to believe he was out of time. That his last minutes would be spent battling waves and weather, two forces he could not hope to beat.

A strong swell picked him up and crested, hurling his body into an outcropping of jagged rocks. Kit lay in a battered heap with cold rain stinging every inch of his body. It took a minute before he realized he was no longer in the water. He opened his eyes, but even the gloom beneath the storm made his head hurt.

He scrambled to his feet and vomited a few times before trying to assess the damage and get his bearings.

He was north of Wolf's Head Point. The Temple of the Moon wasn't very far, but the terrain was difficult. There was no road. There might still have been an old trade path, wide as two horses abreast, from the days when men didn't have ships to carry the goods that the Temple needed. Doubtless, any path as old as that would be grown over in some spots and washed away in others.

Kit took a few tentative steps.

Brutal rocks cut into his paws, and his foreleg was injured, but he couldn't let that stop him. He tried to shift again. It didn't work. Despite his desperate prayers to the Goddess, he still couldn't find his magic.

Yet he was alive.

He was on the other side of Wolf's Head Point.

He still had a chance to find his mate.

He thanked the Goddess and begged the moon he'd be worthy.

Being alive is enough.

CHAPTER 21

*I*ris took Ember through the temple gates, where he was immediately swarmed by well-meaning omegas. Inside, the temple complex wasn't anything like how Ember had imagined it would be. He'd pictured an austere place filled with a few women in sacred robes, moving to and fro silently as though making noise would be an insult to the Goddess. What he found instead was a busy, noisy place, full of light, laughter, industry, and much affection.

After many, many introductions, Ember remembered few of the other omega's names. Certain women were more memorable than others, like Arwen, whose hair was the color of the temple's copper roof, and shy Gemma, who'd floundered for a greeting when they shook hands, and Iris's outspoken omega sister, Violet, who reminded Ember of his sister Nora.

Of course, in a crowd of omega women, Ember stuck out like a cuckoo in a nest of swallows. They were kind, though, and patient with his many questions.

After the first day, Arwen took Ember under her wing. She introduced him to the temple's many industries—wine making, cheese making, their flock of sheep—and pointed out the areas where Ember could help.

While he was able to do a lot of physical work that the smaller women could not, they didn't immediately assign him a heavy workload due to his pregnancy. Arwen passed him to Violet, who took him to the pasture and asked if he could see himself as a shepherd.

"I …" he paused, giving the idea some thought. "I like animals, and I enjoy being outdoors. Why not?"

"It would be wonderful if you'd take the night watch. Would you be amenable?"

"Any time would be fine. I'm happy to help in any way I can."

"Excellent." Violet clapped her hands together. "Three of us mind the flock in shifts, but the nights are rather lonely. I normally do it because I'm a capable fighter and a good with a bow, but I would much prefer to hunt or fish. I would be grateful to have the opportunity."

"If I can have one night with you to learn by watching, you'll be free to switch jobs."

"Thank you." She eyed him. "I know you didn't come here to be part of the order."

"No." Ember glanced down. "I find myself in an awkward position, and—"

"I can imagine! An omega man with child." Violet looped her arm around his, and they continued walking. "We're all praying for your safety. Our midwives are the finest in Helionne, but you're the only one of your kind, and there are bound to be anatomical differences."

He blanched. "Does everyone know about me?"

"I know you're trying to keep things to yourself, but you know how it is. It's hard to hide anything from a group of nosy omegas."

"So *everyone* knows I'm with child?"

"I'm sorry if you never intended for it to get out, but your scent gives you away."

"Ah. How unfair," he complained. "My nose seems to have quit working altogether."

"It's fairly normal to feel as though you've landed in a pile of pepper weed for a while. The insides of your nose are swelling along with"—she lowered her voice—"other important parts of your body. Nature means to ease the passage of the child when it's born."

"Are you a midwife?"

"Oh no. That would be Iris, but it's pretty common knowledge. We often shelter women who have nowhere else to turn."

"Do they keep their babies?" he asked out of curiosity.

"Some do, some don't. In that case, we find parents who wish for a child and are unable to have one."

"So there's no misunderstanding, I will be keeping mine and returning home with it."

"All right," she acknowledged the force of his words. "It's not as if we force women to give them up."

"I didn't mean to imply that. The situation is unexpected, but it's always been perfectly clear to me what I want."

At the end of the path, the two stood on the edge of the cliff, looking toward the sea.

"Iris wants you to join us in meditation this afternoon."

"I'd like that, but I'm afraid I don't know how."

"There's a guided session at four for those outside the order. Many people come to learn and then follow the practice when they leave. A clear and focused mind helps every aspect of one's life."

"Then I would like that very much."

They started back the way they'd come, walking in easy silence. When they reached the doors to the temple's busy kitchen, Violet stopped him.

"There are always chores for those who ask, but if you begin the night watch, no one will expect you to rise until mid-afternoon. Food will be packed for you, and you'll be given a water skin to keep with you. I'll meet you here."

He nodded. "I look forward to tonight, then."

CHAPTER 22

*K*it could barely take one step after another. Concussed and badly dehydrated, every part of his body hurt. Days passed before he was clearheaded enough to keep track. He was so close. He reckoned the temple was only about twenty miles farther. The omega who'd stolen his heart—who had disappeared believing Kit had abandoned him—had to be there, waiting.

John probably thought he'd made a terrible mistake in trusting his alpha. Yet with each painful step, Kit grew more determined to move his broken body in whatever way was necessary to reassure his lover that such was not the case.

His right forepaw gave away beneath him. Putting any weight on that leg produced a pain that made him whine with frustration. He was forced to pick his way over the rugged terrain on three legs, avoiding sharp shards of volcanic rock and sea glass that could cut his paw pads to ribbons.

At one time, he could have crossed a distance twice as far at a ground-eating lope. Now he was forced to stop every half hour or so and rest. It seemed to take him hours to go a single mile. Pain didn't deter him, but it slowed him down.

The sun was too bright, and there was little respite to be found. Only the shade of the occasional wind-twisted tree. Most leaves were gone this time of year. He slept for hours beneath skeletal branches that lifted like fingers to the sky, as if they too were in supplication to the Goddess.

This was a test. It had to be. It was Kit's atonement. He would show the Goddess he deserved the gifts she'd showered him with before his transgression the night of the prince's ball, or die in the attempt.

He needed fresh water. He wouldn't survive without it. He walked the next agonizing stretch of ground sniffing the air. When he found a shallow stream he drank moderately because he knew to drink his fill would make him sick. A few hours after that, he hunted small prey, mice or voles. A rabbit, when he got lucky. For a half-starved wolf, he had little appetite, but he needed sustenance if he wanted to keep going.

His journey seemed never-ending.

His shifter magic was useless. There was no healing his injuries.

He journeyed many more days. He rested to conserve his strength. At last, he crested a hill and saw the Temple of the Moon silhouetted against a darkening, sky.

Kit could have wept with relief, but he now faced another, perhaps insurmountable problem. The temple kept flocks of sheep known as far away as Lyrienne for the quality of their wool. Kit wasn't foolish enough to imagine that he could prance up to the Temple of the Moon in his wolf form and find welcome.

His destiny was so close: his mate, his future. Kit could almost see his omega's welcoming smile. He could almost taste his mate's unique scent on the wind. But instead of racing down this last bit of ground that separated them, Kit forced himself to wait. He had to bide his time. He had to watch, and plan, and choose the right moment to sneak onto the grounds without raising an alarm.

That night, he hid himself in the nearby wood.

In the morning, he found a small, cool stream and drank. Its slow progress allowed him to look at his reflection in the water. Goddess, he barely recognized himself. Along with his inability to shift came torturously slow healing. Blood still matted his fur and he was so thin that for a moment he simply stood staring, wondering how the reflection could possibly be him at all.

Kit's shock was so complete that he almost missed the progress of a hare that skittered through the trees behind him. He gave chase and caught it, gobbling it down with such greed he was ashamed and delighted at the same time. He'd been literally starving, and he'd barely been aware.

He went back to the place where he'd could observe the shepherdess who watched over the temple flock. Another took her place at midday. When a third omega exchanged places with the shepherdess in early evening, every muscle in Kit's body froze, and his heart quickened.

Mate, *mate!* Could it be? Was that his coachman?

The newcomer wore the robes of the temple sisters but was taller than the shepherdess—tall enough to be a slender man. He walked with a purposeful stride, with dark, shoulder-length curls whipping silkily in the breeze.

Kit's senses went mad when his omega's scent hit his nose. His wolf ran wild with joy. He ached to run toward John, he burned to bound into the field and roll in the precious scent of his mate at long last. He yearned to reveal himself and beg John's forgiveness—but how could he? His mate wouldn't know him. He had never seen Kit's wolf. To John, he would appear a desperate, feral beast. To any shepherd, a thin and battered wolf like him would surely be a threat. He'd be met with force if he showed himself now.

Instead, he waited. He watched to see if he'd get a chance to meet his mate alone. Away from the sheep. He rested beneath an oak tree, licking his wounds. Long after the first shepherdess retreated to the temple, he waited and watched.

For once, Kit urged patience while his wolf wanted to go, go, go.

Kit's head pounded with every beat of his heart. His coachman was *right there*, in the pasture. Kit had waited too long after claiming his mate, he didn't even know how to face him. Would John reject him? Was there now another alpha in his mate's heart? And what if there were beasts—other than him— also watching and waiting for a moment to steal the sheep he protected? Was his coachman even safe out there?

Kit lurched to his feet, instantly alert to the possibility that he might not be the only predator in the area. He had to help John watch over the sheep, in case there were other beasts around with malignant intent.

It occurred to Kit that his coachman might come to see him as a friend, even in wolf form.

If that was all the Goddess gave him, he would accept Her will with gratitude.

The Goddess is good.

May I be worthy.

CHAPTER 23

Over the following weeks, Ember's routine became second nature to him. Every afternoon when he awoke, he helped to clean the dormitory, joined the sisters in meditation, and assisted with the evening meal. At dusk, he headed outside to look after the sheep. He'd learned the temple maintained its flock for the production of wool, which they sold to buy things they could not grow or manufacture. The temple sheep's wool was the finest in the world. The softest, the easiest to dye, their wool was said to be a dream to spin and weave.

In the evenings, Ember relieved Urta, who watched over the sheep during the afternoon. He began at nightfall. From the pasture, on clear nights, he could watch the moon rise and create its shimmery path across the sea.

Watching the flock could be pleasure or pandemonium, but Ember's best memories were of spending time outdoors, either with the horses or hunting with Tom in the Carlysle woods. Ember loved all animals, though he preferred horses. He was determined to make friends with the temple's sheep, even though they stank and they weren't anywhere near bright. He found them endearing. Keeping them safe satisfied something deep within his omega nature. Perhaps because of the babe growing within him.

Above all, Ember loved the starlit sky.

Each night, he imagined that somewhere, Domino looked at the moon too. Maybe his alpha enjoyed watching its phases. Maybe he studied its progress across the sky. As the moon waxed and waned, Ember even fancied he could give it messages to take to his beloved. Though Ember acted the lovesick fool, and his wishes were probably futile, he could not stop trying.

During the day he prayed with the other omegas, some of whom had chosen to join the order, and some who were there to take refuge from the world. Several omegas were pregnant out of wedlock like him, and one had already given birth. Much was made of her baby, a boy who was likely to be the most-spoiled beta in history because every omega doted on him.

As time passed, Ember's slim waist thickened, and his flat belly rounded as though he'd swallowed a ball. The robes of the Sisters of the Moon hid his shape and they'd given him a woolen cloak lined with fur to wear at night, which kept him warm. Ember studied the baby's progress with his hands at night, yet it was sometimes more palatable to believe this was all a strange dream.

Despite his many chores, he felt lazy as a slug.

One chilly night when the moon was half full, he sat with the flock and listened to the waves cresting on the shore below. He watched the stars twinkling above him. Like shepherds every-where, he imagined animals or storied people in the clusters of stars. He tried to find some meaning, some sign in the vast inky dome, that all was well.

After a lifetime spent with Tom outdoors, he was more than capable of defending the flock. The hard part was watching, waiting, praying he wouldn't have to face a predator.

Tonight, the sheep seemed agitated. Ember carried a shepherd's crook, wore his knife sheathed at his side, and hid the long slim dagger Hugh made for him in his boot. They were reminders that Ember had people at home who cared about him.

The sheep nudged one another anxiously. Some began to bleat, whether in fear or warning, Ember didn't know. He peered into the darkness but saw nothing out of the ordinary: sea grass, buffeted by strong winds. He saw nothing moving in the darkness of the trees in the distance.

Time passed, but the sheep didn't relax.

A surge of protective anger rose within him for both the flock and his unborn baby. Ember stood tense and waiting for whatever had his sheep spooked to show itself.

Five minutes passed. Ten.

There. A shape manifested. A low, lean shadow, slinking toward him, still outside the light of his fire.

Was that a wolf?

If it was, if it came for his flock, he would kill it.

But instead of charging, the wolf stayed still as a statue. Ember added more sticks to the fire. As the light adjusted, he saw the beast was thin, its ribs visible beneath sparse, blood matted fur. It favored its foreleg.

Was it a natural wolf? Or a shifter in wolf form? These days, with Ember's nose betraying him, he could not tell.

The beast was more than likely a shifter in wolf form. Natural wolves would not abide Ember's presence, and he had never seen a hungry wolf pass up a sheep.

A natural wolf would neither show himself nor leave Ember's flock alone.

This wolf sank to his belly and inched forward slowly. He stayed in the tall grass, but Ember got a better look at him. He was a bloody mess. Ember felt sick for the poor thing but wary as well. Wolves, natural or shifter, were most dangerous when wounded. In a single instant, he could rip Ember apart to get to the sheep.

Ember waited, wishing he had a bow and quiver. No, maybe he was glad he didn't. He didn't want to condemn this scrawny wolf to death any more than he wanted to be eaten by him.

To Ember, it seemed they watched each other. The sun rose. Ember kicked soil over the last traces of his fire. When he looked back, the wolf was gone.

Ember let out a relieved sigh.

He hoped the wolf would show himself in the light of day, in his human form, not as a wolf. When Lyra, the morning shepherdess, came to relieve him he did not hesitate to mention the wolf and its odd behavior.

Lyra was far more alarmed than Ember had been. "We've got to warn the others. Even a human in wolf form is dangerous if he's starving."

"True," Ember agreed. "But the way he simply watched and waited led me to believe he's not here to steal the sheep but for aid of some kind. If he's a shifter, he might have wanted company. If he's a natural wolf, perhaps he's been domesticated in some way?"

"Natural wolves avoid people, especially those who've had prior contact with humans. We're not very nice, are we?" Lyra glanced over the flock. "We'll have to be extra cautious from now on. There's no way that could have been a natural wolf. A shifter who comes in wolf form at night is highly suspicious. Violet would have sent an arrow into him without thought."

"I won't kill a wolf without reason." Ember couldn't make himself do that. "I'll handle him if he attacks, of course. Since he did not, I waited to see what happened."

"Fine, but if he appears on my watch," she muttered darkly, "I won't give him a chance to attack."

"Understood, Lyra. The safety of the temple and those in it is paramount."

"Don't forget that when you're on the fence about this wolf."

"Understood." He picked up his bag and waterskin.

Could he do it? Just kill an animal who so far hadn't threatened him in any way? Probably not. That was not to say that shifters who went wolf for reasons of grief or to evade capture by the law didn't go feral and kill. A man who shifted and stayed in wolf form too long would lose his humanity. The morals and emotions he once had no longer ruled his nature.

A feral wolf was dependent on his instinct to stay alive. People and animals that he'd once known ceased to be familiar. He saw only predator or prey. As an omega, Ember couldn't shift, so he'd paid little attention to the cautionary tales. However, he knew feral wolves could and would attack and kill as nature dictated.

Ember had been foolish. Lyra was right to be alarmed.

CHAPTER 24

The following afternoon, Ember managed to snare a pair of rabbits. He would roast them for himself if the wolf he'd seen the night before failed to appear; but if he did appear, Ember would try leaving them for the starving creature to eat. Would the damaged shifter understand a gift, or was he too far gone? Likely he would run, believing all humans meant him harm.

Yet shortly after moonrise, the wolf came out of the trees some distance away from Ember's fire. Tall grass gave away his movements as he crept near, making no attempt at stealth unless he was a terrible hunter. That could be the reason he was so thin. The wolf's behavior puzzled Ember. He was a true predator, he needed food, and still he made no move to attack. He might have been drawn by the homely pastoral setting—a fire, a shepherd, and his flock. Perhaps he was clinging to wisps of humanity.

The beast acted like no wolf or shifter Ember had ever known. Tonight, he stopped a good distance away and simply lay belly down, nose on his paws, and waited.

Making up his mind, Ember rose from his seat on the

ground by the fire, picked up the rabbits, and took them to a spot between himself and his visitor. The wolf's nose came up, quivering as he scented the air.

Ember backed away, hand ready on the hilt of his knife, until he'd regained his place by the fire. Once he had settled, Ember made his body language as unthreatening as he could. He acted as if he did not notice the wolf was there but marked its every move from the corner of his eye.

The beast practically fell on the rabbits. He tore them to pieces, swallowing big hunks of meat in his eagerness. When he finished he put a distance between them again. He did not leave; instead he sat cleaning his muzzle with his forepaws. Without making eye contact, Ember kept the wolf in sight. Eventually, the beast put his muzzle down. After a few tense minutes, Ember heard snoring.

Ember laughed into his hands. What a *creature*. The wolf was fully thirty feet away and snoring loudly enough to wake the dead.

Though the wolf had melted away with the darkness the night before, Ember feared his reaction to the strange creature was trouble. He should have driven the wolf away or killed it. Instead, he'd fed it, setting a dangerous precedent and one he was sure he would regret if Iris discovered it. The fact remained, the wolf hadn't attacked, even though it was starving.

"You are out of your mind," Lyra scolded after he told her the tale. "You fed it? Are you mad?"

Ember shrugged. "He's obviously a shifter in wolf form who hasn't yet lost his humanity. He's drawn to the fire and human company. He caused no harm. How could I kill him?"

"What will happen when he's healed?" Lyra asked. "What will happen when he regains his strength and realizes that he can dine on mutton instead of a hare, or he fancies a bit of idiot male omega?"

"As long as he doesn't act like an animal," Ember admitted, "I can't treat him like one."

"I must go to the high priestess about this." She patted his arm. "You can't make this decision. You're risking our sisters. Any wolf is a threat, yet you're training it to expect handouts."

Unhappily, Ember agreed. "You must do what you believe is right, Lyra. I'm sorry if you feel threatened, but he comes to me at night, and I feel no fear."

Ember continued about his business by day in the temple then hunted at dusk. Each night he offered the wolf meat. Though Ember never attempted to move closer to his nightly visitor, he could see the food was having an effect. Soon enough, the wolf's ribs subsided and the patches of fur grew in. Before long, his coat appeared glossy in the moonlight.

Among the sisters, angry whispers grew. Where they'd treated him warmly before, now they eyed him with some suspicion. Eventually, he was called to the office of the high priestess to speak with Iris personally.

She got straight to the point. "I hear there's a wolf that dines with you every night."

"I don't invite him. He just drops by."

She crossed her arms. "You feel safe with this creature."

"I do," he admitted. "His behavior doesn't threaten me or the flock. I think he's simply ... lost."

"So you don't believe this wolf presents any danger to you?"

"Of course, he does." Ember sat forward. "I'd be stupid to believe he didn't, but I'm armed and I'm not without skill. I won't allow him to hurt me or any member of the flock."

"What if he comes when you're not around?"

"I truly believe he'll respect your acolytes as he respects me."

"Hmm." She didn't look convinced. Ember studied his clasped hands.

Why did Ember care so much?

Obviously, he was in the wrong here. Wolves were dangerous.

"Look," he said. "I don't know what happened to this wolf, but when I saw him, he acted completely out of character for a feral shifter or a natural wolf. He approached using no stealth. He was so thin he was practically starving, yet he didn't even try to take a sheep."

"So you're not afraid, but you have no guarantee for me."

"In the first fifteen seconds, I was wary," he admitted. "After that, it seemed he merely wanted to be near me. Maybe it was the fire or his memories of home. My guess is he's some poor shifter; perhaps he lost his family. He's fled humanity for the safety of his wolf, and he'll lose his human nature over time, but he hasn't lost it yet. Maybe we can save him from that fate."

"It could be exactly that," Iris said. "He wouldn't be the first or the last lost shifter. But Ember, I have the safety of all the sisters to consider. Those who go out at night to heal the sick or act as midwives are afraid. You have no connection to this wolf. How can you guarantee there's no danger?"

"I can't." He lowered his gaze.

"I must ask you not to feed beasts that could turn around and kill us all."

Ember winced. "It's one wolf who has killed no one."

She placed her hands on the surface of her desk. "My hands are tied, Ember."

"I understand—I truly do—but I cannot kill this wolf. I ask you in the name of the Goddess: Please don't make me harm him. He's done nothing wrong."

Ember felt sick imagining the deed. He wished he had some way to warn the wolf that the sisters were not happy to have him as their guest. He wanted to tell him—somehow—that they would be watching for him with murder on their minds. Would the wolf would understand, or was he too far gone? Ember made up his mind to try.

That night, he couldn't get close enough to speak to his four-footed friend. Every time he made a move toward it, the beast slunk away.

Long before morning, the wolf disappeared into the trees.

Ember slept fitfully that day, anxious that Iris would have someone hunt his wolf. That night, Ember stood by the fire instead of sitting as he usually did. He wrapped his arms around himself, fingers tight with anxiety. He hoped he'd see the wolf approach if he came—when he came—oh, why had Ember believed feeding a wolf was a good idea?

The wolf would surely come for his nightly meal. Who would they send to kill him? Only Violet, whose skill with a bow was unmatched and whose prowess in other martial arts made her the best choice. She'd have no second thoughts or regrets after putting down a feral wolf shifter. Violet wouldn't hesitate to kill Ember's friend.

Wait. Friend?

He'd begun to think of the wolf as his friend. The thought startled him enough that he searched his feelings. The word was accurate. He considered the wolf a friend.

But why?

The beast hadn't attacked, but it hadn't exactly fed from his hand either. How had Ember come to care so deeply for the scrawny, skittish creature? He didn't know what made this wolf special, but he was obviously in Ember's heart. His death would crush him.

Later that night when the wolf appeared for his nightly meal, Ember felt another's presence in the darkness. Was it one of the sisters, going about on a quest of mercy, or was it Violet with her wicked bow, her fierce skill set, and her unwavering dedication to the Temple of the Moon?

Violet would kill without prejudice, without mercy, should she see a wolf on the temple grounds. She'd see it as her duty to the sisters and the high priestess herself, who probably sent her.

Iris was right. Wolves were predators. Ember knew that, but he could not help the queasiness in his stomach when he thought of his friend lying dead at Violet's feet.

Violet stepped into the light, arrow nocked and ready.

The wolf startled, ears forward. His strange, moon-reflective gaze searched out Ember's. He must have sensed the danger he was in. Thank the Goddess. Now he would run into the trees and take cover.

"Stand down, Violet." Ember watched as the wolf leapt up and started running.

"Like balls I will," she said through gritted teeth. He bow following the wolf's progress through the darkness.

"Please, don't kill him. I'll—I'll take him away. I'll find him someplace where—"

"Hush." Violet was still trying to line up the perfect shot.

"Please!" Ember begged.

"Should I wait until he kills one of the sisters?"

"He's leaving. Look." The wolf was too far away. "You'll never bring him down now."

They both watched as the wolf disappeared into the trees.

Violet muttered a curse. "Are all men soft where you're from, or is it your omega nature?"

"It's just me, I think," he replied bitterly.

Ember was used to being called soft, but in this context it annoyed him. He and Violet might not be able to shift, but they *were* wolves. Why was it impossible for her to believe the wolf that visited him was simply taking refuge and desirous of company? If the wolf didn't do any of them harm, Ember was willing to give him the benefit of the doubt.

Violet, he could see, wasn't as trusting. She stood watch with him, eventually sharing his supper of bread and cheese while the waning moon sailed across the sky above them.

"Were you invited to the prince's ball?" she asked suddenly.

"Me? No. My stepmother and sisters attended."

"But you're an omega. Why didn't you go?"

"It isn't very comfortable being a male omega. I've kept my status a secret."

"Are there others like you?"

"None that I ever heard of." Ember toyed with his well-balanced knife. "That doesn't mean there aren't any. Maybe they're as reluctant to come out of hiding as I was."

"What were you afraid of?" Violet frowned. "What did you think would happen if people knew about you?"

"When I was about twelve"—he winced over remembered pain—"I was bullied. The other boys my age reached maturity, and their voices grew deeper than mine. They were taller and more muscular, while my body didn't change much at all. They started to tease and call me Emelia when they caught me alone. I stopped going into the village not long after getting a split lip and a black eye from an encounter with the apple seller's boy."

She widened her eyes. "You're an earl, aren't you? Why didn't you have them flogged?"

"Earls can't just go around flogging people, no matter what you've heard."

"The gentry can do what they like," she said bitterly. "Everyone knows that."

There was a story there. Ember heard pain in Violet's voice, in the way her eyes held his before she glanced away. He threw a few more bits of kindling into the fire.

"I'm not a very good earl," he admitted.

"I guess not, if you've come here knocked up and alone."

Ember smoothed his hands over his rounded belly. "I guess that's a cliché."

"We've had a broken heart or two here. Iris told me to look after you."

"She's probably worried about my sanity." He must have seemed addled, befriending a wolf. "Or is she worried I'll hurl myself off the cliffs in despair? She should take my optimism about the wolf as proof I haven't lost all hope."

"That's a fair point." She snapped a thick stick in two and fed them to the flames. "He's obviously interested only in you."

Ember lifted his gaze. "I couldn't say why."

"The fact that he hasn't shifted is what has Iris worried. We get male visitors all the time. He'd get a room and meals if he took his human form."

"Maybe he can't shift for some reason." Ember was suddenly sure that was true, though he'd never considered the idea before.

In the dark beyond the fire, one sheep bleated and then another. Hooves scraped the grassy earth as the animals nudged each other uneasily.

Other sounds seemed to cease, even the insects.

"You see something out there?" Violet asked as she stood and scanned the pasture. Ember rose with her. Despite their differences, they fell into an easy partnership, back-to-back, scanning the darkness beyond the fire's light.

"Not yet," Ember answered, low-voiced and urgent. "It's not my wolf, they hardly notice him anymore."

"Something's coming." Violet lifted her bow, drew an arrow, and nocked it all in one smooth, almost-seamless movement.

"I don't ... wait—" Ember studied a point between the cluster of trees and the low hills that formed a natural boundary. "Did you see that?"

"Eyes." She nodded. "Looks like a mountain lion. Summer was dry this year. Game hasn't been as plentiful. The cats don't normally come close unless they're desperate."

"And desperate is truly dangerous." He gripped his knife in his right hand while removing the slim dagger from his boot with his left. "I'm right beside you."

CHAPTER 25

Kit heard the cat's approach despite its stealth. He smelled its desperation. He had been watching the humans and the sheep for well over a moon cycle by now, and he knew the normal sounds of the night in the area. His coachman was in danger. Despite the threat presented by the omega hunter, Kit moved to intercept the beast.

At the same time, John and his fierce omega friend noticed the threat.

They rose to their feet gracefully, making no noise as danger stalked toward them. Kit's mate armed himself to protect his fluffy, smelly charges. Kit's heart clenched with fear though he was gratified to see the two omegas stood back-to-back as if they'd both been trained to fight.

His mate was strong and fine. Equal to any task. Yet he was Kit's omega, and he was precious, and—

Sheep scattered, bleating helplessly. Kit didn't bother with stealth. If his mate needed to protect these foul, fluffy creatures, so did he. He raced toward the big cat, despite his bad leg. He shot across the humans' path like a cannonball, barreled into the surprised predator, and caught him by the throat.

What followed was a blur of teeth and claws and blood and pain.

The cat was driven by starvation, just as Kit had been when he'd first seen his mate here. It was determined to kill because it wanted to live. Kit was even more determined to protect his mate.

The battle raged. They rolled over and over. Kit took a painful swipe across his face. Blood ran into his eyes, blinding him momentarily. He went for the cat's throat again, this time with such ferocity he didn't recognize himself.

Mate. He snarled his deadly intention. *Mine. Mine, mine, mine.*

An arrow skimmed his hindquarters. The humans argued.

The woman's shouted reply distracted Kit's quarry for the split-second Kit needed. He lunged forward and chomped the creature's throat. No mercy. The animal's blood spattered everywhere. It gasped, eyes going wide as its life force drained into the earth beneath them. With a last, painful, rattling sound, it stilled.

Kit limped away from the carcass and into the trees where he felt safe enough to take inventory of his many new wounds. He should feel victorious. He'd done what had to be done. Instead he felt sick, not triumphant. He'd killed a beast that only wanted to eat. If he could feel such a human emotion ... be this human ... why couldn't he shift back?

The humans ensured that the cat was dead before coming after Kit. As they advanced, he tried to crawl away, aware that he might be the next predator they put down for the sake of the flock. His head spun dizzily, but he rose and backed away.

Mate put his empty hands out to his side and bade him to be still.

"It's all right," he crooned. "We won't hurt you."

Mate glared at the female omega, and she reluctantly put her weapons away.

"You need help right now, friend." Mate spoke low, his voice melodious and sweet. "I want to help you."

Such a lovely voice. His omega. His mate. Kit took another step back, though he wanted nothing more than to fling himself into his coachman's arms and beg for forgiveness.

"Violet, go back to the temple and bring back a healer."

"Iris will never—"

"Then bring a healer's kit: ointment, bandages, a needle and thread. I'll take care of it myself."

She nodded before shouldering her bow. "I still say you're mad to try befriending a feral wolf."

Kit growled. *Who was she to call him feral?*

He was Prince Christopher of Helionne no matter what form he took!

"Don't goad him," Mate warned. "He doesn't seem to like it."

"He's probably been wolf too long to understand me."

"I wouldn't bet on it." Hesitant, Mate laid a hand on his flank. "Don't eat me, my heroic friend. I'm going to take care of you."

Kit preened at Mate's words. His omega couldn't know Kit was the alpha he'd met in Moonrise Bay. He couldn't know Kit posed no threat to his flock or his friends, yet he'd treated him with the kindness of the Goddess Herself.

Kit had never known anyone like his mate. Strong as a warrior, willing to battle a predator to protect his smelly, fluffy sheep, brave enough to befriend a wounded wolf, and yet gentle as a mother with her child.

Child—Goddess. That was the very thing, the new and different aspect of Mate's scent that had been teasing Kit's nose this whole time.

Mate smells different. Mate carries a child!

Such a bright burst of happiness came over him that he was temporarily blinded by it. Maybe that was blood in his eyes. Probably, since the cat had raked its claws from Kit's ears to his muzzle. He hurt everywhere. Darkness gathered at the edges of his vision. The earth seemed to shift and sway beneath him. Kit could rest. His omega mate would protect him.

Kit had arrived at his destination—found his destiny—at last.

"Don't worry, Wolf. You're not alone," Mate said. "I'm not alone either anymore, I guess. Thank you for defending us."

Kit drifted, carried by the sweetness of his omega's voice and the gentle hand stroking his fur. His human thoughts, his emotions, his very heart were as close to the surface as they would ever be.

Now would be a good time for me to shift.

If I shift now, my wounds will heal without scars.

I'll be human and fit and worthy of a mate as fine as mine.

Kit gathered every bit of his will and made the attempt. Nothing happened. He broke down and whined like a pup when he could not make the transformation. What more did the Goddess want from him? He'd found his coachman. He'd fought off a predator to defend the beasts his Mate held dear.

Kit needed to apologize for taking his mate for granted, but how could he, unless he could use his human voice, his words? How cruel was fate, to let him come so far and still be unable to make amends?

Kit dozed fitfully. He was aware that at some point a group of omegas came with a travois to move him. He awoke, not in the temple, but in a distant abandoned cabin—barely more than a hut—with his mate beside him.

The others were still unwilling to leave the two of them alone. They argued with Mate, tried to talk him out of stranding himself with a dangerous feral wolf—hah—but Mate prevailed.

Finally, the others left.

Kit heard his heartbeat and his omega's. Also, the *rush-rush-rush* of the growing babe. There was no one else nearby who mattered. Nothing that posed a threat. The room was indeed bare, just the cot on one side where Kit rested and a cobwebby fireplace on the other. A dresser held a wash basin. A rickety table with a single chair sat by the only window.

Had the sisters banished his mate here because of him?

"Lie back." With the scratch of a match, Mate lit an oil lamp and hung it on a nearby hook. "I need to be able to see where you're wounded in order to treat you."

He sat beside Kit, who held his breath, fearing the ancient cot would crumble beneath their combined weight. When it didn't, his sigh of relief was echoed by his mate's.

"If you can't shift, you'll scar," Mate said quietly.

Kit whined and tried to rise, to turn away. His good looks would be destroyed, he knew, but he could not shift.

"*Shh.* I know." Mate's hand smoothed down his spine. "I thought as much. I'm so sorry. This will probably hurt."

Kit wanted to be strong for his mate. He tried. But had there ever been a more foolish prince? His arrogance had cost him his mother, his humanity, his mate, his child, and now his looks. The pain of his wounds burned despair into his flesh. It was over. Kit had run his race. He was exhausted.

When he could no longer stand the agony of Mate cleaning and stitching his wounds, he didn't fight the darkness of oblivion that claimed him.

CHAPTER 26

*K*it's sense of time was broken. He awoke to find Mate sitting in a chair beside him.

"Oh, you're finally awake," Mate said. "You slept for a whole day."

Kit opened his mouth to answer, but ... he was still wolf.

Mate used a cloth to wipe his eyes, his muzzle. Kit was so thirsty he could barely move his tongue. He needed water. Badly.

Mate picked up a ladle and offered Kit a drink. He had to lift his head up. "Iris says that sadness and guilt can cause a shifter to get stuck in wolf form. Did something happen to you?"

Kit got in a lick or two before spilling water all over the linens. He scrambled to his feet, angry with himself.

"I know this is very hard for you." Mate stood and moved toward the door. "Do you think you can go outside and walk a little?"

Kit stretched painfully. He needed to go outside unless he wanted to make a mess indoors. Mate opened the door for him. They walked a few feet together. Kit did his business and looked to Mate for clues. *What now?*

Mate smiled fondly at him. "Come inside for food and water."

Kit followed him into the cabin, where Mate placed meat and water in pie tins on the ground next to the table. Kit got a brief glimpse of his reflection in the water before he shoved his muzzle in and drank gratefully.

This was his life now. His muzzle itched with wounds. He had a noticeable limp. The court physicians or their mystical counterpart mages could fix what was wrong if he could shift, but who would bother healing a feral wolf?

Even if he did shift now, everyone would call him the Prince of Scars. They'd say it was his just reward for mating and claiming a coachman—an omega of the serving classes—but they had never seen his mate as Kit saw him. Noble in truth if not in station, his mate was as brave, as fine a man as any that had ever lived.

He let out a long, sad whine.

"Are you in pain?" Mate asked.

Kit grunted and went back to eating.

The omega began to hum a tune that Kit remembered from childhood.

Did his mate know the lyrics? The song was remarkably fitting, about a foolish wolf who saw his reflection in a clear mountain lake but didn't understand it was his own. Thinking a strange wolf in the water smiled back, he was so taken by what he saw—so dazzled by the wolf in the water—that he missed meeting his true mate, who couldn't get his attention and sorrowfully passed him by.

Kit had once been that sure of himself—and his mate, pregnant and desperate, had lost hope and moved on.

Oh, if Mate would only allow Kit to remain by his side, he could be happy forever—even in wolf form. But wouldn't his mate eventually want human companionship instead of solitude with a scarred beast by his side?

Kit wasn't used to being afraid.

Kit was used to being alpha, the man in control. He was a prince, privileged, with every resource granted him by birth and blood and tradition. He had never wanted for anything in his life before, but now he understood wanting in a whole new way. He understood that some people never got what they wanted no matter how hard they tried.

Another mournful cry escaped him.

"I'm sorry, Wolf. I've done everything I know to ease your pain."

There was nothing to be done. Kit's pain was woven into his very lifeline.

A soft knock at the door made Kit's muscles tense.

"Stay here. It's only one of the sisters."

The omega reached for his knife anyway. *Smart, Mate. Careful, Mate.* Mate sheathed the blade after cracking open the door. An older woman and her underlings came inside, bringing baskets of food and a jug of clean water.

Mate thanked the women politely for the gifts and the use of the cottage.

"This cabin was built for those sisters who require isolation for deep thought and meditation," said Iris. "The amenities are obviously limited."

"It's perfect for our use," Mate demurred.

"You'll have to draw water from the well and bathe in the stream. You can't see it now for the mist"—Iris pointed out the window—"but it's there beyond the trees in that direction. The water is clean, but I warn you, it's very cold this time of year. The sisters will bring you food as needed, but you are always welcome to dine with us without your wolf friend."

Iris turned her attention to Kit without approaching him.

"There have always been tales of men whose great burdens render them unable to shift to their human form. It happens to those who have transgressed greatly as well. The Goddess grants such wolves the chance to make amends."

"Do you mean to say they cannot shift until they've atoned?" Mate's gaze moved from the priestess to Kit.

She shrugged. "This wolf of yours could be such a case. Or the human inside him could be a dangerous criminal."

Mate's hand steadied Kit when he tried to rise. "Every wolf is dangerous, but this one protected Violet and me and the flock. I refuse to believe he means me harm."

"If I thought he meant you harm, we would not be having this discussion. Take some time together. Perhaps you can help him find his atonement. Goddess be with you, Ember," she said before turning to leave.

What was this *Ember?* Wait, was Ember the name his omega had refused to give the night they met? Ember. Ember, Ember, *Ember.* The name suited his lovely omega. Warmth and glow, the last gift of the fuel in a dying fire.

Ember ...

Kit watched the sisters drift away from their cabin, and then Ember closed the door.

"You had better be worth all this trouble if I have to sleep with spiders and bathe in a frozen stream." Despite his words, Ember didn't seem angry about being isolated with him. "Let's see what they brought us."

Ember opened the basket and began pulling out food. Kit smelled fresh bread, cheese, smoked ham, and cured sausages. There were apples and grapes and, oh ... honeycomb! How he had loved honeycomb as a boy.

The fare seemed simple to Kit, but Ember laughed with delight.

"I hope those rabbits gave you a good head start. I'll share, but you'll need meat to regain your strength." Ember bit his lip. "I promise, tomorrow I'll hunt for you. You won't go hungry in my care, Wolf."

Kit did not deserve the kindness Ember showed him. He didn't even know who Kit was, believed him to be some feral stray working off a transgression or some kind of trauma, and yet he treated him like family.

Ember had opened his heart to Kit with no expectation of anything in return. He'd given love without any guarantees, not once but twice now, first at the inn and again here, where he didn't know Kit from any other wolf.

Was it because they shared a mate bond, a mystical connection?

Perhaps his mate's wolf recognized him, even though he had shown up in a form Ember had never seen. Kit wanted to believe Ember's actions had been driven by recognition, not altruism, but Ember would probably treat any injured beast the same if the animal proved he meant no harm.

Ember finished his meal and lay down on the cot, facing the fire. He idly cupped both hands protectively over his round belly.

"Goodnight, Wolf." It took no time for Ember to drift into sleep.

Here at last was Kit's chance. He crept forward and sniffed Ember from his hair to his toes. He smelled uniquely *mate* and very pregnant. Kit had no doubt at all. He truly was a royal fool. Kit had allowed Ember to leave the night of the ball assuming it would be easy to find him later and make a formal offer for his hand. But his mother had died, and he'd spent nearly a month running mad with grief. Ember, misinterpreting his silence, had fled. It had taken ages to find him.

Goddess help him, Kit's actions were far worse than careless or entitled. They were a betrayal of everything a man like Kit should stand for. Though he'd had the best intentions, Kit had ruined this wonderful man's life. From this day forward, he vowed to put Ember and their child first. He would live or die to keep the two of them safe and happy and whole.

Kit whined and buried his face beneath his tail.

Goddess, give me strength. May I—at last—be worthy.

CHAPTER 27

$\mathcal{E}$mber loved his life in the cabin. He'd never experienced a time like it. He was free to do for himself without the heartache and responsibility of Carlysle Manor, the stables, or his family. He'd never been alone before but he'd often felt lonely. As the days in the cabin passed one by one, he learned what it was like to be alone but content.

Well. He wasn't alone, precisely. He had Wolf beside him. His constant shadow. Not human but present and reassuringly alive. A living, breathing soul who had a way of communicating his needs and thoughts by the use of his expressive eyes, a yip here, a howl there. Ember got a polite nudge when he needed one, even a nip, when he failed to understand the first time Wolf had something to communicate.

During times of melancholy or self-reflection, Ember had the time and space to work his troubles through. Wolf was a good listener, sometimes playful, sometimes distant. The sisters who brought them food got used to seeing Wolf at Ember's side. Many grew to like him.

Days passed, and the colder winds blew. The sisters made Ember fur-lined boots to go with his heavy cloak. When fall finally tipped into winter, they helped him chop several weeks' worth of wood.

The first morning they awoke to snow, Wolf ran outside with unadulterated joy. He raced back and forth like a pup, trying to catch snowflakes in his mouth. He lay down in the soft powder to make shapes and then shook himself, getting snow in Ember's hair and all over his clothing. He raced around Ember's feet like a mad thing.

The next morning, Ember had to crack the ice on top of his wash basin. He put another log on the fire and waddled about the tiny space with Wolf on his heels. Ember was living for the moment, but a part of him still worried about the future.

Iris had removed him from his responsibilities as they were fast approaching the fifth moon. She told him to rest and ready himself because five moons was the period that used to be called "confinement" for an omega female. Though no one knew if the same held true for male omegas, Iris thought it wise to be prepared.

Ember still had trouble believing he could bear a child. Trouble, and no small amount of fear. How was this going to work? His body didn't seem capable.

Slow, cold days followed one after another.

The temple celebrated Winter's Night in grand style. Ember made an appearance with Wolf, who had been given special permission to enter the building. Try as he might, Ember couldn't enjoy the feast. The sisters gave him venison stew and winter vegetables cooked in a special casserole, but the food proved too rich for him. He tried a bite of treacle candy for dessert, but its sweetness didn't settle well. Ember and Wolf left the celebration early and walked back to the cabin in relative silence. Ember's feet hurt.

"Why couldn't you be a horse shifter?" Ember asked miserably as they approached home.

A few days later, Iris stopped by. Ember waddled across the cabin to answer the door with Wolf by his side.

"We weren't expecting you, Iris. Come in."

"A cargo ship anchored in the harbor this morning." Iris carried a small burlap sack with her. "The captain gave me some things for you."

"Oh, thank you." There were packages and several letters, some dating back to the date he'd left.

"You must miss your family. I wanted to be sure you got these as soon as possible."

"I've wondered how they're doing. I hope everything is all right." Ember set the packages aside. He was far more eager to open the letters, but some desire to be polite made him offer Iris refreshments. He rose. "I'm so thoughtless. Let me get you tea."

"I'll get it. You sit down with Wolf and read." He lowered himself back into his chair gratefully. She got his kettle ready and put it on the fire. Wolf sat to his right. Iris sat across from him. She folded her hands on the table and waited until he met her gaze. "I want a word with you anyway."

He glanced up. "You do?"

"I need to be honest with you, Ember." She seemed uncharacteristically nervous. "I don't know how to assist your birth."

Ember stared at the letters in his hand. "It's not as if I know."

"When your time comes, I'll do everything I can to see your baby safely into the world. But even though I'm a skilled midwife, even though I've been at this for forty years, I've never helped a male omega give birth."

"I understand." Ember had thought this over many times. "My mother died giving birth to my little sister. The baby died as well. If it comes to a choice, I want you to save the child. Will you promise?"

Wolf growled.

Ember automatically motioned for calm, but the wolf's body didn't relax.

"Giving birth is dangerous," said Iris. "Your male omega body is new to me, but that doesn't mean you face greater danger. Your body is known to the Goddess. She gives omegas instincts for a reason, and our instincts serve us well. I'll assist you. The sisters and I will pray for a safe and uncomplicated delivery, but life offers no guarantees."

"I understand. Thank you." Tears fell. Ember brushed them away brusquely.

He'd have liked to be with his family for the so-called *blessed event*. He needed Nora's teasing, Lucy's calm. Even dour Lenore —who was dedicated to brutal honesty—would be refreshing in his time of need.

Iris gave a small smile. "Omegas represent the Goddess's wisdom and her grace. Your rare birth was no mistake. The Goddess brings new life into the world in a myriad of ways. Trust the omega in you. The Goddess has a plan for you."

Some plan. Ember hadn't forgotten his harassment at the hands of three young nobles. Domino had saved him that night and set him on this course, only to abandon him to it.

To his everlasting shame, he could not stop the tears from flowing.

"Your baby's moon is almost upon us. Send Wolf if you need me. In case he's out hunting, take this." She carefully held out a piece of hollow wood wrapped in paper with a string at one end.

"What is it?" Ember asked.

"A ship's captain brings these for us. Take it well away from the cabin, aim it at the sky, and then pull hard on the string." She demonstrated without setting the device off. "Be careful with it. They're quite dangerous. Use it as a signal if there's an emergency. Anyone outside will see it and come running for me."

"I'll do it, thank you." He took the strange item. "If I'm in distress, Wolf will probably be very protective."

"The sisters will bring him treats. They've all taken to him."

"Even Violet?"

"She most of all since he took down the big cat. I know he won't leave your side, but I believe he'll let us do what we need to do. He's a good boy."

Ember snorted. "Hear that, Wolf? You're a good boy. Yes, you are."

Wolf seemed gratified by their words. No. Ember had to stop humanizing the wolf's reactions. When Wolf found his human form—if he found it—the reality was bound to fall short of Ember's ideal. The stuck shifter wasn't some dream alpha. He was only a man with good points and flaws, like any other.

"Now." Iris rose. "I'll leave you to your thoughts and your letters from home."

"Thank you." He rose to see her out, but she stopped him.

"No, Ember. Stay there and rest. All too soon the babe will keep you up day and night, and you'll miss this quiet time. I'm perfectly capable of opening a door." She left him to his letters and gifts.

"Whose letter shall I open first?" Ember asked aloud.

Wolf raised an eyebrow as if to say, yes, whose indeed?

"You're right. I should read them in order." They'd had far too many conversations exactly like that one: Ember, searching Wolf's expressive face for an answer to his questions.

"Good idea."

He opened all his letters and placed them in chronological order.

"This first one is from Nora," he told Wolf.

Dearest Ember, I hope this finds you well, the girls and I were desperately unhappy to see you go and in such circumstances. We cannot imagine your feelings on the matter. I still believe it's for the best, especially since there are soldiers still searching for "the Carlysle Coachman."

The country still mourns the queen deeply. I hope our plans for the winter holidays don't have to change. They will probably be subdued, especially in the presence of the Duke of Ehrenpries. His uncle the king and cousin Prince Christopher are said to be inconsolable.

Wolf gave a whine at this. Ember glanced his way. "I'm sad too, Wolf. Our queen was the heart of the realm. I can't imagine how the royal family is coping with her loss."

He opened a letter from Lenore. No salutation.

Soldiers have been watching our home. Hugh Smith assures me that he saw you to safety, and I've asked him to find out what he can. Perhaps it's simply a case of mistaken identity? No doubt we'll have answers before this painful episode is over. I only hope we know soon.

Nora and Lucy are still over the moon about their beaux. We're making frantic preparations for Seavane but I wonder if your absence will cause a disruption in our plans.

You told me everything that happened while we were at the ball. I cannot fathom what this summons—for that is what it appears to be— can be about.

I tell you frankly that my greatest fear is that your Domino comes from such a highly placed family that they can use the king's men to warn you off. Powerful men may dally where they like, but they must ensure discretion.

"Well, that can't be it," Ember mused. "Can it? I hope not. If that's the case they're being awfully persistent."

Ember picked up a third letter. "Ah, another from Nora."

Dearest Ember, For the past five days we've done nothing but stand for endless fittings. The ball gowns are going to be lovely, and of course, we must have all kinds of day dresses and gloves and stockings and shoes and hats! Oh, you would not believe the fetching hats that mama bought us. I do hope my duke is there when we get to Seavane. I have a lovely travel ensemble.

I haven't received any more letters from him since you left. Mama assures me this is normal as men don't take the time to write as often as women do, but the Duke of Seavane sent two letters for Lucy begging her to remember him. As if she could forget, she's so besotted. He was kind enough to tell her to let me know that as a member of the royal family, Oliver will be spending much time with the king and Prince Christopher during these sad days. I suppose preparations and events must keep the royal family very busy. Every day, we hear about some artistic tribute to the queen or some visitor of state who has come from afar to offer condolences to the grieving king in person.

I like Oliver all the better for spending this time with his family. I only wish our family was together as well.

Hugh Smith sends his best wishes, and Tom and Geoffrey promise they're taking excellent care of the stables.

I hope this finds you well and happy. I can't wait to see you again. You must meet my Oliver and Lucy's Duke of Seavane. You'll like them both, you really will. As soon as I can, I will make Oliver promise to get to the bottom of why the soldiers are looking for you.

All my love, Nora

"I'll bet they've heard about the male omega from those three fools at the inn, and now people in high places curious about me. That can't be good. " Ember stuffed the letter back into its envelope as Wolf curled in on himself. "It must be something to do with the estate. Now that I'm the Earl of Carlysle, perhaps the palace has some plan for me. Wait, no. Why would they ask for the Carlysle *coachman*. Blast. I haven't the faintest idea of what they want."

CHAPTER 28

$\mathcal{K}$it remained absolutely still as Ember read yet another letter aloud. He only caught snippets of words here and there. He was too busy reacting to what he'd heard. *Ember is the Earl of Carlysle?* Goddess only knew why he'd been in the Carlysle livery. Kit wanted to find a hole and pull dirt in after him.

"Look." Ember held out a scarf knitted from a soft wool in a cognac color that matched his eyes. "I've got gloves and a second scarf. I'm going to be warm no matter how low the temperature falls."

How many times had Kit opened a gift from his parents: elegantly tailored suits, shirts so fine you could almost see through the fabric, jeweled cufflinks, and trinket boxes? He'd simply accepted what they gave him and then laid everything aside because he had so much already.

These simple homemade gifts from Ember's sisters brought Ember true pleasure. He tried on each item as though the yarn had been spun by the fairies, and as he did he reminisced about watching his sisters knit while his stepmother embroidered decorative linens.

Inside the last parcel from his stepmother, there was a baby's layette. A tiny lawn gown and cap, a small pillow with a pocket to tuck a lock of baby's hair.

Their baby. Goddess, Ember's time was coming all too soon.

Kit was anxious for the baby's birth but at the same time more frightened than he'd ever been in his life. Ember would suffer. All omegas did. Guilt followed the thought like the specter of death. If Kit only had done the right thing in the beginning, Ember would be in Spindrift Palace, attended by every doctor and mage the kingdom had to offer. Instead, they were trapped in a cabin in nowhere. If anything happened to Ember or the child ...

Kit couldn't bear thinking about it.

In the days that followed, Kit watched Ember grow melancholy. The skies remained gray and daylight hours diminished. Snow continued falling but didn't always stick. Morning would find five or six inches on the ground, but by afternoon it would melt. They should have much more snow by now. Kit worried that true winter would come soon and hit them hard.

Ember kept his anxiety to himself. As if his wolf, his mate, couldn't smell h is anxiety or hear the rapid beating of his heart. At night, Kit lay awake praying: *Goddess, please. Only let them live, and You can do with me what You will.*

~

*E*mber's birthing moon was almost upon them.

The skies were dark, and the air smelled like snow.

Kit hoped the bad weather would hold off. Would it be better if Ember went to the residence with the sisters even if they made him stay in the cabin?

Ember's ungainly body was both comical and worrisome. Even the briefest outdoor walk exhausted him, so he rested and read by the fire most of the time. Kit was content, even happy, to be by his side but their winter idyll couldn't last.

If this was all Kit could have—slow rambles with Ember while they hunted, and quiet, comfortable hours spent by the fire together—it was enough. It was more than he deserved after taking every one of his blessings for granted.

"I wonder," Ember mused, "if my sisters are still at Seavane. The coastal road is difficult to travel in heavy weather, and the area around Carlysle Manor will be blanketed in snow by now. I hope they're all right."

Kit grunted as if he would answer. Seavane wouldn't allow guests to leave unless it was safe. If there was light snow, he'd send the ladies' carriage with a company of men to assess the roads and see to their comfort. If the snow was dense, he'd keep them in his home until spring.

Oliver and Seavane were good men. They had good heads on their shoulders. Ember's sisters would be safe with them. Kit hated not being able to reassure Ember of the fact, but he knew it to be true.

"I'm scared out of my mind, to be honest." Ember caressed his belly. "All of this, the soldiers, the hiding, birthing my babe, it's sick-making in a way. If I concentrate on what's happened to me, my heart races, and prickles of sweat sting my back. I feel like I'll lose what little I've eaten. I need to settle my nerves for the sake of the baby, but—"

Wolf gave a yip, rose to his paws, and moved closer. He rested his muzzle on the arm of the chair to be near his mate, to breathe in the scent of him and offer comfort even though he couldn't help. Goddess, being useless burned him up inside.

When the time came, Kit would be nothing but a helpless mass of nerves and fur. The high priestess would shoo him out the door because even if she would suffer him to live near the temple, she wouldn't let him attend the birth of a child.

"I truly believe the Goddess has a plan for me, and it isn't to end my life in childbirth in the middle of nowhere," Ember said. "But what if I'm fooling myself? Many would call me a freak or a mistake or an abomination. What if all this is the Goddess's way of removing an imperfection from the natural world?"

Kit whined. He couldn't help himself. The thought of Ember being a mistake or any kind of imperfection … no. Ember was a gift—Kit's *perfect* gift—from the Goddess Herself. Kit refused to believe for one second that his kind Ember, his selfless, loving mate, was a mistake.

"The only thing I can do is pretend it will all work out." Kit's hands moved in slow circles over his belly. "So I pretend my omega body will be just as resilient as any other, just as capable of bringing a child into the world. And I pretend that once my baby is safely delivered, I can return home and see my family again. But make-believe is hard sometimes."

Kit tried so hard to shift. He held his human image firmly in his mind, thought of all the things he could do for his beloved mate if he was human, considered all the ways he could make things right for Ember … The shift would not come. He let his muzzle fall to Ember's thigh.

Ember stilled. "I don't want to alarm you, but you're getting pretty cuddly there, Wolf."

If Kit could have frowned, he would have. As it was, he huffed an unhappy breath and closed his eyes.

"All right if I do this?" Tentative fingers touched his head, stroked the area between his ears. Kit sighed with relief. He welcomed Ember's touch. One finger became two, then four, then Ember's whole hand smoothed the fur on Kit's neck, his back.

"Goddess, you're as soft as you look."

Kit moved as if to shrug. He had majestic, royal fur. Of course it was soft.

"Listen to me, complaining as if I'm the only one with problems. You're obviously unable to shift out of your wolf form, but you remain remarkably human. I've never heard of a shifter who didn't succumb to his wolfish needs and desires when in wolf, yet you make human choices, again and again. You did so even when you were hurt and exhausted and starving."

Kit gave a soft groan of pleasure. Ember's hand continued to stroke from Kit's neck to his shoulder blades and over his back. He could have died from happiness. Mate's touch, at last!

"No wolf has ever trusted me this close," Ember murmured. "I quite like it."

I like it too. Love it. Want this forever and ever. Goddess, how he'd missed human touch. He should have closed the physical distance between him and Ember sooner. Should have found a way to let Ember know who he was.

"Whatever happens, I hope you'll stay with me," said Ember. "Carlysle Manor has plenty of room for you to roam."

Kit's ears perked up. Ember wanted to keep him around even after the birth of their child?

"My sisters have serious suitors, and Lenore keeps to herself. We keep a very unusual household, a smaller-than-average staff, and frankly, most of them are family to me. I hope you and I can spend many fine days together roaming my land as we do here. Our woods are good for hunting."

Oh, how Kit wanted that. The company of his mate, a simple life, a place to wander and hunt, and a cozy fire at days' end.

Impossible, if he shifted back to human form.

As Prince Christopher, he had duties and responsibilities. His future was mapped out for him. Yet when he thought about it, his father always made time for Kit's mother and him. Was that what was holding him back? Didn't Kit want his human life with all its responsibilities and fancy dress and strict rules?

Kit's answer was clear enough. Life would be unbearable without Ember. He would stay by Ember's side whether he could shift or not. He and Ember would make whatever life they could have work. As long as they were together, it would be all right.

He laid his muzzle on Ember's knee.

"That feels like a yes." Ember laughed softly. "Excellent. You mustn't be too wolfy around the older staff. Tom's heart will leave his body when he sees you for the first time."

His mate thought him fierce? Well, he was a large specimen. He'd always considered himself pretty fearsome in wolf form. Perhaps Ember had only approached him because he'd been in a weakened state, but he was certain he could cause Ember's entire staff to tremble.

Not that he would. He would earn their trust as he'd earned the trust of the temple's sisters because the most important person in his life was Ember, and to be near him he would do anything. His stomach rumbled fiercely.

"Time to hunt if you want meat." Ember yawned hugely. "'Fraid you'll have to go without me, old friend. I feel quite tired. I don't have a walk in me today."

Kit gave Ember a worried whine.

"It's fine. No pain or anything." Ember opened the door, so Kit could leave. "I'm just tired. I'll rest while you're gone. We have plenty of bread and cheese in the cupboard. I'll not starve."

Kit glanced back, worried, but he walked outside. The sooner he left, the sooner he'd be back.

⁓

*K*it awoke the morning of Ember's birthing moon to find Ember washing his clothes. Dear Goddess, he'd heated the wash water, and his hands were red from scrubbing. What on earth did he think he was doing? Kit gave him a worried yip. He had to chase his mate around until he hung the garment he'd washed and got back in bed.

"All right, all right," Ember huffed as he lay on his side,

rubbing his belly. "I woke up this morning and realized if I was going to have a baby, I'd want something clean to wear after."

Kit gave him a growl.

"It wasn't difficult. I feel quite energized. I suppose that's the effect of the moon."

Kit was glad he didn't have to give Ember the satisfaction of a reply. He was supposed to be resting, everyone said so. Not washing clothes.

Outside, the sky was ominous. Thick dark clouds that smelled of snow curdled over the horizon. It looked like they were in for several inches by nightfall.

Kit glanced Ember's way and found him smiling at some thought that was his alone. The barrier between them had become unbearable in the last few days. Ember had touched him, stroked his fur, talked to him like a friend and companion, and all Kit had to offer in return was longing glances, whines, and yips.

Even in his days as an indolent prince, he'd been more useful.

He'd assisted his parents in governing a kingdom, been on the boards of charities for the poor, collected clothing and food and distributed them throughout the kingdom, and now ...

Now he couldn't bring the love of his life a cup of water.

After making certain Ember had everything he needed nearby, Kit left to hunt before the snow began falling heavily. At first, fat, lacy flakes sifted into downy powder, but all too soon the wind rose. Drifts of snow changed the landscape beneath his feet. There was little game. He caught a vole and a mouse, but he didn't need to gorge himself. There was bread in the cottage. Ember would share his cheese.

Kit made his way back to the cottage by following the scent of smoke from the fire they kept going night and day.

Visibility was so poor, he couldn't see even the cabin until he came right up to it. Heavier snowfall would make it next to impossible for the sisters to come if Ember had need.

They were in danger of a blizzard. Should Ember begin laboring, it might not be safe to call the sisters. It might not be possible to get aid for Ember at all.

Instead of entering the cottage, he changed course and made for the sisters' dormitories in the hopes they'd send someone—a human—back with him just in case. He saw Violet on the way. He yipped to get her attention and nearly found himself spitted on her knife.

"Oh, it's you. Is Ember all right?"

He wanted to growl at the lethal blade but yipped excitedly, circling her as he'd seen dogs do. He glanced back. *Follow me! Follow me!*

"Is it Ember's time?" she asked. "The weather's so foul I believe Iris was planning to go to your cabin, ready or not."

Kit tried nodding. He yipped and ran around her again.

"Well, aren't you insistent. One would think you're the baby's father." Her gaze pierced him. "Fat lot of good you'll do them as a wolf. "

Kit growled as she left for the pasture, laughing at him.

He'd laugh too if it was someone else. He'd find all of this funny if it wasn't happening to him. Must he add *lacks compassion* to his list of faults? His breath clouded around him as he ran the rest of the way to Ember's old dormitory. He got there just in time to see Iris and two of the sisters leave the kitchen doors, bundled up for the cold. They looked like snowmen coming one after the other.

"Wolf?" Iris called. "Has something happened?"

Kit had no way to tell her he was acting preemptively, so he turned and followed the three women as they made their way through the worsening weather.

"It's going to be a wretched night," she called over the wind.

"Better to be safe than sorry. You may need to guide us. Can you do that?"

He yipped and circled. Yes, Yes. Mate. *Mate!*

The three carried blankets and baskets of food and probably medicine. They were prepared, at least. Ready to face anything. The farther they were from the temple complex, the more worried Kit grew. Due to the weather, he'd been gone a long time. He hoped Ember wasn't worried, or Goddess forbid, looking for him.

A whistling noise echoed through the clearing. Even in the falling snow, he couldn't ignore the ball of light that burst in the sky a second later.

"That's our cue. Obviously, we were right to come out," said Iris.

Kit watched the light flare then wink into a spark that fell to earth in silence.

Goddess save them, Ember's time had come.

CHAPTER 29

*P*ain hadn't come upon Ember suddenly. He'd been feeling out of sorts all morning as he'd rearranged the same things over and over. During that time, a kind of intermittent tension had pulled at the muscles of his belly, yet it was only enough pain to make him wonder if he'd been straining previously unused muscles while he cleaned.

Those early, unaccustomed aches had become real grabbers since then, clamping in waves like a giant fist tightening around his belly and then slowly letting go again.

Ember had ignored the early warning signs, which only made figuring out what to do more difficult when the pains grew longer and stronger. He'd kept his feet, paced and turned, paced and turned again.

A burst of viscous fluid flooded the floor at his feet. Suddenly terrified, he'd barely made it to the door, much less out into the furious snow to signal for help. The kick of the device that Iris had given him shocked him. Its brightness burst above the tree line and lingered. He told himself someone had to have seen that. Now he could wait for them to come before panicking.

It did no good to tell himself that.

Wolf wasn't back yet either.

Ember's fears painted all kinds of horrible pictures for him. Wolf, lost, freezing in the dark woods. Iris, unable to see his flare or leaving him alone to his fate because of the terrible storm. Him, dying in the cottage when the fire went out. His child, barely born and crying alone or worse because he had been a fool to think he could do this.

Ember sagged into bed still wearing his wet garments. His legs quivered. He couldn't stand any longer. His mind clouded with fear and exhaustion. Between cramps, he drifted on each wave of brief relief only to feel the next awful twisting pain begin.

Ember had spent all his energy making sure everything would be ready if the babe came with the moon as Iris had warned it might. Now he doubted he had the strength to labor and deliver. He couldn't measure the time that passed between spasms, but it seemed they'd been coming closer together.

He closed his eyes and prayed, "Goddess. If I am to do this, show me how."

～

The scrape of boots outside—the scrabbling of paws— told Ember that Wolf was back and he'd brought more than one of the sisters with him. Thank the Goddess, Ember had been about ready to lose hope.

The candles guttered when Iris burst through the door. Wolf stuck his head inside, gave a whine, and huffed a frosty breath into the air.

"Come inside, Wolf, but sit well over there," Iris instructed. "Gemma, Irina, get those wet things off Ember before he freezes to death."

Ember couldn't help the awful moan he gave when one of

the sisters tried to help him sit. Sitting was easier to do between cramps. He asked them to wait until he could get himself up. They let him. Then without so much as a by-your-leave, Iris lifted his robe, and Gemma stripped him of his smallclothes.

"Don't fuss, Ember," she chided. "I've seen a man's penis before."

Ember's cheeks filled with heat.

"Just not on someone about to give birth." She pushed his knees apart so she could see what was happening between his legs. Ember wanted to die when the other two looked on with interest.

"Must we be this ... inquisitive?" Ember asked. The women laughed at him.

"We're all curious," said Iris. "If I'm right and there are more male omegas out there, we need to learn, don't we?"

Irina winked at him. "I have five alpha brothers, and none of them could do what you're doing. Of course, none would want to."

"Irina, put some water on to boil." Iris ordered.

"What should I do, Sister?" asked Gemma.

"Let's make Ember more comfortable." Iris found a mug on the table. "Can you fill this with snow and bring it back?"

"Yes, ma'am." The girl grabbed up her cloak and ran to do Iris's bidding.

Wolf whined.

"Hey. It's all right, Wolf." Ember lifted his head. "We knew this was coming."

"Ember's fine right now." Iris reassured.

Another cramp hit him and his back bowed. He wanted the comfort of his Wolf, but didn't call him over. Iris had been magnanimous enough to let Wolf stay inside during the storm. Ember dared not call any more attention to him.

Iris prodded Ember in places only his mother and Domino had ever seen.

"Hmm. I begin to see how this is going to happen. Your body has been softening, and now muscles are pulling between your anus and an orifice you probably had no idea you had. It's much like what happens to a female omega except for how the seed is planted, so to speak."

"I know you're delighted by the discovery," Ember told her, "but please stop talking."

"Oh, goodness, you're dilating at the same rate as any female omega in your situation. This is fascinating."

"Don't. Just. Help? I don't need to know everything. Or anything, really."

"Squeamish?" Iris backed away and gave her hands a wash in something that smelled like spirits. "I plan to write a scholarly paper about this. Other male omegas will be much safer if we learn as much as we can about you."

He wanted to cry. "All right."

"I'll keep my observations to myself." She smiled down at him. "Spend this time picturing yourself holding your beautiful, healthy baby."

Another pain caught Ember, lower this time. He felt like ripe fruit being pressed by Victoria during the summer jam-making.

"Goddess," he moaned when it was over.

"Here, open." Irina fed him a spoonful of snow.

If Ember lived to be a hundred, that frozen, crunchy goodness melting deliciously on his dry tongue would rank among the best things he'd ever eaten.

"More," he croaked.

Irina fed him snow, Iris watched over him, and Gemma kept the kettle boiling. Every so often, he heard Wolf whine.

Hours passed. Maybe they did. Ember was only aware of the pains that lifted him, drained him, and let him go, one after another. His was dazed, his body losing strength, but his heart was filled with hope. He couldn't wait to see his baby. His child by his true mate. Hugh had said it would be a girl, and Ember clung to that. He imagined greeting her by morning.

Outside, the snowstorm raged. Icy wind-driven snow hurled into the against the cabin walls. It occurred to Ember that they'd have to dig their way out in the morning. They were completely cut off. There was no way for the sisters to go back for supplies or aid. There would be no one coming to check on them.

Ember had never, ever felt so alone. He would never leave home—never venture away from those he loved—again.

Another pain hit. Along with Ember's unmanly scream, there was a plaintive whine from Wolf, who had curled into a ball in the farthest corner of the room and tucked his nose under his tail. Obviously, Wolf knew Ember was in trouble, and it affected him. Ember would be just as distressed if anything should happen to Wolf.

What would Domino make of Wolf if Ember returned with him? Would there be problems between the two alphas in his life? If Wolf ever found his human form again, there very well could be.

Would Domino even show his face after this long?

The future was too much to think about. It was too hard to see where his path would lead him. All Ember had now was a rising tide of pain, the blessed release of tension after it was over, and the icy delight of sweet snow in the respites between.

"What's that?" A jolt of unexpected awareness startled Ember. He opened his eyes in surprise.

Iris sat forward. "What does it feel like?"

He examined what had made him so suddenly alert. "I think she's coming. Oh, Goddess—"

"Does it feel like you need to push?" Iris put her hand *down there* again. This time, her fingers were actually inside him. He couldn't keep his right eye from twitching.

"I do now," he growled angrily. If Ember could push Iris's

questing fingers out, by the Goddess, she would be in the next county by now.

"All right, then, it's time to get to work, Papa." She grinned at him. "Now watch me and breathe as I'm breathing."

She panted, and he copied her, feeling like the world's biggest fool.

"Next wave, here it comes, give me a big push."

It didn't seem to matter if he didn't know what he was doing. When the next wave crested, he planted his feet and gave everything he had. It was instinct, just as she'd said when they first met. His body guided him. Push after push, wave after wave came over him then receded. He lost all ability to count.

"Look at that!" Gemma squealed when she saw the top of the baby's head. "It's coming! It's coming!"

Ember's body seemed ready to tear apart, but from there he was a passenger. His body did all the work. There was pain. So much pain he couldn't quantify it. But in the end … Oh, in the end, Iris placed a bloody, filthy, squalling baby in his arms, and all he could do was cry.

"She's beautiful." Iris told him. "An omega, like her papa. Take a look, and then Gemma will take her for a minute while we get cleaned up."

Ember sobbed while Iris took care of business below. There seemed to be more to do before she was willing to help him get cleaned up and into a new nightshirt. Through it all, he didn't take his eyes off his baby and Gemma, who cleaned her and placed her in a simple sack of a gown with a drawstring at the bottom. Irina swaddled her in a blanket and Iris placed the babe in the crook of his arm.

Ember had never seen anything so beautiful in his life.

Iris pulled the chair back to his side and sat, hands folded in her lap. "Have you thought about names?"

"Charlotte," he croaked the word. "Charlotte Bella Maria, to honor my mother and the late queen."

"What a lovely, meaningful name. May she wear it in good health."

Charlotte's eyes opened narrowly. She seemed to stare at Ember.

"Can she see me?" he asked.

"Of course she can. If she doesn't see clearly, she's warm and comfortable and wanted. She scents you."

"I didn't have any idea how much I wanted her until now. I think I was afraid to believe in her."

"Like a lot of new parents, you were afraid you might lose her." Iris touched the baby's tiny fist. "Don't let it affect how much you let yourself love."

"Thank you, Iris." He glanced up at Gemma and Irina. "I am so grateful all of you were here to help."

The scrape of a claw on the floor drew their attention to Wolf, who seemed to be belly-crawling toward the cot.

"Looks like someone else wants to see the new baby," whispered Irina. "Do you think it's safe?"

"I believe so." Iris shoved a cushion behind Ember's back, so he could sit up a little. "If we watch carefully."

Ember switched Charlotte from his right arm to his left, which was farther from the edge of the bed—and Wolf—just in case. He didn't know how Wolf would react to an unknown creature the same size as the hares he hunted. Did he understand the difference?

Maybe befriending even a benign wolf wasn't a great idea.

Wolf arrived at the foot of his bed. He seemed to know he should peek at the baby from a safe distance. He whined unhappily, his dark eyes so lost and sad that Ember wondered if he was reliving the event that stole his ability to shift. Perhaps he'd lost a wife and child, and this moment was causing him to relive it. Ember wanted to comfort him in some way, but he couldn't move.

"Wolf. Meet Charlotte Bella Maria," he spoke gently, hardly daring to make a sound in the silence.

Ember and the three sisters watched Wolf for any sign of aggression, but instead he sank to his belly with a cry that sounded so human Ember looked to Iris in distress. Wolf rolled into view, jerking spasmodically. His bones cracked. Muscles stretched. His back bowed horribly and he let out a strangled cry. Iris and Gemma and Irina fell back to give him room ...

Wolf's transformation didn't come easily to him. Ember winced with every groan, every jerk of his flesh as his hair retreated and his human skin appeared. The souvenirs from a long time spent in wolf form, scars from his fight with the cat, didn't fade.

When at last Wolf lifted his scarred human face, it was streaked with tears.

Ember gasped. "Domino?"

Goddess, Wolf was *Domino!*

No wonder he was crying. He must be so relieved to be free. How could Domino be here? How had he gotten trapped in his wolf form and more importantly, why? The high priestess and her acolytes seemed equally shocked.

It took an eternity for anyone to speak.

"This is ... an unexpected pleasure, Your Highness." Iris rose and curtsied deeply, as did Gemma and Irina, who giggled nervously and slapped her hand over her mouth. "It's a good thing Violet didn't shoot you."

"Wait—" Ember gaped at the man he knew as Domino. "You called yourself Domino. Who are you?"

"Mate." The word tore out of Wolf's unused human throat. "I'm your mate, Ember. My name is Christopher Ehrenpries."

"But." Ember tightened his grip on his daughter. "I thought—"

"Domino was a jest, because of the mask. I didn't go to the ball.

I switched places with my cousin." Wolf—the man, Kit—bowed his head as tears streamed down his cheeks. "He used a simple illusion charm to appear as me, only it turned into a huge mess."

"You didn't go to your own ball?" Irina seemed to feel that sort of thing was beneath a royal prince. Ember didn't disagree. "What about all the omegas who went to meet you?"

"Goddess forgive me." Kit shrank back very much like Wolf did when he was ashamed. "I was an arrogant fool, and it will take me a lifetime to apologize."

"You couldn't shift all this time?" asked Iris.

"I lost my magic," he confessed.

Ember let took Charlotte's tiny hand. "Is your magic back?"

"I don't know. I think it was Charlotte Bella Maria. Her magic called to my heart." He inched forward to stroke the tiny baby's forehead with one finger. "It was her magic—and yours— that saved me."

Charlotte chose that moment to let out a wail. Swallowing hard, Kit pressed his forehead into Ember's side.

"What do you say, Kit." Ember reached out to stroke his alpha's hair. "Our daughter needs us."

"May I be worthy," Kit whispered.

"Me too." Ember closed his eyes. "Goddess, may I be worthy also."

CHAPTER 30

Spring flowers blossomed over the temple grounds before Kit was able to send a letter to his father. In it, he laid out what had happened during the prince's ball and afterward unflinchingly. He begged his father's forgiveness.

He had no idea how his letter would be received, or even if the king would choose to read it. Had his father given up on him, or did he still believe Kit might be worthy of his blood and royal heritage?

Kit was more worried about his father's love than any royal title he might wear in the future. He missed his father deeply. He still grieved for his mother. He wanted more time with his family. Whether they removed him from the line of succession was nowhere near as important to him as returning home to spend time with the people he loved. People like Oliver, whom he'd probably gotten into serious trouble with his prank. He wondered if Oliver had given up on him too.

His first step toward making amends was to ask the high priestess of the Temple of the Moon to perform a handfast ceremony for Ember and him. In this way, he conferred the power of his name—what little power he had left, anyway—and his worldly goods on Ember and Charlotte.

Lotte, as everyone called her, had grown fat and happy under the care of all the sisters. Kit needed to take his family to Spindrift Palace to meet the king, and to Carlysle Manor to be coddled by Ember's family.

There were many hurdles to overcome, first. After the cargo ship left with his letter, his anxiety was such that he barely ate or slept. Ember had cornered him in their cottage, away from prying eyes, and scolded him for not taking better care of himself.

"Kit, everything you've told me about your father tells me he'll greet you with open arms." Ember wrapped his own arms around Kit's waist from behind. They stared out of the tiny window together. "You'll see; everything will be all right."

"You don't know that. I was unforgivably rude when my mother was only trying to help me find a mate. I should have told her I wanted a consort. She would have understood. My parents would have found a way."

"But if she had, you wouldn't have met me."

"I know." Kit turned and lifted Ember's hands to his mouth. He kissed each knuckle, one by one.

"I'm your true mate, Kit. Even if your mother had gone looking for a consort for you, she would never have considered a savage country earl like me."

"You don't know that. Anyway, once I told her you were my mate, she'd have loved you as much as I do."

"Then you agree; the Goddess knows what she's doing. Your father will see we were brought together by destiny, and he'll lose his mind because our daughter is *perfection*."

"You're right about that." Kit pressed a kiss to his hair. "As soon as he lays eyes on Lotte, the point will be moot."

"Your father is going to be helpless against her baby wiles, just as we are." Ember dropped kisses all along his jaw. Down his neck. They were newly handfasted after all, they had a standard to uphold.

"You named her for my mother. Why?" Kit turned and cupped Ember's jaw with his hand. "Why did you do that?"

Ember blinked up at him. "I always admired our queen. She seemed to be the kind of person I'd want our daughter to be. My mother was lovely and good, but sometimes I don't remember her. Everyone talks about your mother in such glowing terms ... I feel like I knew her."

"Queen Bella Maria Filomena was the heart of our kingdom. Everyone loved her," Kit said proudly.

"I saw her once when my parents were alive. They took me to watch a royal procession; I think it was probably your birthday."

"You saw me?" Kit's eyes widened. "What did you think?"

"You sat atop a white stallion far too large for you, wearing a helmet with gilded wings. I thought you looked silly."

"Wait—oh no. Those were wolf's ears I'll have you know. That procession celebrated my first shift. You're absolutely right, I looked ridiculous."

"I liked the horses," Ember admitted. "And your mother was the most beautiful woman I'd ever seen, besides mine, of course."

"Of course." Kit wrapped his arms around Ember's shoulders.

"There was something about the way the queen waved from the carriage. She knew her subjects. She cared about us. It's as if she was the Goddess made flesh."

Kit had to clear his throat before speaking.

"She was good. I wish I'd known it was the last time I'd talk to her. I'd have said so much more."

Ember nodded. "My father said goodbye to us at breakfast on the morning he left. I didn't want him to go. I ran to the gate to get another look at him, but he'd already gone."

"It's up to us to learn from our losses. I will never waste a moment with you. Not a single second."

"Nor I." Ember laid his head against Kit's chest. "I can hear your heart."

"Oh no, it's yours. You stole it the first moment I laid eyes on you."

"Then this"—Ember pressed Kit's hand to his chest—"must be yours."

"Mm. I wonder what other parts of you belong to me." It had taken time for Kit to find his balance in this new human reality of theirs. At first, he'd been anxious that he'd lose Ember again, or that their little family, their happiness, was some cruel dream and he'd wake up. He must have truly turned a corner because being able to tease, to be lighthearted and romantic and carefree with his mate, was entirely new.

Kit had regained hope for the future.

He'd stopped punishing himself for the past.

Now, he wrapped his hand around Ember's nape and brought him in for a kiss that began soft and sweet then deepened—like their love had deepened—into something compelling and rich and everlasting.

Ember parted his lips and swept his tongue out to play with Kit's. Each mingled breath and gasp and moan held the promise of more. Ember's cock connected with Kit's thigh, making his heart race.

"Ember?" Kit slid his hands down his lover's back. They landed on Ember's gorgeous ass. "Do you suppose we have time?"

Ember looked toward the window. "It's still early. Iris has Lotte until supper."

"Then—"

A rapid knock on the door froze them in place. Ember looked at Kit, who shrugged and went to answer.

"Your Highness." Gemma offered a nervous curtsey, "Begging your pardon—"

"I've asked you to call me Kit," he reminded her. "There's no need for formality between us."

"Sir. *Kit, sir*," she said breathlessly. "There's a ship here for you."

"I—" Kit looked Ember's way, confused. "A ship?"

"It's His Majesty the king. He's come. Here! And we hardly know what to do. Iris told me to bring you because she thinks you should be the one to present the little princess to His Majesty."

"Of course." Kit straightened his spine and held his hand out for Ember. "We'll be right there."

"I'll tell Iris." Gemma spun on her heels and ran ahead, looking like nothing so much as a bird who'd forgotten it had wings.

Kit exhaled slowly. "This is it. Now we find out if he forgives me."

"Your father wouldn't have come so quickly if he was angry with you."

"You don't know that."

"I know he must have missed you terribly. He's here now." Ember's expression softened. "Let's go say hello, shall we?"

Kit rocked his head from side to side. "I did say I'd never waste another moment."

Ember gave him a sly grin. "How very wise you are, Your Highness."

Kit gave his bottom the lightest swat. "Don't think I've forgotten what we were doing."

"As if I'd forget you owe me a tumble."

Kit leaned over and placed a kiss on Ember's cheek. He held out his hand.

"Let's go."

CHAPTER 31

*T*he royal family's pleasure yacht, *Invicta Ventus*, had dropped anchor in the brilliant, sun dappled waters of Temple Harbor just after ten that morning. She was a sleek, three-masted schooner with lacy decorative woodwork and a saucy mermaid figurehead on the bow.

"Oh my." Ember slowed his steps when he saw the grandeur of the canopied skiff carrying passengers to shore.

"Don't be nervous, darling." Kit kissed his hand before tucking it under his arm and moving to greet the visitors. "My father will adore you."

"Even though I'm a rustic earl?"

"You're my true mate, and we're married. What can he say?"

"We're handfasted, not married."

"Oh, you'll hate the very sound of the *M* word when you realize how bone-crushingly boring a state wedding is. Preparations will take months, and then you'll spend weeks smiling for strangers and accepting gifts and tributes, all the while wishing people would spend their money helping the poor."

"We'll help the poor, won't we?"

"Of course, dearest. We'll bring all of my mother's most

radical social programs to fruition. You're very like her, you know. Good inside and lovely out. Unlike me."

"Hush." Ember pulled Kit's hand away from the left side of his face, where three still-red scars went from his forehead to his lip. "You vanquished the dangerous predator that tried to kill me and our baby. You were handsome before, but now you're also fierce and dashing. I might swoon."

Kit tried to tame his delighted smile. "Really?"

"Too bad I don't have time to show you how much I admire you right now."

Kit was different from the man Ember had met the night of the ball. Steadfast and patient, with noble ideas he wasn't afraid to share. It pained Ember that the queen would never see how wonderful he'd become.. She would have been very proud.

"Oh my." Ember got his first look at the king. He never expected the robust, handsome, silver-haired alpha to leap from the skiff to the sand with his arms stretched wide.

Behind him a man in livery and two sharply dressed noblemen debarked. The three carried Lenore, Nora, and Lucy to shore so they wouldn't get their slippers wet. Ember's heart lurched with joy.

"Christopher." The king's voice carried over the crash of waves. "I should beat you, but you're alive, you're well, you've found your mate, and you've brought a brand-new royal princess into the world. I guess you did fairly well." The two alphas came together in a bruising hug. The King pushed him back playfully. "No. I still want to beat you!"

Each royal took a fighting stance that stole Ember's breath. They tussled playfully for a few seconds before hugging again.

"Oh, son," the king's expression darkened. "How I wish your mother could see you so happy."

"Forgive me, Father. I never meant to—"

"Hush. The past is past, boy." The king knuckled tears from

his eyes. "Take me to your consort and prepare to hand over your daughter until I'm satisfied that I'm a grandfather."

Iris had come from the residential complex carrying Charlotte in the fabric sling she—and now Ember—preferred. While they waited for her, the king looked Ember over.

"Father," said Kit. "I'd like you to meet Ember, the Earl of Carlysle and my Goddess blessed mate."

Ember bowed deeply. "Your Majesty."

"I am very pleased to meet you." The king took his hands. "I knew your father very well."

"Yes, I know, Your Majesty. He always spoke fondly of his time at the palace."

"A good man lost too young."

"Thank you, sire." Ember longed to greet his family. He'd missed them terribly, but protocol dictated that his impromptu audience with the king took precedent. Ember bit his lip and glanced to Kit. *Protocol.* He'd have to be patient and learn, if he wanted to fit into his new life.

Kit reached out to take Lotte from Iris. "Princess Charlotte Bella Maria Ehrenpries, meet your grandfather." He whispered into her tiny pink ear, "Don't be fussed about his title, I swear he's a pushover."

The king took the baby with a heavy sigh. His huge hands practically enveloped her, but he was gentle as a kitten when he held her to his heart. Everyone stilled. They all pretended they didn't notice that His Majesty was quite openly crying. Kit put his arm around his father. They touched foreheads.

"Please forgive me. I was foolish, arrogant, and spoiled."

"Son—"

"Let me finish," Kit said earnestly. "I promise you that if you ever place your faith in me again, you won't regret it. I will accept your guidance and listen to your counsel. I'll be a son you can be proud of."

"Oh, you idiot," the king said fondly. "You *are* a son I'm

proud of. Moreover—despite what you believe—there was never a single moment when I doubted you. I only wanted to find you so I could tell you to your face. *I love you.*"

"I love you too, Father. So much."

The two men embraced, careful not to squish the baby between them.

The king broke away first. "Come, Lotte Bella. I must ask High Priestess Iris all about her marvelous baby sling."

Ember's alpha and his father-in-law were so much alike. Kit's face bore scars. The king's was etched with lines worn by time, by sorrow, by the contemplation of weighty matters of state. His would never be a carefree face, but just now it had softened into one of soul-deep happiness.

The end of Kit's painful adventure had truly justified the means.

Ember gave Kit a moment to gather himself. He knew what the king's words of love and pride meant to his mate. Ember would never intrude on such a private time between them.

Kit noticed Ember hanging back and wasn't pleased.

"Is it our turn?" Lucy stage-whispered to the man standing beside her. "May we approach our brother now?"

Ember stepped to the side only to have his two sisters throw themselves into his arms. They looked wonderful bundled up against the chilly sea air in fur-lined cloaks with little round fur hats to keep their heads warm. Dressed equally carefully, but in the dark colors she preferred, Lenore stood back with a satisfied smile on her face.

"Oh, Ember, we've missed you horribly." Nora squeezed him so hard it hurt. "And now you've gone and had a baby! I thought I'd be the first."

"Ow—" Ember kissed the top of her head. "Where did you get these brawny muscles?"

"We've been at Seavane. There's ever so much to do there. Archery, riding, hunting." Her eyes traveled to her beau, Oliver.

Kit couldn't help the double take he gave the man. The resemblance between Kit and his cousin was remarkable. No wonder the got away with their pranks. Even scarred, Ember preferred Kit's looks. Oliver was handsome, but Kit was simply devastating.

"I went on a hunt," said Lucy, "but like His Grace, I prefer spending time with the pups at the kennels." She flushed deeply. "Your Grace, meet my brother Ember, the Earl of Carlysle. I hope someday you'll be great friends."

"Seavane." The Duke sketched a bow. "Your family is a delight, I must say."

"It's a pleasure to meet you." Ember bowed in return. "Call me Ember."

"I've told His Grace all the things you did to make certain we could attend the ball," said Lucy.

"My darling girl." The duke lifted her chin with one finger. "Didn't we decide you're to call me Lawrence?"

"But in front of the king?" Lucy's cheeks grew pink. "It seems a bit bold."

"No need to be shy, darling. You'll be my duchess soon." Happiness seemed to surround the sweethearts. It was as if no one else was around. Ember was thrilled for them.

"You look remarkably well, Lenore," said Ember.

"My daughters are both blissfully engaged to wonderful, titled gentlemen, and my stepson has married a prince." Her smile was slightly wicked. "I *feel* remarkably well."

Ember might have been embarrassed by this mercenary recap of events, except ambitious mothers were a cliché for a reason. Every mother wanted her child married off well and happily.

"Ember, really. You caught Prince Christopher!" Nora prodded his chest. "You didn't even attend the ball, and you walked away with the prize!"

"I believe I did that." Kit draped his arm over Ember's shoulders. "I found the real treasure that night—greater than all the riches in the world."

"Oh." Lucy covered her heart with both hands. "How romantic."

"And dashing," Nora added. "He's very dashing, isn't he? Good job, brother, though I wouldn't trade my Oliver for anyone."

"I should hope not," said Oliver. "Ehrenpries, at your service, Lord Carlysle."

"Ember, Your Grace." They gave each other tight little bows.

"You ran Kit a merry chase."

Ember shrugged. "I have apologized for everything."

"Don't do that." The duke sent Kit a teasing grin. "Everything has come so easily to my wretched cousin. He deserves to work for love like the rest of us."

"Now, now. I have worked for my happily ever after, and then some." Kit clapped Oliver on the shoulder before turning to Ember. "Come along, my love. Father's waiting."

"Don't you want to go ahead?" Ember glanced toward the king, whose jiggling was making Lotte squeal with delight. He didn't mind putting off discussions with his mate's formidable father for a while.

"Without you?" Kit asked.

Ember felt his cheeks heat. "I thought you and your father might want time alone."

"Did you, or did you not promise to spend all your days by my side?" Kit lifted an imperious brow.

"I *might* have said something like that." Ember hid a grin. "Were those my exact words?"

"Yes. So?" Kit laced their fingers together. "There. Must I do everything for myself?"

"Mm." Ember gave him a long, slow perusal. "Perhaps not *everything*."

"Saucy consort." Kit glanced skyward. "What have I let myself in for?"

"Destiny, Kit." Ember squeezed his hand. "I promise from now on, I'll stand beside you always."

"Wait—" Oliver snapped his fingers. "I nearly forgot."

He spoke to one of the king's men, who turned and ran back to the skiff.

"I've brought you something." Oliver smiled. "You'll never guess in a million years."

Kit looked as puzzled as Ember felt. "What is it?"

The king's attendant handed Oliver a black velvet sack from which the duke pulled Ember's battered coachman's hat. "Here. Back to its owner at last, courtesy of your brother-in-law to be."

"Heavens," said Lenore. "Is that—"

"The hat Hugh gave me!" Ember clapped with delight. "I thought I'd lost it forever."

"You left it at the Red Wolf Inn." Kit gave the ratty thing a brush with his coat sleeve. "I carried it all the way to Carlysle Manor in my mouth only to see you ride off with that farrier. Goddess, you'll never know the despair I felt that day."

"I'm so sorry, Kit. I didn't know."

"We found each other and we're together now, dearest. I love you so much." Kit made a great show of placing the coachman's hat on Ember's head. He adjusted the thing so it sat at rakish angle. Kit pressed his lips to Ember's, taking in the tiny gasp and moan Ember gave him. "I thank the Goddess every day for bringing me to you," Kit said.

"As I thank the Goddess for you, my love," Ember answered solemnly.

"May I be worthy," they spoke the words in unison.

Ember's sisters and their beaux laughed at the royal sweethearts. They cooed like doves and made teasing kiss noises.

"You're ones to talk." Kit pointed at them. "We're all sweethearts here."

"Hear, hear!" Oliver clasped Nora's fingers while bashful Seavane merely met Lucy's gaze with longing. Lenore sighed with satisfaction.

Holding Charlotte, the king looked upon the three couples with great fondness.

~

The Goddess had blessed them all, quite thoroughly.
And they were worthy all their lives long.

EPILOGUE

$\mathcal{E}$mber's wedding day began with morning fog, but by the time the procession took off, the summer sun's golden rays pierced through a smattering of small fluffy clouds in a fathomless blue sky. A fresh breeze blew in from the sea, cooling the throngs who waited to see their royal family make the journey from Spindrift Palace to the Ehrenpries summer home.

The wedding ceremony was scheduled for moonrise at Sea Glass Palace, which featured the Ehrenpries family temple.

Though the king still mourned the queen deeply, he made the decision to hold the prince's wedding before her official year of mourning for Queen Bella ended. This was partly due to the unpredictability of autumn weather and partly because Prince Christopher got a head start on his family.

Exactly one year had passed since the prince's ball.

The Prince's carriage took off at four o'clock, with Prince Christopher dressed in his formal uniform as commander of the Helionne Mounted Guardians. For the procession, the elite cavalry formed teams, each of which surrounded the royal carriages. By the time they reached Moonrise Bay, it seemed as if every citizen of the kingdom lined the streets to cheer them on.

The citizens of Helionne were ready for revelry after their subdued year. The palace had sent coin and supplies to every baker in the kingdom for the making of Ehrenpries buns— sweet rolls with dried citron and cherries, marked with an iced letter "E"—to be given out freely so every citizen could feel as though they were part of the wedding feast. Taverns and Inns did brisk trade in beer and wine. If the raucous cheering and laughter was anything to go by, the celebrations would go on all night.

Following the prince in his own carriage, Oliver Ehrenpries, Duke of Solistenne, waved to a giddy crowd. He was joined by close friend Lawrence Kilmer, Duke of Seavane. Both wore the formal uniforms of officers in the Helionne Royal Navy.

Pipers and drummers heralded the palace guards, and several members of the peerage followed in their own fine carriages, along with more pipers and Prince's Christopher's true mate.

Ember originally worried about his wardrobe, or lack thereof, but of course Kit brought in half fae master tailor Inigo Bertille-Rodrigo, whose sartorial guidance had been sought after by royalty for generations. If Lenore's seamstresses were indignant pigeons, Master Inigo was a great Helionne eagle, and his assistants lessor raptors determined to do his bidding or die trying.

At their first appointment, Master Inigo posed him on a box in front of three mirrors in his small clothes, while his assistants sat in a semi circle around him. Each one studied Ember like a new insect specimen. They sketched him from every unflattering angle for their master. After an hour and a half of this, the great man finally spoke.

"Pale blue, I think. Ermine." He pursed his narrow lips. "A silk corset, studded with gemstones—"

"A corset?" Ember's face heated. Did this man see him as a girl?

"My dear boy," Master Inigo had said kindly "I simply wish to accentuate the unique, goddess-given features of your body. A slender, elegant man can be both beautiful and masculine. You wish to outshine the moon on your special day, no?"

"I guess I do."

"Then trust me." Because the old tailor was kind to him, Ember didn't hesitate to give a free hand. He did not regret it.

As his valet had dressed him that morning, Ember couldn't help admiring the results in the mirror. He wore silk lace small clothes that made him blush, a nearly transparent collarless shirt, a corset in lieu of a waistcoat, and the most magnificent pale blue silk cutaway coat with trousers to match.

Though he'd feared looking feminine, the corset showed off his—proportionally—broad chest and tapered down to his slim hips. Even tightly tied, the garment didn't cut off his air supply. It featured handmade lace, intricate embroidery, and had been studded with sapphires in every shade of blue from light to dark. In the open carriage, the sun struck sparks among the gemstones, making his corset twinkle like a constellation of stars. Even his boots were new, hand crafted, and polished to a glossy black shine.

To signify Ember's upcoming royal status, a pale blue velvet capelet lined in ermine was fastened to his shoulders with chunky, celestial-themed brooches—the sun on one side and the moon on the other. He wore the very diadem of the only other male consort in Helionne's history, a gold circlet composed of gold and silver leaves with clusters of large ruby cabochon berries.

As enchanted as Ember was with his wedding garb, he was far more delighted with the company in his carriage. His sisters sat opposite, each dressed regally. Nora wore her favorite shade of blue and Lucy, a pink that picked up the blush blooming in her cheeks. They both waved cordially to the people they passed.

Lenore sat beside him wearing a look of intense satisfaction. Though the girls chattered gaily, she offered little more than her reassuring presence at his side. Having landed the top three bachelors in Helionne, their little rustic family had become notorious among the peerage, but from the way ordinary citizens cheered their carriage, they'd also touched a lot of hearts.

Everyone, it seemed, liked to see Goddess-blessed couples in love.

In the last carriage, King Leander sat holding Princess Charlotte Bella Maria. His Majesty had dressed most somberly—black from head to toe—in honor of the late queen. It was doubtful he'd ever wear colors again. Indeed, his grief at her passing was so great that he often said he would never *see* colors again. Those courtiers in a position to know said if it weren't for the Prince, Ember, and Lotte, the King might never have found his smile.

Ember had intimate acquaintance with grief. He'd lost the most precious people in his life. But Ember had gained Nora and Lu, and Lenore. They were equally precious to him, as were their husbands and his mate and King Leander. He'd come to the conclusion that if one's family members died, it wasn't an act of betrayal to add more. A man could mourn the dead while finding new love among the living. The king could not replace his mate, but he was smart enough to enjoy his grandchild. Since that was the case, it was a good thing Kit and Ember had plans to fill the nursery to overflowing with children.

At the very least Ember wanted much more of what it took to make them.

Since Ember hadn't wanted to arrive at his wedding fat with baby number two they'd been circumspect with regard to carnal activities. Kit had refused to knot him. Ember had extracted Kit's promise to sate Ember's body to exhaustion—and knot him—after their wedding ceremony and every time either of them felt like it in the future. Thinking about it now, Ember shivered deliciously. Ember expected Kit to knot him as many times as it took to create the large family they both desired.

"You look like the cat who swallowed the cream," Nora said, while waving pertly.

"Er—" Ember choked on what was very likely drool over the idea of a night of uninhibited love-making with his husband. "What?"

"You're blushing, brother. What on earth are you thinking about?"

The girls tittered together. Lenore turned to him.

"Ember, since this is your wedding night, perhaps I should be frank. Since you're already a father, I assume you don't need me to—"

"No ma'am," Ember said quickly. "I'm perfectly fine."

"Because there's nothing you can say that will shock or—"

"It's—" He cleared his throat. "It's all good."

Lenore seemed to be hiding a smile. "Don't hesitate to ask me anything."

"I won't." Ask, he meant. *He would not ask.*

"Ember! You should see your face."

"Stop it." He turned to look behind, to see if His Majesty's carriage was close enough for him to see Lotte. It wasn't, but the cheering behind their carriage was thunderous. The people truly loved their king, who was still a very striking figure. When he held Lotte in his arms, the tenderness that came over him, the fierce pride, was both beautiful and noble. His subjects responded to his joy. They knew their king had the best interest of future generations at heart and they lined up in droves to see him anytime they knew he'd leave the palace, rain or shine.

Kit worried about the shoes he would have to fill one day, but Ember wasn't worried for him. Kit had been a bit juvenile—

and spoiled—before the ball, but he'd acted princely and responsible since. It seemed to Ember that after Lotte's birth, he'd become the prince—the future king—that Helionne deserved.

Ember's arm was killing him from waving. His diadem was too heavy. The metal bit into his forehead and pulled his hair. When at last, their carriage slid beneath the portico at Sea Glass Palace, he sagged with relief, but it was short-lived.

The wedding coordinators had already taken Kit and his attendants. Now they bustled Ember into a cool, breezy lounge to fuss over his clothing and refine his hair. An artist applied a bit of kohl to his eyes, pinched his cheeks, and bade him bite his lips. This was no time to exercise his independence, so he took direction before pacing back and forth, waiting for his turn to show himself to the crowd.

"Knock, knock," Lenore called from outside.

"Come in," he answered.

"These are for you, my dear." She entered with a large bouquet of white roses. "Read the card."

Ember read, "Here's something borrowed for you, with love, Lenore."

"Thank you?" He didn't know what the card meant, should he ask? "Something borrowed?"

She opened the door, and in walked Hugh Smith. "Hello, Ember."

Kit practically threw himself at his friend. "You're here!"

"Whoa, little wolf. Warn a man, will you?"

"I'm so glad to see you." Kit pulled back and got a look at him. Though Hugh wore no uniform, he was dressed as fashionably as anyone in the wedding party.

Lenore smirked. "I borrowed Hugh from his forge for a day. I knew you wanted him here."

"Oh thank you, Lenore, what a wonderful surprise."

"I'm to be part of the wedding party," Hugh said. "I must go take my place with Prince Christopher's attendants, but I wanted to see you and wish you every happiness."

"Thank you for coming. We'll talk after, won't we?"

"Not of your husband-to-be has anything to say about it, I'll wager." Hugh winked. "He'll want you all to himself."

"He'll have to wait," Ember gave Hugh a final embrace, and let go. "I owe you everything."

Hugh met Lenore's gaze. It seemed to Ember that they shared some joke.

"If you mean you asked for my counsel and then went out and did the opposite of what I told you to do, then you're right," Hugh teased.

"It turned out all right,"—Lenore shrugged—"but he didn't listen to me either."

"My wolf knew what we were doing," said Ember. "You did tell me to listen to my wolf."

"I did," Hugh admitted. Trumpets sounded outside, a warning for guests to take their seats. "I should go."

Hugh left just as a flurry of attendants came to put on *final* finishing touches.

For the ceremony, Master Inigo had commissioned a white lace mask from Rhielôme's finest dentellière, to be worn over Ember's eyes in lieu of a veil. At a certain point in the ceremony, one pull by Kit on a thin strip of ribbon would be needed to remove it. Ember found wearing the mask arousing. It reminded him of removing Kit's domino mask the night they met.

He imagined that their gazes would meet for the first time as "married" men and with a kiss, they'd seal their union. Despite his corset, Ember's breath quickened and his heart rate picked up.

His attendants pronounced him ready. Dowager Countess Lenore walked down the aisle with him. She stood to one side when he got to the place where Kit waited with his men.

Kit. Looked. Glorious.

Prince Christopher of Ehrenpries was magnificent beyond anything, anyone, Ember could have imagined for a mate. High Priestess Yanlain officiated the ceremony under the authority of King Leander and the Council of Elders. It didn't make Ember feel more married than he had when he'd promised himself to Kit before Iris at the Temple of the Moon, but he endured, knowing that Helionne royal protocol required the ceremonial words he and Kit exchanged.

After their vows, the temple's bells rang and the guests cheered. The clamor was taken up by others, distant bells rang out in celebration, fireworks that began over Sea Glass Palace were joined by those of Spindrift Palace, and presumably, others places all over the kingdom.

All knew Prince Christopher and Ember were Goddess Blessed and the celebration went on and on, in every city, every town, in Helionne.

After the fireworks, everything blurred in Ember's mind. He must have eaten. He'd had a lot of wine, even if he'd only taken a sip when guests toasted their union. He'd watched King Leander carry Lotte around in his elaborately decorated sling carrier until it was time for her nurses to put her to bed. Ember and Kit kissed her plump cheeks, and watched them go, though they'd rather have taken her themselves.

King Leander left the party shortly after. He went for a walk on the family's private beach. At Kit's frown, Ember told him he should follow.

Kit scoffed. "I can't leave you alone at our wedding feast."

"It's time for me to retire anyway, Your Highness."

"Numpty." As always, Kit met any formality between them with a frown. "Obviously, my place is at your side."

"Not while I'm relieving myself. Go, sweetheart. Talk with your father and then join me in the bridal suite." He wagged his eyebrows. "I'm afraid you'll have to help me out of my clothing.

It's very complicated. There are laces and ... lacy things to consider."

"You make a very good case for leaving."

Ember kissed his cheek. "Come soon."

The two stood, hoping against hope they could sneak away. They couldn't.

"Oh ho," Oliver's voice boomed. "Where are you two skulking off to?"

"It's late, and my husband is very tired." Kit said.

"He doesn't look tired." This from Seavane, the bastard. "He looks newly energized."

"In the pink of health," Nora added. Everyone laughed. They accepted the teasing with good humor.

Their guests continued catcalling until Lucy stood and began to sing a folk song about courtly love. Ember was both relieved and surprised to see his shy Lucy had become a leader in so short a time. Of course, the potential had always been there. Like Ember, maturity had given her confidence. Her husband gazed on her with a wonderstruck expression. Oliver and Nora seemed lost in their own world, singing the words to each other.

The rest of the guests joined in, standing, lifting their glasses in one final toast to the new husbands. Kit and Ember bowed then left. Kit followed his father, and Ember retired to his rooms.

~

Though his attendants greeted him warmly, Ember asked to be left alone with the moonlight as the room's only illumination. His attendants had outdone themselves. Masses of flowers and greenery filled every corner of the room. The sweet fragrance of lilies and gardenias, fresh from the palace hothouse. mingled with the greener scents of ivy and eucalyptus. Whenever Ember closed his eyes, he could easily believe he was in a lover's bower from a fairy story.

He removed his crown, rubbing the irritated skin beneath. He'd have to get used to that, he supposed. Kit's eyes when he'd donned it for the first time were both possessive and passionate. Ember guessed it was a symbol of ownership. Wearing it meant he belonged to Kit. Ember was his consort. His mate. Ember didn't begrudge Kit that. He liked belonging to Kit.

Ember decided to put on his little lace mask because he wanted Kit to remove it. Here in their private room, Ember was free to act on the thrill wearing the little veil gave him. He lay on the bed fully dressed, thinking he'd rest his eyes for a moment, believing that when Kit came in, he'd welcome him with open arms.

The bed shifted, the weight of a body waking Ember from sound sleep.

"Wait. What?" His lips were gummy.

No, that's not how this was supposed to go!

"I'm so sorry I woke you." Kit lifted himself to his elbow and looked down at him. "You obviously need your sleep."

Ember disagreed. "There are things I need more, husband. You promised."

Kit tried to cover his laugh. "I'm not denying you. You seemed so peaceful. I thought—"

"Come here," Ember ordered. "And make love to me, husband."

"Okay, wow. Yes." Kit played the role of henpecked mate. "At your service."

"Unless your talk with His Majesty went poorly."

"No, no. He was simply remembering Mother." Kit's eyes lost their sparkle. "He told me that a year from now, he plans to hand the reins of the kingdom over to us. He'd like to spend more time with Lotte, and in the gardens. He wants to paint, he says. He said the burden of sovereignty is too great without my mother beside him."

"No." Ember's mind reeled. "A year? Goddess, no."

Were they truly only giving Ember a year to learn everything it took to be a royal consort? There wasn't enough time. Queen Bella was beloved by all. Never mind Kit filling his father's shoes, how could Ember fill hers?

"I can see your panic." Kit cupped his face with both hands. "The matter isn't set in stone. Father could change his mind, but even if he doesn't, we'll still have him to guide us. He won't leave us to find our way blindfolded."

"Please stop talking."

Another laugh, this time, Kit pulled him close. "You are going to be a magnificent consort, dearest. You know that don't you? You had all the qualities you needed before we met. Noble, loyal, self-sacrificing, kind, generous. You'll be dressed differently, is all. We only want you to be yourself."

"Is that the royal we?" Ember asked, feeling slightly better. "Already?"

"No, my father and I both adore you. He even told me he couldn't have wished for a better man to stand by my side."

"He said that?" The part of Ember that had been tightly wound since Lottie's birth, since he'd found out who Kit really was, unfurled a little. Kit's love made him feel confident. The king's praise was heady.

"I'm sorry we didn't have a secretary there to take down his words for posterity. He loves you as much as he loves me."

"I can't imagine."

"You don't have to. He'll show you. That's the thing about my father. He shows his love for his family a hundred different ways every day. I wish you could have known him when my mother was alive."

"I wish I could have too."

"I plan to show you how much I love you right now. Do you want that?"

Ember's cheeks heated. "Yes."

"So, it's this little ribbon here?" He gave a tug. Ember's heart fluttered as the scrap of fine lace slid to the bed between them. "Oh my. What a beautiful mate I have."

"Don't tease."

"I would never." Kit began to unbutton Ember's coat. "This outfit is very enticing. Master Inigo wrapped you like a gift for me."

Ember lowered his gaze, suddenly shy.

"Guess I have to help you out of this jacket. Kneel up so I can get it—"

"All right." Ember rose to his knees. It felt very right.

"Mm. I like you on your knees for me." Kit pushed the silken fabric off one shoulder and then the other, exposing the corset and the nearly sheer blouse beneath. "Oh, look at you."

He threw the expensive garment aside and caressed Kit's shoulders.

"Look how broad your shoulders are. How slim your hips. You were made for me."

Ember flushed deeply. He didn't disagree, but he had no words, given the look in Kit's eyes. Kit's alpha gaze made the omega inside Ember quiver.

"Turn." Kit backed up, and Ember turned. He sat on his knees while Kit undid the laces of his corset. "This ... You need to wear corsets for every formal occasion from now on."

"Except—"

"Except when you're with child. I know." Kit's hands moved beneath the loosened garment. He cupped Ember's belly. Though his abdomen was flat again, it wasn't the same as it had been before Lotte. "I love your body."

"Thank you." Ember said breathlessly.

"I love everything about it. How you move, how you smell,

how you accept me inside you and swell with my child. My god, you're a miracle. Didn't I tell you that? You're my miracle?"

"Don't be so silly." Ember could hardly bear this man's words of devotion. They undid him in the best possible way. "You're just as miraculous."

"Maybe." Kit kissed his neck. "But I'm used to me. You surprise me every day."

"Oh, hush." Ember didn't want words right then. He wanted action. "Shut up and prove it."

"Arms up." When Ember did as he was told, Kit lifted his corset away and discarded it with the same casual abandon as the jacket.

"You know, my clothes are works of art. I'm even thinking of establishing a museum with all the wonderful clothing I've found in storage at the palace."

"They're just clothes."

"Don't be a spendthrift Prince."

"This is my wedding night, sweetheart, I promise I'll be financially responsible tomorrow."

"You have no idea what clothing costs. I had to sell my horses to dress my sisters for the ball you didn't even bother attending."

This stilled Kit's hands. He leaned over to see Ember's face.

"I've been meaning to mention we have a few new additions to our stable, since the prince consort is such a horse fancier."

"Really? You bought horses?" Ember couldn't help himself. "May I work with them? I love horses. I used to train—"

"Yes, I've heard about your expertise with the beasts. One of your neighbors told me all about it when I purchased two of his horses—a mare and a colt named Beauty and Beau—I hope you'll enjoy them."

"You—" Ember threw himself at Kit. "You bought Beauty and Beau? I can't believe it. How did you know?"

"I wanted to buy you a wedding gift, so I asked Lucy what you'd wish for if money was no cost."

"Of course, Lu would understand. You've made me so happy. I can't wait to see her."

"I hope you can wait until morning. I'd rather not spend my wedding night with a horse, if I can avoid it." Kit began on the buttons of Ember's collarless shirt. "How many buttons are there, my God, it's like a Lyrienne puzzle box. They're said to be nearly unsolvable."

"I have faith in you."

Eventually, Kit lifted the fine lawn shirt over Ember's head. He made quicker work of Ember's boots and trousers. "Oh, my."

Ember smirked when Kit finally got a look at the ... *thing* ... Master Inigo had conceived for Ember to wear under his clothes. Barely a scrap of the finest silken lace, held up with a drawstring, it had to be the most scandalous garment Ember had ever seen. Kit's eyes widened with apparent appreciation.

"Goddess, what are you wearing?" he asked.

Ember lifted a shoulder. "I'm not sure."

"We are buying you a whole wardrobe of those." Kit pulled on the bow and helped Ember out of them. "For all you'll only be wearing them for seconds at a time."

Ember's whole body flushed.

"I mean, how am I supposed to help my father run a kingdom if I know you're wearing something like that."

"They'll probably make council meetings more interesting."

"And shorter. Much, much shorter."

Ember laughed at the absurdity of ... everything. He was a royal consort for Goddess's sake. He had a child. He couldn't seem to stop laughing once he started, and Kit joined in, both of them laughing so hard tears blurred Ember's vision.

"What are we"—Kit gasped—"laughing about?"

"I don't know." Ember fell to his back on the bed. "Everything. Nothing. The fact that we're here, together, despite all the reasons we shouldn't be."

"Ah," Kit sobered. "There are no reasons against us. Not if the Goddess wills for us to be mates."

"May we be worthy," Ember muttered. After a long, deep look into Kit's eyes he said, "Make love to me. Give me your seed and your knot."

"Oh, Ember." Kit began by kissing Ember softly on the forehead. Both eyes. Jaw, neck, and shoulder. His hand slid over Ember's chest. It roamed over his belly, stroked down from his hip to his thigh to his knee.

"There has never been a more beautiful omega," Kit whispered, moving down.

Ember gripped Kit's hair while his mouth did dangerous things to his naval and the hollows of his hips. He gasped when Kit nuzzled into his curly hair, when he kissed Ember's cock.

Kit pressed maddeningly slow, soft kisses over his balls and his taint. He licked over Ember's tightly furred hole while Ember made helpless mewling sounds. It went on and on, Kit gripping his hips and lifting them to gain access, all the while using his tongue to drive Ember mad. A dozen times, Ember was close to orgasm. So close, so close, only to be denied his release by his husband, by the intimate knowledge Kit already had about his body.

That was all right. Ember didn't want to slip into his climax with Kit's mouth on him, he wanted to roar into it with Kit inside him, with the light pain and fullness of Kit's knot binding them together in the aftermath.

"Please."

Kit ignored him in favor of bringing him to the brink again.

"Kit, Goddess, please, *please*. I need you inside me. Now, please."

"Bossy," Kit rose above him. "You want me? Want my knot?"

Ember could have smacked him. Instead he said, "If it's not inconvenient."

"It's not. *Knot.* Get it?"

"Goddess," Ember groaned.

Smiling, Kit reached for the pot of oil their attendants had thoughtfully left for them. He dipped his fingers in, and used them to prepare Ember, who was just a little too on edge for much more than a casual handshake by that point.

"Now, if you don't mind."

"But—"

"The next words out of your mouth had better be 'Yes, Ember, now is perfect for me,'" Ember warned.

"Oh, how demure you are." Kit's hand left and he lined up his cock. "Such a shy, delicate omega."

"Kit."

Kit pressed inside slowly but steadily, robbing Ember of the next few breaths. "You were saying?"

"Ngh." Ember groaned. His head fell back against the pillows. *"Yes."*

Kit started to withdraw, but Ember had something else in mind. He gripped Kit's hips and pulled him closer, while wrapping his legs around Kit's waist. Kit groaned as he bottomed out inside Ember's body.

"I'm guessing—"

"Do it," Ember urged. "Fuck me like you mean it."

"Who is alpha here?" Kit asked, though he changed his pace to please his lover.

"You are my alpha. You owe me." Ember wrapped his arm around Kit's neck. He met each thrust, until he was gliding on each wave of pleasure building inside him. This. This is what he was made for. He welcomed his alpha, rode him, shivered and pushed him until they were both taut and sweating and ready to come.

Ember exploded first. He spent all over his chest and belly, his body spurting with each new thrust of Kit's cock. Kit shuddered into his own climax a moment later. He gave one last wild cry and deep inside Ember's body. Kit's cock thickened, his knot stretching Ember's hole to impossible fullness. Still clinging to him, Ember let Kit pull him to the side to keep from crushing him.

"That's what I needed." Ember sighed against his neck. "Goddess. I love you, Kit."

"I love you." Kit kissed his forehead. Kit ran his hand from Ember's pert bottom down the back of his thigh to his knee. "It scares me sometimes how much I love you."

"How so?"

"If my father hadn't welcomed our marriage, if he had expected me to marry a woman—"

"But he didn't." Ember said gently.

"But if he had, I would have taken you and left the royal family. Left the country. You're the most important person in my life. Without you, I couldn't even begin to understand love."

"Nonsense. Your parents loved you to the stars, Kit. You're full of love."

"No, I mean I know what love *is* now. I know how to show love. I recognize all the times I was confused because it seemed to me that love was so much more complex, harder than it really is."

Ember blinked up at him. "I don't understand."

"Love is the best of me, sweetheart," Kit eyes shone. "I want to give the best of me all the time. I want to be the finest prince, king, husband, and father that I can be, and it's only possible because I carry this endless well of love for you inside me. I can love everyone, because I love you."

Ember placed a hand on either side of his face and kissed him gently. "Oh, sweetheart."

"I know it doesn't make sense when I try to say it."

"It doesn't matter. My wolf believes in you."

"Even if I mess everything up?"

"Yes."

"Even if I'm a lousy king?"

"You won't be."

"Even if I get stuck in my wolf form again?"

"I'll find you," Ember promised. "Or Lotte will."

"I am the happiest alpha alive, because you're my omega."

"I'm happy you're my alpha."

"When it suits you." Kit teased.

There is some truth to that.

Ember glanced up at Kit from beneath his lashes. "Maybe?"

"Don't ever change."

Ember wouldn't. He didn't have to. He had people who loved him exactly as he was, he could show his true face to the world, and the Goddess had blessed him with this man.

Would he and Kit live happily ever after?

Yes. Yes, they would.

~

*W*hat's next in Fiona's Faux Fairy Tales?

When he's forced to play bait after a series of grim murders, a naive omega must decide whether his fated mate is a philanthropic outlaw, or a psychopathic killer.

Preorder Yours!

Thierry Toussaint has no choice but to don the crisp white dress and red cape of the Sisters of the Merciful Moon and act as bait to catch a killer. As a male omega, he's considered a freak —a mistake of nature—and therefore expendable. He's dispatched to deliver food and aid to an old woman deep in the shelter of Bois des Voleurs forest, where picturesque, mostly benign outlaws, and a homicidal maniac, await.

Yves, the bandit of Thieve's Woods, has enough on his mind

without some murderer giving him and his pack a bad name. He's sworn to serve the poorest citizens of Rhielôme as well as the red-cloaked Sisters of the Merciful Moon who act as counselors, nurses, and midwives to families displaced by Rheilôme's impossibly high taxes.

When Yves saves Thierry from becoming the third victim of the "Red Cloak Killer," they discover a fated love so powerful nothing can tear them apart.

In the sun-drenched kingdom of Rheilôme, appearances are more important than reality. There are laws on the books protecting all omega citizens against forced marriage and trafficking, but justice often comes at a high price. In a country that sees him as less than nothing, Thierry must risk everything—even the freedom of his fated mate—to catch a killer.

ABOUT THE AUTHOR

Fiona Lawless is the pen name of a multi-published author of gay romance.

As Fiona, she can combine her love of traditional storytelling and folk tales with the modern concept of an ABO universe, mpreg, fantasy paranormal, and shifters.

You'll find she doesn't necessarily stick with the original plots and characterizations of the fairy tales she uses.

Aren't those wonderful, familiar tales more like guidelines, really?

Writing these stories makes her feel connected to all storytellers everywhere, and she hopes you enjoy these fanciful retellings as much as she enjoys writing them. Let her know what your favorite folk tales are. She'd love to explore them with you.

There's a whole, wide wonderful world of story out there. As they say in the Peter Pan ride at Disneyland (still Fiona's favorite after all these years) **Here we go!**

COPYRIGHT

Made in the USA
Monee, IL
10 January 2022